S0-BYY-448

www.carolynarnold.net

POLICE PROCEDURALS RESPECTED
BY LAW ENFORCEMENT.™

"Carolyn Arnold's love for law enforcement and providing an accurate depiction of their job is clearly evident in her writing. She is eager to have police procedures spot on, both in tactics and investigations. It's this enthusiasm paired with her knack for storytelling and her realistic portrayal of police work that makes her an author that mystery readers would enjoy reading, including those with a law enforcement background.

"You experience the emotions, distractions, frustrations, and successes of the characters in every chapter of *In the Line of Duty*. I found her heartfelt details to be spot on with a line-of-duty death. Being able to put such a tragic situation into words, is difficult in itself, but she does it with compassion, knowledge, and respect for those in uniform who know what it is like to lose a brother or sister in blue."

— *Carl J. Harper, Training Officer, ERT (SWAT), Lower Merion Township, Pennsylvania*

ALSO BY CAROLYN ARNOLD

Brandon Fisher FBI Series

Eleven
Silent Graves
The Defenseless
Blue Baby
Violated

Detective Madison Knight Series

Ties That Bind
Justified
Sacrifice
Found Innocent
Just Cause
Deadly Impulse
Life Sentence

McKinley Mysteries

The Day Job is Murder
Vacation is Murder
Money is Murder
Politics is Murder
Family is Murder
Shopping is Murder
Christmas is Murder
Valentine's Day is Murder
Coffee is Murder
Skiing is Murder

Matthew Connor Adventure Series

City of Gold

Assassination of a Dignitary

CAROLYN ARNOLD

IN THE
LINE OF DUTY

HIBBERT & STILES
PUBLISHING INC.

In the Line of Duty (Book 7 in the Detective Madison Knight series) copyright © 2016 by Carolyn Arnold

www.carolynarnold.net

2016 Hibbert & Stiles Publishing Inc. Edition

This is a work of fiction. Names, characters, places, and incidents are the products of the author's imagination or are used fictitiously. Any resemblance to actual events, locales, or persons, living or dead, is entirely coincidental.

ISBN (e-book): 978-1-988353-22-7
ISBN (paperback): 978-1-988353-24-1
ISBN (hardcover): 978-1-988353-25-8

*To all the fine men and women who serve
or have served in law enforcement, and
in memory of those who have made the
ultimate sacrifice...*

CHAPTER 1

I LOVE YOU. Three words that possessed the ability to change everything—your beliefs, perceptions, decisions. They also had a way of transforming whatever previously mattered to you and replacing it with this warm feeling that melts away your defenses, leaving you completely vulnerable.

Until now, Madison Knight had avoided such vulnerability at all costs. And she had been good at it. Maybe it came from her job as a major crimes detective and all the lying criminals, but it more likely had to do with the fact she'd been engaged before and it had disintegrated before she reached the altar. A bias toward men and romantic relationships was always born when the first one you gave your heart to was a cheater. Call it *once bitten, twice shy*.

To compound the issue, her ex, Toby Sovereign, was a fellow detective with Stiles PD. This should have taught Madison to date outside of law enforcement, but she'd failed to grasp that little lesson. Currently, the man in her life was Troy Matthews, SWAT team leader and hot-blooded American male who turned the heads of most women. But the good news for Madison was that he didn't seem to notice their attentions. Well, maybe he noticed, as in *he was aware*, but he certainly didn't care.

He said that he only had eyes for Madison, and for the most part, she trusted him when he told her so.

There were still times that doubt about his loyalty would creep in, but she would acknowledge them and then release them. In the five months they'd been dating, he had never given her actual reason to distrust him. It was just her past recycling back, trying to tell her that all relationships were doomed to failure. In her defense, finding your fiancé in bed with another woman wasn't exactly an image that went away quickly. And really, Troy had just as much reason to be suspicious of her, seeing as his marriage ended because his wife cheated on him with his best friend.

She looked over at Troy lying beside her. She was in his bed, at his house. These days she was at his place more than she was at her own apartment. Even Hershey, her chocolate lab, was snoring loudly on the floor at Troy's side of the bed. It made her smile and her stomach flip-flop.

And there it was. The gushy side of her…

What had he done to her? What had those three words done to her? After Sovereign, she'd become good at keeping any man in her life at a distance. Less chance of getting hurt that way. And she'd usually put an end to things if it they got close to being meaningful. But Troy was just about as stubborn as she was. He wasn't going to let her go easily; he'd said as much. His determination and loving perseverance were actually wearing down her defenses. Maybe there was a benefit to existing in a state of vulnerability. It meant she had someone she could rely on.

She wanted to wake him up, but the sun wasn't streaming in around the drawn curtains. She glanced at the clock on the nightstand. *5:35.*

And it was Saturday.

She let her head fall back against the pillow, surprised that she was even awake. They hadn't turned out the light until after midnight, and she loved sleeping.

She rolled onto her side, trying to abstain from touching him. But he was so beautiful... His jaw was angular and had the hardened edges of the alpha male he was. She should have turned away from him right then, but he was lying with the sheets crumpled at his feet, wearing a pair of boxers. His chest was a work of art—six-pack abs, a speckling of dark curls across his pectorals—and lower down were groin lines.

Her breath caught and tremors coursed through her body just remembering his flesh against hers, his hands on her skin, the sex they'd had last night before collapsing into a heap of sweat. His love made her high in a way she had never experienced before—as crazy as that sounded, even to her. And maybe that's why her mind sometimes got carried away thinking Troy might be the one.

Her heart raced at the thought. Or maybe it was just Cynthia's romance getting to her. Her best friend and colleague had recently set a wedding date, and Troy and Madison had just had dinner with the lovebirds the night before.

Really, who needed marriage when everything was going so well? They had the love, the romance, and their independence. It couldn't get better than this...

Something niggled in her gut. What if it *could* get better?

She hated that damn niggling. It *had* to be the fact that she was immersed in party and wedding planning for Cynthia. Madison was the maid of honor, and the responsibility had her immersed in taffeta, cake decorations, guest favors, and flowers. And if that wasn't enough, she'd been working with Cynthia's fiancé and Sovereign's partner, Lou Stanford, and Samantha—a technician from the crime lab that Cynthia managed—on a surprise engagement party. It was something that the groom wasn't typically involved in, but Lou had graciously stepped in and initiated the plan. But with the caseload at work, it had taken them months to put together.

At least the party would be behind her come next Saturday. Until then, there were only a couple of last-minute details to work out: checking in with the caterer and making sure the florist would have Gerberas, as they were Cynthia's favorite flower. Today, though, Madison had to go dress shopping with Cynthia.

No wonder she was thinking about marriage—she was drowning in it!

"Someone's up early," Troy said groggily, opening one eye at a time as if he was adjusting to the light. He looked over at her and smiled. "Good morning, beautiful."

Madison returned the smile. "Morning."

"Why are you up already? It's Saturday. You should still be snoring," he said.

She raised both brows. "I don't snore."

"Yeah, okay," he stated drily.

She playfully hit his shoulder, and he grabbed her sides and started tickling her. She squealed and squirmed, trying to get out of his reach…but not really.

"Stop it…" It was a weak protest, but it was the best she could manage.

His hands were resting on her hips, and his green eyes were peering into hers the way they always did. It was as if the man had the ability to read her mind. And based on what he'd say and do sometimes, she wondered if he really could.

She'd never tell him how the M-word wasn't as scary *some* days, though. Why risk scaring him off? Besides, he probably wouldn't believe her anyway. Her and marriage? Laughable.

"My mind's awake," she said, finally answering his question. It was simple, precise, and honest.

"Is that all?" He moved over until he was against her, *hard* against her.

Her eyes playfully narrowed to slits, and her gaze fell to his lips. He took her mouth with hunger, yet she felt like the one feeding on him. Heat grew in her belly…and lower.

His cell phone rang, and his moan was deep-seated as he pulled back from her.

"Let voice mail pick it up," she whispered.

Troy lifted his phone. "You know I can't."

As part of SWAT, he was on call twenty-four hours a day, seven days a week.

She dropped the back of her head onto the pillow, panting and disappointed.

Then her phone rang.

Strange… This was her day off, and she *wasn't* on call.

She reached for her phone. Her superior Sergeant Winston showed as her caller. First Troy's boss, now hers? This couldn't be good news.

She answered and listened to Winston, only the odd word making it to her ears. "…a shooting…Officer Weir is down…fighting for his life…"

Madison swallowed, her mouth thick with saliva, her eyes full of tears. Her heartbeat slowed and her chest seemed locked in expansion.

"When?" She managed to scrape the one word from her throat as she looked over at Troy. He was still on the phone, staring at the far wall.

"Just over a half hour ago."

"Where— Is he—" The question only partially formed when Winston's earlier words sank in.

Fighting for his life.

"Outside a gas station on Hamilton and Highbury," the sergeant responded. "He's at Peace Liberty Hospital."

"I'll be right there." Madison hung up, otherwise frozen in place on the bed, her heart beating fast for a different reason than before. Barry Weir was more than a fellow officer. He was their friend.

Troy ended his call.

"Barry was shot," she said in disbelief.

Troy's face was pale as he got out of bed ahead of her. "I know. We've gotta go."

CHAPTER 2

THE HOSPITAL WAITING ROOM WAS A SEA OF BLUE. **Regardless** of their rank, all the officers in the Stiles PD were awaiting word on their brother. Even those on duty would be taking turns stopping by. The energy in the room was one of both grief and desire for answers.

Madison and Troy walked in together and were greeted with embraces. Their fellow officers had solemn expressions on their faces, and while tears filled the eyes of almost all who were there, most were refused the right to fall. Honor and determination made that a requirement. And just as with a blood family in the case of an emergency, all their differences disappeared.

She even hugged Officer Tendum, in that moment letting go of the anger she had been harboring against him for the last six months. Tendum had accompanied his training officer, Higgins—who was also her former TO—on a call that had resulted in Higgins being shot. She'd held Tendum responsible, attributing it to his negligence, but maybe she had rushed to judgment. Tendum hadn't caused the shooting, and at least Higgins had recovered fully.

Speaking of Higgins… She looked around the room but didn't see him anywhere.

"What's the word on Barry's condition?" Madison

asked Tendum, aware of Troy's hand on her lower back and finding comfort in his touch.

"He's…" Tendum's chin quivered and he bit his bottom lip.

Madison squeezed the officer's shoulder.

Tendum swiped a finger under his dripping nose and sniffled. "It's not looking good. He hasn't come to since the shooting. We're all trying to be optimistic, but the doctor said it's too soon to tell. He's in the operating room now. The bullet hit his lungs." Tendum's gaze fell to the floor briefly. "That's all we've been told. He was wearing his vest…but they're not one-hundred-percent—" Tendum locked his gaze with hers, apparently thinking better of trying to educate her, and took pause.

Vests only helped so much. Bullets could still penetrate the Kevlar despite the fiction of movies, and even in the cases when they didn't, the impact alone could cause fatal internal bleeding.

"The bullet entered the meaty part under his left arm," Tendum added.

Madison swallowed, suddenly aware of Troy's silence, and pressed on. "Did they catch the guy who—"

Tendum shook his head. "He even hit the panic button. The closest cruiser to his location was five minutes out."

Every police radio had a red button that would clear all radio traffic and alert dispatch that an officer was in trouble. They could tell who and where with that one push.

"Weir didn't say anything in that time. It's believed he didn't have the strength." Tendum cleared his throat and then went on as if trying to assign some sense or reason to what had happened. "He was just filling the gas tank." He shook his head. "A car pulled up and fired off rounds."

Madison's mind snapped into investigative mode. Had this been random or targeted? That was one of the first things they would need to figure out. "And his family?"

Barry Weir was married with three daughters, ages six, twelve, and fifteen.

"Joni's over there." Tendum pointed to Barry's wife, who was seated at the edge of the waiting area closest to the doors that led to the operating rooms. She was surrounded by officers, leaning forward with her head in her hands, her dark hair falling to the sides, hiding her face. Joni sat back as if she sensed new eyes on her and connected directly with Madison's gaze. Joni's eyes were bloodshot, her cheeks streaked with tears.

"Where are the girls?" Madison asked Tendum.

"Officers are with them at the house."

Madison nodded and then looked over her shoulder at Troy. His eyes were glazed over, his focus on Joni. It was rare to see emotion etched into Troy's features, but it was clearly visible now.

"Excuse us," Madison said to Tendum.

When they were a few feet away from Tendum, she put a hand on Troy's arm. "I'm sure he'll be fine. We have to think posi—" His cold gaze quieted her. The pain in it was tangible. She swallowed roughly and nodded. He wasn't in the mood to be placated.

They silently walked over to Joni, Madison leading the way.

Joni's eyes were full of shock and confusion, and while they had been looking in Madison's direction, she didn't really seem to see Madison until she squatted in front of her.

"We came as soon as we heard," Madison said softly.

Joni's gaze went from her to Troy and back to Madison.

She wrapped her arms around Madison's neck, and in that moment, Madison nearly lost it altogether. Tears did fall, but to hell with it.

She cupped the back of Joni's head. "I'm so sorry, Joni." Madison's chin quivered as she struggled to regain control of her emotions. Joni was sobbing, and Madison just held her until Joni pulled back.

She swiped her palms down her cheeks, wiping away the tears, only to have more fall in their place. "I need to be strong—" the hiccup of a sob "—think positive. The girls…" Joni broke down for a while and then managed to get out, "They need their father." Joni held out a hand for Troy to take.

"Anything you need, we're here for you," Troy reassured her, his voice gravelly as he squeezed her hand.

Joni nodded, chewing on her bottom lip.

At least Troy could speak now. Madison didn't have confidence in herself at the moment. All she wanted to do was take Joni's worry away and guarantee that Barry would pull out of this. But she couldn't. There was, however, one thing she could promise. "I'll make sure we find his shooter and bring them to justice."

Joni's gaze latched on to Madison's, and in that moment there was only purity—a vow spoken that Madison would ensure was fulfilled.

She took a deep breath, exhaling from her mouth as she tried her best to pull herself together. Detachment was the toughest part of the job—the separation between the job and what was personal was hard to distinguish. Madison didn't even like to refer to murder victims by that label, preferring to use their actual names. But Barry was blood… Rage, the desire for vengeance, and heartbreak blurred together. She dried her cheeks with her hands.

More officers came up to Joni, and Madison put her hand on Troy's back. Others wanted to speak with her. Troy was hugging Joni when Madison turned to see Sergeant Winston stepping through the doors. Their eyes met, and she found herself moving toward him, regardless of their history, which usually saw them blending about as well as oil and water. Madison stopped about a foot in front of him.

They stood there facing each other for less than a few seconds before Winston hugged her, and she found herself reciprocating. A flood of emotion now made it almost impossible to swallow the tears, to refuse them free rein. But she managed. She held them back, tamped them down with righteous indignation.

"We've got to find this guy, Sarge," she said.

"Oh, we'll get this son of a bitch." Winston's voice took on a gruff edge.

She felt relief at his choice of words. "So we're going to handle this?" In some cases, line-of-duty deaths were investigated by nearby police departments due to how emotionally taxing it could be on the fallen's colleagues.

"Yes. Officers are on scene now, of course. But there will be a briefing downtown in thirty minutes. Every detective-grade officer is expected to be there. We can't miss a thing, Knight. That means keeping everyone up-to-date."

"You got it."

He blinked slowly, almost as if he expected an argument. Normally, she'd buck at his requirements for communication, but not this time. They were going to catch the bastard who shot Barry, and the best way to go about that would be to approach the investigation as a team, in an organized fashion, armed with knowledge.

Winston bobbed his head. "What's the update?"

She relayed what Tendum had told her, finding her training and experience kicking in as she went, her heartbreak for Joni now superseded by the drive to not just get answers but to pin whoever did this to the wall.

In the midst of her mental planning, a quiet fell over the waiting room. A doctor was standing next to Joni, who had gotten to her feet. He was talking to her, his face pale, his shoulders slumped, and he was moving his hands around, restless, as if he couldn't decide where they should go—in his pockets, out of his pockets, in his pockets, out of his pockets.

Joni wailed suddenly, and her legs buckled. The officers near her buoyed her and helped her back to her seat.

Madison rushed over to her and stood next to Troy, who was still there. Other officers had their arms around Joni's shoulders as she cried.

The doctor scanned the crowd, then spoke a bit louder even as he directed his words to Joni in a tender voice. "We did everything we could to stop the internal bleeding." The doctor paused. "I'm sorry that it wasn't enough."

A heavy, suffocating silence fell over the room like a cloak, stealing Madison's breath. Suddenly, it was as if she were watching everything from a distance. The adrenaline was kicking in, attuning her senses to what was around her. People became still, and words were spoken in whispers, sentiments were offered. Then everything fell silent. An impromptu and instinctual moment of silence, in remembrance of their fallen brother.

In this solemn state, the inherent scents of the hospital became noticeable—antiseptic and the faint hint of flowers. The smells transformed into an unpleasant coating on her tongue. She sensed pain all around her, blossoming within her.

Troy's green eyes were glassy, and it didn't seem like he was focused on anyone or anything. Madison touched his arm, but he felt cold beneath her hand. Without looking at her, he pulled out of her reach and left the hospital.

CHAPTER 3

TROY GRIPPED THE SINK IN the men's washroom at the Stiles police station with both hands and stared at himself in the mirror. He'd lost men close to him before. The last one was two years ago, and the officer had been killed in a car accident while off duty. He'd left behind two kids and a wife. But Barry…he was different. Life always equaled death, of course. It was a simple equation to accept until it touched close to home. And that's what Barry's death was for him—personal.

Losing Barry made it clear just how dangerous this job could be and how fragile life was. One minute here, the next gone. Barry had just been pumping gas, a routine thing, something people did all the time without any thought to their safety. Those on the outside would say that's the risk he took being in law enforcement. Yes, there was the chance any one of them wouldn't return home from a shift, but it wasn't something Troy consciously thought about before heading to work.

In fact, when serving in a SWAT capacity, he'd say it was one of the safest positions within the Stiles PD. SWAT had the toys, and when they showed up to manage a situation, it was often brought under control rather quickly. Even the majority of criminals didn't want to tango with an AR-15 and armored vehicles. Besides, dwelling on one's mortality wasn't healthy. But when something like this happened to one of their own, it spurred on such self-reflection. It could have easily been him in the morgue, or one of his team members. Or Madison…

His insides quivered with rage as his heartbeat slowed with his grief. He squeezed his eyes shut.

"I've got Dad's car tonight," Barry says. "We'll take it out on the back roads and see what she's really capable of."

"Your dad's a cop, Barry," Troy reminds him.

"So? What he doesn't know won't hurt him." Barry takes a few steps down the hall of their high school but stops and spins when Troy doesn't follow. "Come on, man. Don't make me take Lyman."

Troy came back from his thoughts and opened his eyes to find himself staring at his reflection.

That night had been one of the best ever. Barry had sent the car airborne by racing over the railway tracks on the outskirts of the city. They'd even conned some seniors into getting beer for them and drank it by the tracks later that night.

Barry had made Troy feel alive…

Pain knotted in his chest, the regrets over skipping drinks with Barry last week paired with losing a part of his childhood somehow.

Troy pinched the bridge of his nose as the memories continued to rush over him.

"I just got my acceptance letter." Barry holds the envelope in his hand. "This college has the hottest chicks… Not that it would matter to you."

"What does that mean?"

"It's Lauren and Troy sitting in a tree…" Barry sings.

"Seriously? You're like a girl sometimes, you know that? A big, emotional girl."

"Hey!" Barry punches him playfully in the arm.

Madison punched him in the arm sometimes, too…

God, what would he have done if Madison were the one who'd been killed? His heart knew the answer, and his mind willingly accepted what it meant. He had fallen for her hard and fast—at least as it might be seen from the outside. But he'd had a soft spot for her ever since he'd helped out with one of her cases eight years ago, one involving a young defense attorney who had been targeted by the Russian mafia.

Another memory churned.

"We're in the academy together!" Barry dances around Troy. "It doesn't get better than this."

"Graduating might."

"Ha-ha. You always have something smart to say."

Troy's eyes grew wet with this recollection, and he swallowed the grief that threatened to destroy him. Entering the police academy was the point when the two boys became men.

Troy needed to go see Joni at home, he knew, but he couldn't face her. Not like this. And the girls? He needed time to compose his emotions, to pillar himself against the wind of this tragedy. But there was someone he needed to call first.

He pulled out his phone and hit the quick key to dial his older sister, Andrea Fletcher, who also happened to be the police chief. She should be back from her vacation this morning, and she'd probably already heard what had happened. He just didn't want to initially discuss this with his sister face-to-face. Talking about it over the phone would make it easier.

One ring.

Two rings…

The washroom door opened, and Sanchez came in. He slipped into a stall, and Troy took that as a good sign to get out of there. Sanchez loved Mexican food.

In the hallway, Troy leaned against a wall and waited as the ringtone drilled into his ear.

Answer the damn phone…

"You've reached the voice mail for Chief Fletcher…"

He hung up and redialed. She should be back from her vacation by now. What time had she said her flight was getting in?

Someone picked up on the other end of the line. "Chief Fletcher here." She sounded groggy, as if he'd woken her up.

"Where are you?" he rushed out.

"Hotel near the airport. We just got in. What's going on?"

"Something has happened." The words came out soft-spoken and dry.

"That doesn't sound good." He could imagine his sister sitting up in bed and turning on the light on her night table.

"It's Barry…" His throat constricted. This would be his first time verbalizing what had happened.

His sister's voice was gentle and caring. "What about Barry?"

"He's dead." He delivered the news directly, unable to water it down no matter how much it hurt.

"What? How?" she asked, her tone switching quickly to one of shock.

"He was shot this morning while on duty." He got through telling her the basics, the facts draining so much from him.

"Wake up, Robert," his sister said distantly. He heard

his brother-in-law moan in the background.

"We're leaving now. I'll be in as soon as possible. Has there been a briefing yet?"

"In ten minutes."

"Has the shooter been caught?"

At his sister's question, his insides pulsed with adrenaline and determination. No matter what it took from him, he would find Barry's killer.

"Troy? Has the shooter been caught?" she repeated, a subtle beep in the background of the line.

"Not yet."

Another beep. "Someone's calling. I better let you go." Her voice was withdrawn, and Troy imagined her pulling her phone out to consult the caller ID. "It's Winston. See you soon." His sister hung up before he could say anything else. He put his phone away, the ache in his chest now almost unbearable.

CHAPTER 4

OFFICER RANSON WAS SITTING AT the front desk of the police station when Madison entered, and Madison wondered if the woman ever had a day off. Usually Ranson was beaming and greeting Madison with a smile and a "good morning." There was none of that today. Simply a subtle nod and a somber face.

"Everyone's in the squad room," she told Madison.

That made sense. It was where officers were briefed before each shift. "Thank you, Ranson."

Another nod.

Madison walked through the station, feeling as though time was moving in slow motion as she first headed to her desk. Once there, she took a seat and opened the bottom drawer, nausea swirling in her gut as she pulled out a clear plastic Baggie. It was where she kept her mourning band. She'd hoped to never need it again…

She pulled it out, and for a few seconds, she held onto it, letting her fingers dip into the thin ribbing in the half-inch-wide black cloth. She unclipped her badge from its holder and slipped the band on, carefully placing it so that it ran horizontally across the center of her badge. As she stared down at the badge, thinking about what that simple band of black meant, a single tear crept down her cheek. But she didn't have time to dwell on her fallen brother and grieve right now.

She swiped at her eyes and returned the Baggie to the drawer and headed for the briefing.

Even with her detour, she beat Sergeant Winston there. Sovereign and Stanford were already in the room along with about sixty officers. It was standing room only, and Madison scanned the crowd for Troy. But there was no sign of him or of her partner, Terry Grant. She didn't see the police chief, either.

Andrea Fletcher, Troy's older sister, had taken over the position almost seven months ago. To say she was a vast improvement over her predecessor was putting it mildly. Patrick McAlexandar was a chauvinist pig who had been in bed with the Russian mafia—the same mafia that almost killed her five months ago. And she was certain there was still a hit out for her. She couldn't allow the passage of time to lull her into thinking it had gone away. If McAlexandar's track record wasn't bad enough, he also had aspirations to be the city's mayor, but Madison would do whatever she could to sabotage his efforts.

Terry walked into the room then and came over to her. She hugged her partner without hesitation. As much as they teased and rankled each other, he was like the brother she'd never had.

"I didn't see you at the hospital," she said as she released him.

"We must have just missed each other. I got there as soon as I could. Dani's still not sleeping through the night."

"She *is* only two months old," she reminded him.

Spoken like someone who knew kids…which she didn't.

"That's what Annabelle tells me, and she's such a good

mother. Besides—" Terry gestured around the room "—complaining about the lack of sleep doesn't really seem like a big deal in light of everything." He fell silent for a few seconds and then added, "I can't believe he's gone."

"Me neither." The nausea that had settled into the pit of her gut didn't seem like it would be going away anytime soon.

Sergeant Winston entered the room, his mourning band also on his badge. Terry was working on getting his band in place, too.

The sergeant stood at the front of the room. He cleared his throat, and all the chatter stopped. "As you may have heard, Officer Barry Weir was shot and killed this morning." His voice cracked as he delivered the message. "We will be keeping the investigation in-house."

Madison looked around the room, seeing the relief on the faces of her fellow officers.

"Chief Fletcher has been notified," Winston continued, "and is expected to be here in about two hours. She's requested that I be the point person for this investigation." Winston paused, seemingly allowing that to sink in. The other divisions and units typically reported to their own sergeant, but with this being a murder—and one of such a sensitive nature—it made sense for the major crimes sergeant to take the lead.

"Weir was shot in what seems to have been a drive-by," he added.

Madison heard Winston's words, and while part of this felt like a hazy dream, her desire was set on getting to the crime scene itself. She'd never been a fan of secondhand information. And another thing preoccupying her was that she hadn't seen Troy since he'd left the hospital without saying good-bye.

With these thoughts running through her head, Winston's words just sank in.

"Wait. It *seems* like a drive-by?" she asked. "Did the vehicle come to a standstill, or did it keep rolling forward?" Terry put his hand on her shoulder, urging her to let it go for now. But why should she? The details mattered. She was just about to press the issue when the door opened and Troy walked in. He came over and stood next to her.

"As I was about to say," Winston went on, "Weir was filling his cruiser's tank at Rico's Gas Station on the corner of Hamilton and Highbury when he was shot."

Highbury Street was one of the main arteries that led to a major interstate, and that intersection was one of the busiest in Stiles. Businesses were positioned on the four corners where Highbury Street met Hamilton Road. Rico's was on the northwest side, and residential properties lined both sides of Highbury going north.

"Weir had radioed in 'away from car' when he stopped at the gas station. His next stop was likely going to be the station to finish his reports," Winston added.

"Do you believe that Officer Weir was targeted because he was a cop?" Lou asked.

Winston paled. "We do. An eyewitness told responding officers that the shooter yelled out 'Die, cop!' before opening fire."

"How many rounds?"

"What ammunition?"

"Do we know the make of gun?"

Speaking of open fire…

The questions were coming at Winston fast. He held up his hand. "One thing at a time."

"An eyewitness?" Madison proceeded, disregarding

the sergeant's obvious preference to leave the question round until the end of the briefing. "Did they see the shooter? Do we have an ID?"

Winston shook his head. "We have a description of the car, but that's all from that witness's viewpoint. We're told the passenger window of the shooter's vehicle was only open enough for the gun barrel to show through and the tinting was dark. The vehicle was a sedan, black, with silver rims."

"So no make or model on the vehicle?" Terry pressed.

"No. The eyewitness was a young woman by the name of Janet Hines. She was the cashier on duty at Rico's. Apparently, she's too stressed to remember anything except for the fact the car was black. She's twenty-two and was on the midnight shift."

Terry leaned over to speak in Madison's ear. "That should be a crime in and of itself. A woman manning a gas station at those hours."

Madison turned to her partner. "What's that supposed to mean? Women can't take care of themselves?"

"That's not what I meant. I just wouldn't want Dani working that late. Or that early, depending how you look at it."

Now that he was a father, he was the defender of all daughters everywhere. She put her attention back to Winston and hoped they hadn't missed anything crucial.

"There is a traffic camera at the intersection where Rico's is located," Winston was saying, "as well as security cams at the gas station. Paperwork for the warrants has already been started."

What the general public didn't realize was how much was involved in requesting a warrant—forty to seventy-five pages of details and information regarding why there was sufficient cause to have the warrant signed.

"Someone from the DA's office should be here by eight, and I anticipate their full cooperation. I expect to see the video footage come through this morning."

Madison glanced at the clock. It was only 6:33 AM.

"The owner, Rico Beck, is out of town, and he won't be back until Tuesday. The manager was visiting family nearby, but will be back and at the station about seven." He paused for a beat. "To get back to some of your questions, we were able to determine three nine-millimeter rounds were used. One bullet found its way into Weir, one lodged into the pump beside him, and one was embedded in his cruiser. The make or model of the gun has not yet been determined."

Madison recalled the sergeant's earlier words about the window: *only open enough for the gun barrel...* If they were looking for a weapon that fired 9mm rounds in the compact space of a car, it was likely a semiautomatic handgun.

"Question, Sarge," Madison spoke up. "Was Barry able to return fire?"

Winston shook his head. "He had pulled his Glock, but all the bullets were accounted for between the chamber and magazine."

Barry likely drew with intent to fire but then hesitated. Stiles PD had upped the government minimum of weapon training from once to twice year, but this still left officers with limited experience handling live fire. To maximize their ability to stop the threat, they were taught to aim at the torso, the center of mass. With only a cracked-open window, Barry's chances of hitting the subject would have been pretty slim. And officers were responsible for every round fired. Taking a shot would have been too risky. His bullets could have passed through the suspect's car windows and injured or killed innocent parties. Barry had made the right call.

"Was he hit with the first round?" a detective from Gangs asked. Madison was drawing a blank on his name right now.

"Too early to say." Winston looked at the detective who had asked the question, who sat with other members of the gangs unit, and he also glanced at members from Guns & Drugs. He spoke to both units when he said, "I want you to reach out to your informants—see if we can find out who's behind the shooting. If this was the work of a gang, someone out there is bragging about it."

The thought cinched Madison's gut tighter. *Bragging about taking a life... Awful...*

"Members of SWAT, you'll also be serving in an investigative capacity, unless you are called in for SWAT services. I want you reviewing all of Weir's reports from his final shift to see if the shooting could tie into anything there. Be sure to review his notepad for what might not have made it into the laptop in his black-and-white. If you haven't found anything of interest there, go further back with an eye for people who might have gang affiliations or a strong reason to target Weir."

Troy nodded and so did the other men from his team.

"Officers are already canvassing the area, knocking on residential doors," Winston went on. "Knight and Grant, I want you speaking to the eyewitness from Rico's and talking to the manager at the Bean Counter across the street. Stanford and Sovereign will take the managers from the other two businesses at that intersection. Officers are already in position to talk to their customers from the time of the shooting, and a tip line will be set up and an appeal made through the media for anyone else who might have seen something."

Winston had so much to relay he hardly had time to come up for air. "Also, as you likely know, it is proper etiquette to wear a black mourning band when an officer dies." He paused as his gaze traced the room, stopping briefly on those who were already wearing them. He bobbed his head in Madison's direction when he noticed hers, Terry's, and Troy's. "If you don't have one, come up here and get one before you leave this room."

He paused a few seconds, his jaw clenched as if fighting back emotion. He cleared his throat. "We've seen this sort of violence going on all around us—police officers shot down in the line of duty, lured out and assaulted, not to mention the rampant disrespect and seeming random acts of violence. Now it's touched our city. But we will not hide from it." Winston's voice echoed through the room, his timbre deep and steadfast, and growing more confident. The energy of the officers began to ramp up, and a tempest was brewing inside Madison. "We will not shrink away in fear. We'll rise up—higher than before— and we'll fight back. We'll claim our city and make it clear that any level of disrespect or violence against an officer of the law carries the heaviest penalty. We run toward the gunfire, not away. We stand united and unmovable. We become their worst nightmare!"

Everyone applauded, including Madison. Not only was Winston's speech getting her geared up to take down Barry's killer, but hearing her boss speak like that shed a new light on his character. Maybe he wasn't as bad as he sometimes seemed… And they really were in the search for justice together, even though at times it felt like they played for different sides. He had an old-school mentality that led to the belief that the best cops were men. She was practically a women's libber in his eyes.

Winston wasn't done yet, though. "Our first priority right now is finding out who killed Officer Weir, and all overtime to that end is approved." He cleared his throat again. "On another note, a memo is going out to all officers—even civilians working for us in administrative roles—that, effective immediately, everyone must ensure that any evidence of working with the Stiles PD is removed from any personal belongings. Strip anything and everything that will tie you to the Stiles PD during off-hours. Don't wear logoed shirts or pants when you take your morning jog. Don't leave printed gym bags in your car. Take down your parking pass for the station lot from your rearview mirrors. We will also wear our vests whenever we are on shift. This is not a response of fear, but one of power, one of precaution. Until we know exactly what prompted the shooting this morning, we treat this situation as if we are at war."

Madison's heart was beating fast, renewed with fiery zeal. A war had started. Only it wasn't nation against nation. It was on American soil being waged among Americans. It was the red-blooded against the blue-blooded.

A life of sacrifice to the higher good was what she had signed up for. She'd defend the innocent and protect and serve if it took her life to do so, and she'd do it despite the way the media painted things to make officers look like the bad guys more often than not. They applied too much use of force to a situation, or they shot someone who wasn't armed. Meanwhile, it wasn't disclosed that the officer approached a subject in the dark of night and the subject was holding a bicycle pump extended in the fashion of a gun. The officer had to make a split-second decision that, if it had been a loaded gun, the officer or his backup would have been shot.

And rarely did the news share the stories of courage and bravery—how the actions of officers saved lives and put criminals behind bars. They never reported about the officers who resuscitated a woman who was clinically dead, saving her life while waiting on the local paramedics to show up. No—law enforcement always fell under the microscope of scrutiny and judgment, and yet she and her brothers put their lives on the line every day because it was what many of them believed they were born to do. Of course, there were some who viewed the job as simply that, but not her. Donning her badge wasn't something she gave thought or consideration to each morning. It wasn't an option. It was the same as putting on a pair of pants or brushing her teeth.

Winston clapped loudly, jolting her from her thoughts. "Now go! Stay safe."

Everyone started out of the room, including Terry, but she turned to Troy instead. While he did look at her, his demeanor seemed rigid and guarded.

"If you need to talk, you know I'm here for you," she said softly.

Troy didn't respond.

She felt guilt snake in for even saying Barry would be fine when they were at the hospital, but she had just been trying to stay positive. "Are you sure that you're—"

His eyes were ice as he narrowed his gaze on her. "You're not going to ask me if I'm okay or if I can handle this investigation, are you? Because you should know me better than that."

His tone surprised her, and her defenses shot up.

"Right. You're Troy. You're untouchable."

"I've got work to do and so do you," he snapped.

Her heart ached at the way he was pushing her away. He wasn't himself, and he was holding something back. She could get criminals to confess to murder, but she couldn't get her own boyfriend to let her in.

"You're right. We do." She heard the vulnerability in her voice, and he would have, as well.

He pulled her in for a hug, but his body was stiff. She touched his face gently.

"Keep safe, Bulldog," he said to her.

Her gaze flicked to meet his, and she nodded. Given the day, he'd get a pass on using the pet name he had for her. He always defended it, saying it was being loving, while to her, the underlying meaning was that she was stubborn like a dog with a bone.

A quick look around the room showed it was now empty except for the two of them. She tapped a kiss on his lips, but he pulled her close and stole another before leaving her standing there.

Madison touched a fingertip to her lips. She just hoped she'd have the strength to get through this.

CHAPTER 5

IT WAS HARD TO BELIEVE this was really happening, that it had *happened*. But everyone going through a tragic situation probably thought the same thing. Madison could only imagine how Joni was feeling right now. She wasn't going to dwell on that, though. She couldn't afford to. She had made a promise, and she intended on keeping it.

Rico's Gas Station was a fifteen-minute drive from the police station for the average citizen. With lights flashing, she made it in five, somehow managing not to scare Terry, who normally clung to the oh-shit bar or passenger-seat drove.

Public Works would be called in to set up a detour, and while it would create havoc for commuters, it was necessary. But until the city came through, officers had established a perimeter and cordoned off the immediate area.

Madison scanned the intersection. On the east corner was the Bean Counter, an independently owned coffee shop whose success challenged the local franchises. The place never saw an empty lot or drive-through. South of that and kitty-corner to Rico's was a McDonald's, and across from the fast-food restaurant was a sandwich shop.

She zeroed in on Rico's. The gas station had two entrances—one on the east side and one on the south, and there were two lanes of pumps, which ran north and south. There were spots for four vehicles per lane, two on each side.

Madison slowed the sedan and parked just outside the cordoned-off area. Two cruisers were angled lengthwise to block both southbound lanes. Beyond them was the crime lab's forensics van. It housed everything necessary for collecting evidence.

Madison expected that Cynthia would have brought in the three investigators who reported to her: Samantha Reid, Mark Andrews, and Jennifer Adams. Each of them had a specialized skill set, as did Cynthia, who was great with technology, documents, prints, and other patterned evidence. Samantha was firearms and ballistics; Mark, trace evidence; and Jennifer, forensic serology.

Madison and Terry got out of their car and entered the crime scene. Weir's cruiser was still positioned next to the pump on the outside, closest to the street, the hose leading to the vehicle, the nozzle inside the tank.

The observation made Madison's stomach churn, but determination compelled her forward, even as grief threatened to immobilize her.

He had been pumping gas, so Barry's torso would have been visible above the trunk, making it easy for the perp to shoot him where he had. And based on what Winston had told them, they were most likely looking for two perps—a driver and a shooter. If the passenger window had been lowered only enough for the gun barrel to stick out, it would have been next to impossible for someone to shoot and keep driving. This was why eyewitness testimonies and obtaining camera footage were key in verifying evidence.

Madison took a deep breath as she and Terry headed toward Cynthia, who was hunched over taking photographs in the middle of the street. The lights from the cruisers were casting color over her. She straightened up when she saw them approach.

Cynthia's eyes were wet and glistened in the growing daylight.

Madison thought about what their original plan had been for the day and made eye contact with her friend. "Did this day ever take a turn…"

Cynthia pulled Madison into a hug. "I can't believe this happened."

"Me neither. I keep thinking I'll wake up."

Cynthia moved on to Terry, an awkward endeavor that had them both initially going to place their head on the same side. They eventually embraced but it was brief.

"You hear about this stuff happening…" Cynthia's words dried up there. She didn't need to finish her thought, as it was one they were all probably thinking.

Madison pointed to where Cynthia had been working. Tire marks marred the pavement. "Are they from the shooter's vehicle?"

"Based on eyewitness testimony, this was the location of the shooter's car and the tracks are fresh, so most likely."

Madison looked at the marks. To lay that amount of rubber, it would have made a loud squeal. "Did the eyewitness testify to hearing the tires squeal?"

"That I don't know. You'd have to ask Gardener. He was first on scene."

Gardener was an experienced cop and a training officer. "Does he have a trainee with him?"

"Yep," Cynthia said, "and he's shaking like a leaf."

Madison nodded. "What do you get from the tire marks?"

"Well, based on the speed they would have gathered tearing away and how close they are to the intersection, I'd say they kept heading south toward the highway. I'd also conclude the car had rear-wheel drive."

"Is there any way to determine the length of the wheel base?" Terry asked.

"Unfortunately, not in this case. But I would say the evidence indicates that the car came to a complete stop, the shooter fired off the rounds, and then they sped off."

Madison turned to Terry. "So much for a drive-by shooting."

"It still has some elements of one," Terry said. "An unnecessary amount of bullets, for one."

And yet, *she* was like a dog without a bone? Had Troy met her partner?

Madison shrugged. "The shooter had bad aim."

Cynthia shook her head. "So this might have been planned?" Her voice squeaked. "God, I hope not."

"They were obviously prepared to shoot someone, anyhow," Madison reasoned. "I believe we're being targeted."

"*We* or Weir specifically?" Cynthia asked.

"We still need to figure that out. Winston's asked Troy and the guys from SWAT to look into Barry's reports from his final shift to see if anything stands out."

"But if they were after Weir, how would they even know he would be here?"

Madison let her eyes drift from her friend to her partner. "Call in to accounting at the station and find out if Rico's was a regular stop for Weir at this time of day."

"It's Saturday," Terry said.

"Leave a message," she ground out.

He nodded and pulled out his phone to make the call.

She hated to admit it was too soon to know for sure, and she refused to dwell on the budget issues that made it so the Stiles PD officers had to fill their tanks at public gas stations. So many departments were upgrading to vehicles that ran on propane, adding filling tanks on department property, but that request had been quickly overturned at the last budget meeting. The costs had been considered too high. She wondered how the committee would feel about the cost now.

She took a deep breath and looked around as Cynthia went back to photographing the marks on the road.

Madison considered what she knew so far. It didn't seem the perps were worried about drawing attention— they'd yelled out, fired three rounds, and squealed away. Drive-by or not, it could point to a gang-related crime given its brazen nature. Most of those people didn't fear anything, not even their rivals within the city.

Terry hung up and turned to Madison. "Message left."

"Okay, good. Hopefully, we'll hear back sooner rather than later." Her eyes went back to Cynthia. "Have you guys found any shell casings?"

Cynthia shook her head. "The ejection port of the gun must have been inside the car."

Madison turned to Terry. "Winston mentioned that the window was down just enough for the muzzle to go through, but that would have made for a difficult shot given the recoil of most handguns."

Terry shrugged. "Or the shooter knew what they were doing."

"Then why such bad aim?" Madison wondered aloud

before addressing Cynthia. "Do we know which bullet struck him yet? What make of gun?"

Cynthia bobbed her head toward Samantha. "She'll need to analyze the bullets back at the lab."

Samantha was next to the pump, which towered over her under-five-foot frame. Madison nodded, and she and Terry left Cynthia and jogged toward Sam.

She was working to extract a bullet from the pump, but she stopped and acknowledged Madison and Terry with a quick, "Hey."

Madison's eyes drifted to the hole in the C-pillar of Barry's cruiser and down to the pool of blood next to Sam's feet. Madison pinched her eyes shut and took a deep breath. She hated the sight of blood, odd as it was for a cop. But it wasn't so much its appearance that affected her right now as it was the knowledge that it belonged to Barry.

God, he must have been so scared.

Madison cleared her throat. "Can you run us through exactly where and how he was struck?" As she waited on Sam's reply, she observed the pump read $22.10.

Sam plucked the bullet from the pump, put it into an evidence bag, and then placed the bag into a collection case that was off to the side of the pump. "I can." Her hands now free, she stood next to the pump, her left side to the road. "Officer Weir was facing the station, his arm slightly elevated as he held onto the hose."

Terry nodded. "So he was holding the hose across his body?"

"Correct," Sam responded. "The bullet hit him here—" she pointed at her torso under her left arm "—and traveled straight to his lungs." She lowered her arm.

"Have you determined the firing sequence?" Madison

asked.

"I'll need to recreate the scene and factor in the trajectories of the fired bullets. That takes time."

But time wasn't something they had a lot of, especially if someone out there was targeting cops…

CHAPTER 6

THROUGH THE GAS STATION'S WINDOWS, Madison could see Gardener and his trainee speaking with a young woman who Madison assumed was Janet Hines. She was leaning against the counter, shaking her head, and gesturing toward the ceiling. She paused her flailing and laid one hand over her forehead, the other on her stomach.

Terry grabbed the door for Madison just before she reached the handle. The door sensor buzzed, drilling an irritating tone right through Madison's head. She shook it off, then acknowledged Training Officer Gardener and the trainee at his side, who really was visibly trembling, as her strides took her across the room.

She held up her badge to the woman. "I'm Detective Knight, and this my partner, Detective Grant. You're Janet Hines?"

The woman sucked in her bottom lip and nodded. Her eyes were wet, and her gaze was filled with a mixture of shock and fear. She was flushed and blinking rapidly.

Madison looked around for someplace Hines could sit, but there was nothing. "I need you to tell me everything you saw and heard."

Hines's gaze slid past Madison toward Gardener and the rookie, who were now near the door. "I told them everything…"

"Now I need you to tell me." Madison held eye contact with the woman until she took a heaving breath and turned away. "Start at the beginning," Madison prompted.

"He— I knew him… He died, didn't he?"

Madison nodded slowly.

Hines fanned herself. "I—" Her eyes rolled back in her head, and her legs crumpled as if she were a rag doll.

Madison raced behind the counter, hoping to stabilize the woman's fall, and caught her just in time. Terry helped lower Hines's dead weight to the floor.

"Call an ambulance," Madison called out.

"On it," Gardener said.

Madison and Terry positioned Hines in a seated position against the wall. Madison stepped back, and Terry put his hand to Hines's neck.

"She has a pulse," he said, "and she's breathing."

Seeing the cashier sitting there somehow made Barry's death sink in even more. Madison took a few more deep breaths.

Police training prepared one to detach, and to a point, she was able to do that or the job would have eaten her alive years ago. When she was a rookie, Officer Higgins had told her that everyone was an empty glass. Certain aspects of the job would cause water to pour in, and depending on the person, the glass would fill up at its own speed, some faster than others. But the point was that everyone's glass would overflow eventually. It was just a matter of when. Investigating the murder of a close friend and colleague had the water coming into Madison's glass at full speed.

She looked out the window at the gas pumps, noticing the clear line of sight the cashier would have had. Then she turned to Gardener, who had finished up his call.

"Tell me what she told you," she said, making an exception to her rule about secondhand intel. She'd rather hear something than wait who knows how long for Hines. She stepped out from behind the counter while Terry stayed with their witness. "I need to know everything."

"We hadn't finished taking her statement, but I can share what I have." Gardener consulted the notepad in his hand, and Madison sensed it wasn't because he had to, but rather because he was struggling to restrain his emotions. He cleared his throat. "Hines said that Weir got to the pumps at five-oh-five," Gardener stated. "She said he prepaid fifty dollars."

"And he got as far as twenty-two ten," Madison stated, remembering the amount on the pump.

"That's right," Gardener began. "Hines described a black sedan, said it pulled up, and she heard three pops. She said she hit the floor after the first one."

"Huh." Madison glanced at Terry. "Either she's got good instincts or she was ready for the gunfire."

"Do you think she was involved?" Terry asked incredulously.

"It's really too early to conclude that she wasn't," Madison responded.

"My name's Caldwell," the trainee spoke up, easing his way into the conversation. "I ran a background on…" Caldwell looked at Gardener, his nerves seemingly getting the better of him. It was probably his first time dealing with the loss of an officer—possibly the loss of anyone. At least it looked like his shaking had stopped.

"Nothing of interest got our attention in her records," Gardener said. "She's single. No criminal charges."

Madison nodded, taking in the information being

given her, but was still determined to check Hines's record for herself. She might even request a deeper history that would provide her a full family background. Before that step, she'd speak with Hines directly. Of course, that meant she'd need to come around…

"Now the sarge mentioned that she heard the perp call out, 'Die, cop'?" Terry asked.

"That's right. Just before he opened fire," Gardener said.

"She identified it as a man's voice?" Madison asked.

"She did."

"Any characteristics to it? An accent? A lisp?"

Gardener shook his head. "She said nothing stood out to her."

Madison paced a few steps and stopped about a foot in front of Gardener. "The driver spun his tires when he drove off. Did Hines say anything about hearing tires squeal after the shooting stopped?"

"Not that she noted."

Madison's mind drifted, thinking over all she knew. A smooth stop wouldn't have alerted Barry. But then calling out before the shooter opened fire took away that element of surprise. And squealing away ensured that the perp drew attention to what he had done. Or was it more likely that it had been his instinctual fear kicking in and he didn't want to get caught?

"Uh, Maddy…" Terry said.

"Yeah, what is it?"

Terry pointed to the monitor. She went behind the counter, careful of Hines, but stopped in her steps at the sound of an approaching ambulance.

Seconds later, two paramedics were sweeping into the store, the door buzzing again. One of them had a flat board under his arm along with a medical bag.

Officer Gardener directed them behind the counter. The equipped paramedic acknowledged them with a bob of his head. Madison and Terry got out of his way. The other paramedic stopped in front of Gardener and shook his hand, then Caldwell's, before moving on to Madison's and Terry's.

"My name's John Price. I'm sorry to hear about Officer Weir," he said as he shook Madison's hand, but his statement was clearly meant for all of them. News traveled fast, especially when it involved a fallen cop. Part of it had to do with the fact that their jobs tended to intersect with other emergency responders—paramedics, doctors, firefighters.

"I knew Barry for six years," Price continued. "We'd have beers together sometimes. He and Joni even came over with the girls for barbecues on a few occasions."

"Sorry for your loss, too," Madison said. The strength she had mustered to focus on the investigation was slipping away fast.

Price gave her a quick nod and then joined his colleague, who was taking Hines's vitals. He had a hand on her wrist to check her pulse, and it seemed he was satisfied as he quickly went into his case for a stethoscope and put it to her chest.

"Anything you need from me," Price added, "I'm stationed with Fire Station 2."

The other EMT was listening to Hines's breathing when she let out a moan and her eyes fluttered open.

"Hello. Do you know where you are?" Price asked her.

"I…" Her eyes flitted backward.

"Come on, stay with me."

Price put a blood pressure sleeve on her arm, and the

store was silent except for the sound of the blood pressure pump and the hiss of air as the cuff deflated.

Hines's eyes opened again, and this time it looked like they were going to stay open. "I have a headache." She went to reach for her forehead, but Price stopped her.

"Just move slowly," he told her.

Madison, Terry, Gardener, and Caldwell watched them work on Hines for about fifteen minutes. Hines's eyes were open, and she seemed aware. They got her to her feet, but she was still holding on to the counter for balance.

"Your vitals look fine now. You just had a mild syncope," the first paramedic said.

"You passed out," Price clarified. "It's up to you if you'd like to go into the hospital."

"No, I think I'll be fine…"

Price must have noticed her grip on the counter. "Actually, why don't you just come with us? It will be quick."

Not that anything at the hospital was ever quick, Madison thought. She'd lose her eyewitness for at least a couple more hours.

The paramedics helped Hines out to the ambulance and loaded her up in the back.

"Gardener, call in and have someone stay on Hines," Madison directed.

Gardener made the request over his radio as the back of the ambulance was shut. A minute later, they pulled out of the lot, Madison's witness in tow.

She looked over at Terry to find him back behind the register, gesturing for her to join him.

"What is it?" She moved up next to Terry, and he pointed at the screen.

Right. That's where they had been before the EMTs showed up…

On the monitor was a snapshot of the pumps labeled one through eight. Next to each was a time stamp noting the last time it was used.

Pump seven, which was where Weir had been, remained active, although frozen at $22.10. The sale was listed as prepaid for fifty at five-oh-five this morning.

"Look at pump two," Terry said. "The last completed sale was at five-oh-seven. Whoever was there was here when Weir was shot," Terry punched home.

Madison looked out to the lot, her gaze on pump two. No one was there. Only Stiles PD employees were on the property. "So where are they now?" She turned to Gardener, about to ask if Hines had said anything about another customer, when a woman was escorted toward the door by an officer.

"Probably the manager," Terry said. "The sarge said they'd be here at seven."

She looked at the clock on the store's wall. *7:20.*

So much for showing up on time.

The woman was probably in her early twenties with shoulder-length brown hair that she wore down. Bangs framed her face. She walked at a brisk pace and rolled her eyes when the officer opened the door for her.

"This is Melody Ford. She's the manager." The officer made the introduction and left.

The woman looked around the store. "Where's Janet?"

Madison approached her, and Officers Gardener and Caldwell excused themselves. "I'm Detective Knight, and this is my partner, Detective Grant."

The woman's eyes traced over to Terry, then back to Madison. "Where is Janet?"

"She fainted and is being taken to the hospital to be checked out," Terry answered.

Ford's balance faltered, but she kept upright. "So she's okay?"

"I'm sure she will be." Terry sounded convincing.

Ford released a drawn-out exhale, the air pushing up her bangs. "I got a call from my boss, who received a call from a sergeant. A cop was shot here?"

"And killed," Madison stated coolly.

Ford's face paled. "Oh."

Madison wasted no time. "We'll need the camera footage from the past several hours, and we have a question about a sale."

"I knew about the surveillance, but the sale?" Her gaze bounced between Madison and Terry, disclosing her confusion.

"It looks like someone was at pump two at the time of the shooting, but as you can see…" Madison gestured to the lot. "No one's there."

Ford's gaze landed on Terry, who was still behind the register.

"We'll need to know what method of payment they used." Terry stepped to the side to let Ford in front of the register.

She clicked some buttons on the keyboard and moved a mouse around. "It looks like they prepaid cash."

"For how much?" Terry asked.

"Twenty dollars."

"Did they pump that full amount?"

Ford shook her head. "Fifteen seventy-five."

"Did they get their change?" Madison inquired.

Ford consulted the screen. "It doesn't look like it."

Madison had been hoping for a credit card, as that

would've made it a lot easier to track the person down, but whoever had been at pump two would have at least come into the station to prepay. "Do you have cameras in here or just outside?"

"Both." Ford pointed to a corner in the ceiling across from her where there was a small black dome. She started to turn around, but Madison noticed it before Ford pointed out the second one mounted behind the counter.

"We'll need that footage, too."

"And you will have it," Ford said. "After I receive the signed warrant."

Rage surged through Madison. The proper channel dictated a signed warrant, but if the information was volunteered, that made for an exception. "You're not going to budge on that, are you?"

Ford's cheeks flushed. "I can't or I'll lose my job. Rico, the owner, told me to get the warrant first. Do you have one?" Her tone took on a hopeful pitch.

If I did, would I be trying to pressure you into handing the footage over?

"A police officer is dead, Miss Ford. That footage outside could have captured his killer," Madison said with heat. "And the cameras inside could provide a lead on the person from pump two."

"Yes, I know—" She rolled her hand "—the situation. It's just that this is a good job. The economy, as you know, might be on the upswing, but it's still not—"

"A wife and three daughters will be burying their father and you're…" Madison sensed Terry's eyes on her. She took a deep breath. "Well, you can be certain we'll be back with a warrant, and in the meantime, you tell Rico that the business is closed until this investigation is wrapped up."

"Un-until…" Ford stammered. "How long? What should I tell—"

"It will take as long as it takes."

"I'm sorry for the officer's family." Ford took in Madison and Terry, too. "All his family."

Madison had to leave before her emotions betrayed her. There was nothing more this woman could do or say to help them until the warrant came through. And someone from the DA's office wouldn't be in until eight.

They were still looking at the better part of an hour, and things never moved that fast. And she certainly didn't have time to just sit around waiting for the answers to come to her. She had made a promise. Her eyes caught the Hershey's wrapper on a candy rack. She grabbed the chocolate bar and went to give Ford a couple of bucks.

Ford waved her hand. "It's the least I can do."

Madison lowered her head in thanks. "Come on, Detective Grant," she said, using Terry's surname due to their company.

Ford's brow wrinkled. "And what about me?"

"You just stay put." Madison made eye contact with Gardener, silently indicating for him and Caldwell to stay with her. Looking back at Ford, she said, "Get the video footage ready to roll because there *will* be a warrant. And soon."

CHAPTER 7

MADISON STEPPED OUTSIDE. The sun was fully out now, and the streetlights had gone out. She unwrapped the chocolate bar and took a few huge bites. Her stomach was in knots, but to her, a Hershey's bar was what a cigarette was to a smoker—a stress reliever.

She looked over the gas station property. Cynthia had finished up taking photographs on the road, but yellow evidence markers speckled the pavement. More were laid out around Barry's cruiser, but the hose was now out of its tank.

Samantha was writing on another evidence bag, and then she placed it into a container. Hopefully, she'd be heading back to the lab soon. Land and groove impressions could do more than lead them to a type of weapon; it could lead them to a specific weapon. Of course, they'd have to find the weapon to make the match. In the meantime, though, striations were as unique as fingerprints, and if the gun used in this shooting had been used before, they might lead them to the firearm and the killer.

Terry came up beside Madison, rubbing the back of his neck, something he often did when there were more questions than answers.

"Let's get over to the Bean Counter," she said.

They crossed the street into the coffee shop's busy parking lot. Madison tossed her now-empty candy bar wrapper in a trash bin outside the shop's door as she and Terry entered. A few officers looked their way. Their notepads were in hand as they questioned people.

One of them raised a finger to excuse himself and walked over to Madison and Terry. "Detectives? We're working our way through the customers to take their statements. It's slow going."

"Anything standing out yet?" Madison asked, knowing it might be too early to know if a tip they were provided would even factor in to solving the case.

"A few have commented on hearing the gunfire and seeing Officer Weir go down." He paused, his voice shaky. "Someone said she heard tires squealing afterward, like a car was peeling away."

Madison looked at Terry, then back to the officer. "There are tire marks on the road indicating that did likely happen." Madison scanned the patrons of the shop. There were a few people crying, but most of them wore weary expressions as if they were in shock.

Wait until the adrenaline wears off, when what you saw really sinks in.

"Anyone speak to the manager yet?" she asked the officer.

He shook his head. "We were leaving that for you."

Madison and Terry thanked him and then headed for the blonde behind a register. Madison held up her badge. "We need to speak to the manager on duty."

"That would be Kayla. One second." The blonde stepped back and ran straight into a twentysomething redhead. The latter put her hands on the cashier's shoulders to offset their collision.

The blonde walked away and the redhead came to the counter. "I'm Kayla Ferguson. Please follow me." She led them to a small office in the back. The place was barely big enough to accommodate a desk and a chair, let alone the three of them.

Terry closed the door, and Madison made the formal introductions. Partway through them, Kayla's eyes filled with tears, and she looked from Madison to Terry.

"What did you see?" Madison asked, sensing that the woman must have personally witnessed something.

"I was just on a break…" She pinched the tip of her nose, not like she was about to sneeze but as if trying to prevent it from dripping. "I was sitting at a table right beside the window, looking out, mostly in a daze." She blinked rapidly, and a tear fell down a cheek. "I tend to daydream."

"What did you see, Kayla?" Madison pressed gently.

"I saw all of it." Kayla's statement was released on one breath as if in an effort to get it out, to move on.

"Tell us what you saw," Terry said, his voice soft and calming.

"Well, I didn't see the cop pull into the station. At least I wasn't really paying attention at that point. But I did see this black car show up and stop. No one was in front of it, and it was some ways back from the stoplight. It was green, and I remembered thinking he didn't know how to drive. But then I saw a flash of light."

From Kayla's perspective, even though she was facing the driver's side, it was quite conceivable that she'd seen the flash as the burst of gunpowder would have bloomed above the height of the car's roof.

Kayla went on. "I hardly had a chance to wonder what it was when I heard *pop, pop, pop, pop*."

Madison straightened up and leaned forward. "Four shots?"

"Uh-huh."

Winston had said that one hit Weir, one hit the cruiser, and one was stuck in the pump… Even Hines mentioned only three shots. "Are you sure?"

Kayla nodded. "Positive."

Terry walked to a corner of the room, putting his phone to an ear. Madison heard him sharing what Kayla was telling them. He was likely talking to Cynthia to let her know they were missing a bullet.

"The shots happened so close together, but it was like everything was in slow motion, too." Kayla's eyes glazed over. "I saw the cop go down."

"Was there any pause between the shots?" Madison wanted to ensure they weren't looking for a 9mm automatic pistol—one trigger squeeze and a spray of bullets.

"Yeah, I think there was a pause. But not much of one."

"Do you know at what point the cop fell? After which bullet?" Madison clarified.

Kayla pinched her eyes shut. "The third."

Terry hung up his phone and shook his head at Madison, indicating that a fourth bullet hadn't been found yet.

"After you saw the cop get shot," Madison said, although she hated referring to Weir by the label, "what happened?"

"I was under the table by that point," Kayla said, "but I couldn't stop watching. Why is that? Why do people need to watch horrible things as they unfold?"

"It's usually because of shock," Madison explained.

"I mean, I didn't really know what was going on. Or

why."

"Did you hear anyone yelling anything?" Terry asked.

Kayla gave his question consideration and shook her head a few seconds later. "No, I don't think so."

"You're sure?" Madison inquired, wondering if Hines had lied to them or if Kayla just hadn't heard the yell from inside the coffee shop. The latter was entirely possible.

"I'm sure."

"Did you happen to notice if there were other vehicles at station?" Terry asked.

Kayla averted eye contact and wrung her hands. "I did."

"Can you tell us anything about the car? The person?" Madison pressed, hoping for a lead they could use to track down the missing vehicle from pump two.

It was the same thing with every murder investigation: the delicate dance, the questioning, the following of evidence, the piecing together of the clues. But somehow, when it came to hunting down those responsible for killing a fellow cop, it almost felt tedious. She wanted to rush it along even more than she usually did. The pursuit of justice that she lived for was starting to feel like a dangling carrot she'd never reach.

"It was a newer car," Kayla began. "A Chevy SS. I only know because my ex-boyfriend used to have one."

"What color?" Madison asked.

"Cherry red."

"Did you also notice the make or model of the shooter's car?"

"Uh-huh. I don't know the model, but it was a BMW."

Madison's heart was beating fast. "So after the shots fired, is that when this car left?"

"Yeah. And I don't blame them. They left from the

south exit and headed west."

Pump two was located closer to that exit and away from the shooter, so it made sense that the driver would leave that way.

"Did you happen to notice if the driver was a man or woman?"

Kayla shook her head. "No, sorry. The streetlights and the station lights were on, but it was still too dark to see from here. And I hadn't really even noticed them until I saw the car leaving."

"Back to the shooter's car," Terry said, shifting the conversation. "Did you get a look at the people inside?"

"The windows had a really dark tint. Oh! Wait a minute." Kayla pressed a couple of fingertips to her temple as if a headache were setting in. "The driver's window was cracked slightly, and he—or she—was smoking a cigarette. I remember seeing the amber glow. I almost forgot about that. I saw that before...well, you know."

"Assume we don't," Madison said.

The manager swallowed and nodded. "As soon as he stopped the car. Just before the gunfire."

Madison's stomach swirled. Kayla's recounting indicated a driver who was calm enough to smoke a cigarette while his passenger shot a cop. The driver likely had a criminal history. He didn't care who saw them because he feared no one. He wasn't worried about the person from pump two identifying him as he was cocky enough to believe that would never happen. The blatant lack of discretion was the mentality of gangs. But was this a one-off or was something bigger going on? She wondered how Guns and Drugs and the gangs unit were making out with their informants.

Madison clenched her jaw, trying to control the

stewing emotion.

Terry flicked a glance at her and continued taking the lead. "And after the shots were fired, what happened?"

"That other car left, and then the BMW screeched away." Kayla sounded confident and sure.

"In which direction?" he asked.

"South."

That was consistent with what Cynthia had said the tire marks indicated.

Terry nodded. "Did they keep going that way or turn to follow the Chevy SS?"

"Kept going south."

So the shooter wasn't interested in the people in the Chevy. It was, however, also possible that the driver was hopped up on adrenaline or drugs and hadn't even noticed it. It was also entirely possible that the subjects weren't concerned about eyewitnesses.

"Thanks for all your help, Kayla," Terry said. His hand was already on the doorknob, clearly anxious to get this new information to the rest of the team.

Madison held up a finger to her partner. "One last question," she said to the manager.

"Sure."

"Was the driver smoking the entire time?" Maybe the driver flicked the butt, and they'd get a lead through DNA.

Kayla closed her eyes for a few seconds. "Yeah, I think so."

Madison nodded. They might not have a cigarette butt to find, but they were still walking away with more information than they had come in with: the missing car was a Chevy SS and the driver left the station and headed west, the shooter's car was a BMW and the driver was a smoker.

CHAPTER 8

MADISON CALLED STANFORD TO LET him and Sovereign know about the possibility that four bullets had been fired as she and Terry hurried back across the four lanes of traffic to the gas station.

They found Sam still next to Weir's cruiser.

"Have you found the fourth bullet yet?" Madison asked.

Sam shook her head and gestured to Cynthia and Mark, who were combing the west edge of the property near a wood fence. "No bullet yet, and there are no holes to indicate one had traveled through the fence."

What if there wasn't one to find? Or what if it traveled and hit an innocent civilian or the person from pump two? Even if shot, a person's adrenaline could keep them moving depending on where they were struck. Madison knew of a man who had taken a bullet to the heart and kept coming at the officer. Sadly, it took the officer firing another round to stop the threat.

She pulled out her cell phone and dialed Winston. She filled him in on the fact that they were looking for a black BMW and a cherry-red Chevy SS, and from there she got to the real reason for her call. "I need you to contact the hospitals and clinics in Stiles, see if anyone's come in with a single GSW this morning."

"They're always reported," Winston stated.

Always... That word left a lot of room for disappointment.

"How are the warrants coming along for the security tapes from the gas station and the video from the city?" she asked.

"The DA just got in within the hour, Knight. He's sorting it all out now."

Amos Buchanan didn't seem the type to busy his hands doing something an ADA could take care of, but a high-profile case like this probably had his personal interest from a political standpoint.

"Keep me updated." Now she was telling him to communicate with her? Their roles had truly reversed. Usually she would run forward in a case without discussing each step in the investigation with him. It was the main source of their contention.

"Will do," he said and then hung up abruptly.

She held her phone toward Terry. "The DA's working on the warrants for the security footage."

"Buchanan himself?" Terry asked incredulously.

"Yep."

Terry pointed to her phone. "You asked Winston to have the hospitals watch for gunshot wounds? You think that the missing bullet found its way into the person at pump two?"

She nodded. "Either that or their vehicle." She turned toward Jennifer, who was searching the ground near pump three. "Was there any blood found around pump two?"

Cynthia joined them and answered before Jennifer had the chance. "We looked there immediately after I got off the phone with you."

"Not even a drop?" Madison asked.

Her friend shook her head. "Nothing. *If* there was a fourth bullet and it struck the person from pump two, there's nothing here to confirm it. It's possible it entered the vehicle itself."

Madison nodded as Mark, the only man on Cynthia's team, came over, shaking his head. "There's nothing to indicate a bullet went that way—" he pointed back toward the fence on the west side of the property "—or that way." This time he stabbed a finger toward the north.

"Sadly, I think we've got everything the scene has to offer in terms of evidence," Cynthia said.

Heat blanketed Madison's earlobes and her chest tightened. "You owe it to—"

Cynthia held up her hand to stave off Madison. "I know, Maddy."

"Yeah," Madison said on a sigh. "I know you know." She didn't verbalize the apology, but it was no doubt clear in her voice.

Cynthia's entire team was now standing around, and Madison wished they'd get back to processing the evidence. And that Sam would get to the lab to examine the bullets closer and, hopefully, get them the gun manufacturer.

"There's also some tough news you're probably not aware of…" Cynthia's voice tapered off at the end, tinged with sadness.

Madison slid her eyes from Jennifer to Cynthia. Based on the sorrow in her friend's gaze, she wasn't sure she wanted to know the *tough news*. Hadn't there already been enough of that?

"We found this on Barry's passenger seat." Cynthia directed Mark to go to the evidence box, which was still near pump eight. He jogged back to them with a bag in his hand and passed it to Madison.

She peered into the bag to find a card with roses on the front and the words, *To a special wife*.

"What's on the inside?" Madison asked, trembling. Barry was talking from beyond the grave...

"His handwriting. He wrote that he loved her and thanked her for being such a good mother to their girls. He went on to say that Emily was going to have the best birthday ever."

Madison glanced at Terry, then back to Cynthia. "When's her—"

"Tomorrow," Cynthia interrupted.

How could Madison not have known that when she claimed to know Barry and his family?

The six of them passed odd glances at each other in silence, all seemingly lost in their own thoughts. Or at least Madison was...

Barry figured things were going great and then *boom*! One second here, the next...

She swallowed the emotion.

"Emily... Is she the youngest?" Terry asked.

"Yeah." Madison's heart was breaking for the girl.

"I wonder what he meant when saying Emily was going to have the best birthday ever," Terry added.

Cynthia shrugged. "Don't know. I'm thinking he probably found the perfect gift for her. What that meant for Emily specifically, I wouldn't know."

"All right, well, we can't just stand around here feeling sad. We've got a killer to catch." Madison lifted her chin. What she really meant was that she couldn't handle dwelling on Barry's death any longer. All cops serve to protect their communities. They expect that if they go down in the line of duty, it will be during a confrontation with a perp. But Barry was simply pumping gas. It was tragic and senseless.

"You're right." Cynthia turned to her team. "Let's get back to it. Do another sweep of the area. Sam, why don't you get a ride back to the lab now and start analyzing those bullets?"

"Wait," Madison said, and the three stopped in their steps. "Sam, I know I asked this already and you said you were working on it, but do you know which of the bullets struck Barry?" They hadn't yet shared with Sam that Kayla had testified to it being the third bullet.

"The bullets were fired from the street and at the appropriate level for someone sitting in a sedan. Based on where Weir was standing, and taking the blood pattern into effect—" Sam shifted her eyes to Jennifer, silently crediting her colleague with this conclusion "— the location of the bullet in the pump indicates Weir was already down, otherwise it would have hit him in the head. The round lodged in the cruiser's C-pillar. That's the panel between the rear door and the back window, and it was at the same height as where Weir was struck under the arm. I'd say that the first bullet hit the car, the second Weir, the third the pump. But now that you've brought up the possibility of a fourth bullet, it's harder to say for sure since I can't exactly triangulate without knowing what happened to said fourth bullet."

"The eyewitness from the Bean Counter said that she saw Weir go down after the third shot," Madison said. "But she also said that the rounds were fired in quick succession."

Sam frowned. "Not sure what to say to that right now."

Madison turned to Cynthia and didn't care if she

sounded repetitive. "It would be really helpful to know the gun type we're looking for."

Cynthia nudged her head toward Sam to have Madison look at her for the answer.

"I should know that soon."

CHAPTER 9

PATIENCE IS A VIRTUE, just not one Madison possessed. Even "expedited" warrants weren't coming fast enough for her liking.

She and Terry were in a department sedan heading north on Highbury Street. "Hope you don't mind, but I'm going to stop by Troy's for a second and pick up Hershey. I'd like to take him to the kennel." Madison took the first turn necessary to go to Troy's house.

Who knew what their schedule would be for the next while? She'd periodically board Hershey at Canine Country Retreat Boarding while she was working so he could play with other dogs and not be alone during the day. Hopefully, they'd have space for him on this short of notice.

"Aw, Hershey. I haven't seen him in a bit."

Terry was the one who had gifted the chocolate Lab to her for Christmas a couple of years back. And despite her initial resistance, she'd fallen for the soft fur, the velvet ears, and the loving brown eyes. At the time, though, Madison could have killed Terry for getting him without speaking to her first. They had talked about his beagles on enough occasions that he should have known how she felt about dogs. But Terry had been insistent, saying that he wanted Madison to have someone to go home to every night, and had promised that the chocolate Lab would become family. She'd never told him that he'd been right, of course. Why let something like that go to his head?

Terry looked over at her from the passenger seat. "So Hershey's at Troy's? Huh." He paused briefly. "So when are you moving in with the guy?"

"Hush it."

"Well, it's a fair question. You sleep there a lot, don't you? And you're picking up Hershey there. I just figured…"

"Figure again." She narrowed her eyes at him and then looked back at the road. She wasn't even going to ask her partner how he knew she was spending most nights at Troy's.

"Have you guys talked about getting married?"

Madison choked on her saliva, starting a coughing fit as her eyes began to water. The thought had entered her head *on occasion*, but no one else needed to know that. After a few seconds, she managed to get out a single word. "Marriage?"

"Ah, look at you. You're getting all emotional. That's what women—"

She punched him in the shoulder—a tough maneuver while driving, but she made it work.

"Hey!" He rubbed his arm, at first pouting and then smiling. The latter expression didn't last long, though. It was as if Barry's death swept in to fall like a weight between them.

She pulled into Troy's driveway.

His house was a Craftsman-style bungalow with olive-green siding and thick wooden columns supporting a front overhang. A picture window accented each side of the entry, and two dormers projected from the roof above those. A double-wide stamped concrete path cut through the front lawn and led to the door.

She unclipped her seat belt. "You stay right there." The last thing she wanted was for him to see all of Hershey's toys in the living room.

"Sure."

Madison keyed in the four-digit code to open the key lock box, retrieved the spare house key, and let herself in. She led Hershey into the backyard and waited for him to do his business. After a few minutes, she was picking up Hershey's steaming gift and tossing it into a black garbage can kept there for this specific purpose.

Maybe Terry was right about her relationship with Troy. But what was going on with her? She used to be so strong and independent.

But lonely.

She had to accept that was the truth. Before Troy, she had been all about the job. She still was, but now she had someone to talk to at the end of the day. She justified her weakness by reasoning that if she became engaged, that was one thing; setting a date and following through was another.

Thinking of Troy, she pulled out her phone and texted him to let him know she was at his house to pick up Hershey. She'd just hit SEND when her phone rang.

It was her younger sister, Chelsea, although in their mother's eyes Chelsea was deemed more mature than Madison. After all, she had the husband and three daughters. The first strike against Madison was her career choice. Second was that Madison's grandmother left Madison everything when she'd passed. And the third was that Madison wasn't married with kids.

She was tempted to ignore the call because of the effort

it would take to convince her sister that she was fine and safe. To top it off, Chelsea would probably want Madison to call their mother. But at least it wasn't her mother calling, and maybe Madison could convince Chelsea to pass along the message that she was fine.

"Hey, Chels," Madison answered.

"I heard it on the news. A cop was killed! Madison, tell me you're okay. Did you know him? What happened?" Chelsea was talking even faster than she normally did.

"I'm fine. Calm—"

"Don't tell me to calm down. One day that could be you. Then what? What would I do then? What about Mom? Dad? Your nieces?"

"Please." Usually her sister was levelheaded and respectful of Madison's career choice. She oftentimes even served as referee between Madison and their mother.

Madison wanted to say something reassuring to her sister, but the words were failing her.

"What happened? He was shot filling his gas tank? That's what they're saying on the news."

"Yeah." Madison couldn't help the sadness that crept in with that admission.

It wasn't missed by her sister. "Oh… I'm so sorry, Maddy. You did know him, didn't you?"

Madison nodded as if Chelsea could see her.

"Maddy?"

"Yeah… Both Troy and I were rather close to the family. He seems to be having an especially hard time with it."

"Sorry, sis…"

There was a pause on the line, and it had Madison's eyes filling with tears. She cleared her throat. "I better get going."

"Yeah, of course. But…please be safe."

"I will be." Madison hung up, wiping her eyes and sniffling. She remembered then that she'd meant to ask Chelsea to pass along a message to their parents, but shook aside the passing thought. If they were worried about her, they'd call her. "Come on, buddy," she said to Hershey. "Time to go."

Any other time, she might have found some humor in what she had said given what Hershey had just done, but she led him somberly through the house to the front door, where she leashed him up. "You're going to go see the girls."

Sometimes moments like this would make her realize just how much she had changed. For starting off with no desire for a dog to talking to him as if he were a person… And now the employees at the kennel were "the girls."

She shook her head. Before Hershey, she thought dog lovers went a tad overboard, especially those who referred to their pets as children. What really used to get her was when people called their dogs people names, such as Max, Lexy, Todd, Chelsea… Her sister's name was Chelsea. It was hard to imagine a four-legged animal responding to the same name. But since Hershey had wormed his way into her heart, she now understood the attachment, the bond between animal and owner. She was even to the point where she didn't like to refer to herself as Hershey's *owner*. She was his *person*. Yeah, that's what she was. Although a lot of days she'd catch herself referring to herself as "Mommy."

She locked up Troy's place, replacing the key to the lock box, and opened the back door of the sedan. Hershey jumped in without issue. He sat behind Terry, sniffing at the air, and stretched out his neck to reach her partner.

His pink slip of a tongue came out and got Terry from the base of his neck up to his ear.

Madison couldn't help but smile at that. She closed the rear door and then got back behind the wheel. She looked over at Terry to find him facing the backseat, rubbing Hershey's head and mumbling words that sounded an awful lot like baby talk.

"He's getting big," Terry said, returning to adult English.

"Tell me about it." Before she'd starting sleeping at Troy's so much, she'd been considering buying a king-size bed, but with Troy's one rule being that Hershey slept on the floor, space was no longer an issue.

Terry stopped petting Hershey and turned around to face forward. "Troy's got quite a nice place. He probably has a fenced backyard, too. It's a good neighborhood to raise a—"

Images flashed through her mind of her in a wedding gown standing at an altar, then a montage of photos of her and Troy smiling in some exotic location. Their honeymoon? And then her with a round—

She slammed on the brakes.

"Are you trying to kill us?" Terry rubbed the back of his head where it had hit the headrest.

"We need to talk." She put the car in park. They were still in Troy's drive. The back end of the sedan was probably hanging over the road, but oh well. "You're like a brother to me, but so help me, if you say one more thing about me and—"

"It's obviously a sore subject. You want him to propose and he hasn't, is that it?"

"Terry." Her tone cautioned him against saying any more.

He held up his hands. "Sorry. Not another word." His statement hung in the air. "I'm just trying to get my mind off what happened to Barry." He held her gaze for a while longer before turning to face out the windshield.

"Which is next to impossible," she said.

Terry nodded. "It feels like we're living in a nightmare."

"Ain't that the truth."

CHAPTER 10

HERSHEY WAS ALL SET AT the kennel when Madison had gotten the call that Hines was already home from the hospital. She and Terry were headed there now and were hoping to get some of the inconsistences of her story sorted out. Specifically, the squealing tires and the number of shots fired.

"Do you think we should dig further into her background before we go to her place? An officer has an eye on her," Terry said from the passenger seat.

"Gardener told us the basics. That should be enough for now at least."

She spotted the police cruiser as soon as she turned onto Hines's street. It was parked in front of a single-story brick house. Iron railings lined the steps to the door and the square landing. A narrow paved drive—barely wide enough for a car—led to a shed.

Madison parked behind the cruiser, and she and Terry walked up to the door. Before Madison even reached the doorbell, the door swung open.

"What do you want?" Hines snapped. She crossed her arms.

The young woman who had been frightened and sad at the crime scene was different now. She was aggravated, inconvenienced, and clearly not open to conversation based on everything from her wording and tone of voice to her closed body language.

"We need to come in and ask more questions." Madison wasn't going to wait for an invitation and stepped past the girl into the home.

Hines sighed and moved over to give Madison the space to get by. "I told everything to the officers at Rico's."

The stress of fainting had left a mark on the woman's body. Her eyes were red and puffy, her complexion pale. And while Madison felt for Hines, she had to stay focused.

"They hadn't finished taking your statement before we showed up," Madison pointed out. "And then you passed out."

"Uh-huh, and the doctor said it was brought on from *extreme stress*. I saw a man *get shot*…" The last two words came out through clenched teeth. "Killed…right in front of me."

Madison couldn't allow herself to get pulled into Hines's emotional state. "Let's sit down."

The living room was to the left of the entrance, and Madison helped herself to a spot on the sofa. Terry opted to sit next to Madison while Hines chose a chair across from them.

"I should be in bed sleeping. That's what the doctor suggested." Hines pulled her legs up under her.

"How many shots did you hear fired this morning?" Madison asked, delving right into things.

"Three," Hines huffed out, apparently exasperated from needing to repeat her statement.

"Will you just close your eyes for me for a second?" Madison asked. Victims of traumatic situations—directly involved or witnesses—oftentimes had images that would replay in their heads over and over. Madison was hoping to tap into Hines's.

"Okayyyyy… Why?"

Terry looked over at Madison, but she remained steadfast. "I want you to put yourself back there and—"

"You want me to relive all of this again?" Hines's pitch took on a high octave, and her eyes widened. "I just want to forget all of it."

It took all of Madison's self-control not to respond in haste. *She* wanted to forget? Wow, they should stop asking her questions right now. If only forgetting was an option, a solution to reverse time and consequence. And really, at the end of the day, how did Barry's death truly impact her life? He was just a customer to her. Meanwhile, Barry's family didn't have the option to *forget all of it*.

"How well did you know the officer who was shot?" Madison asked, somehow managing to detach further and pace her words.

"I didn't really. He was married, though, wasn't he?" She added the last part as if an afterthought, and her face seemed to pale even more. "I remember him talking about his wife. He said something the one day about their anniversary coming up and how he wanted to make it special." She wasn't looking at Madison or Terry; her eyes were sort of drifting about the room.

"Did he regularly fill his cruiser at Rico's?" No one from the Stiles PD accounting department had gotten back to them on that yet.

"He did," Hines said with a nod.

"At the same time of day? About five in the morning?" Terry asked.

"Not always. Sometimes at night."

"You normally work the midnight shift?" Terry

sounded concerned.

Fury licked Hines's eyes. "Are you implying that a woman can't take care of herself at that time of night?"

Terry shook his head. "That's not what I meant at all."

His response and calm demeanor doused her anger, and she shrugged. "It pays better."

Madison let a few seconds pass in silence and then broached the subject of the shots again. "Will you please close your eyes?"

"Fine," Hines complied. With her eyelids closed, they appeared more purple than red. She really did need her rest. Hopefully, they could get their answers quickly.

"How many times did you hear the gun fire?" Madison asked.

"One, two." Tears streaked down her cheeks, and she wiped them with her palm. "Three..." Her brow compressed. "Four." Her eyes shot open.

"Four?" Madison's heart beat faster, knowing this supported Kayla's statement.

"Yes. It was four." Hines's eyes drifted to Terry. "I'm not sure how I missed that."

"It would have been a traumatic thing to witness," Terry offered, his voice comforting.

"It was." Hines fell quiet for a few seconds. "And I didn't realize how loud guns were before..."

"Do you know when the officer fell to the ground?" Terry asked.

Hines looked at him. "I don't know. I was on the floor after the first shot."

"Did the shooter yell at him and then fire right away?" Madison asked.

"No." Hines's eyes widened. "He yelled— Well, I thought it was just before he fired, but it all happened

so fast. He might have even yelled out as he fired. I don't
know…"

Hines didn't sound certain, but if the shooter didn't
yell *before* firing, it would explain why Barry hadn't hit
his panic button sooner. But if the gun fired at the same
time as the man yelled, Madison found it hard to accept
that Hines heard him say anything. It seemed most
plausible that the shooter yelled and quickly fired. Hines's
recollection could be off due to stress.

"You're certain that the shooter yelled out, though?"
Madison asked. "Even though the gunfire was so loud?"

"Yes." Hines clenched her teeth. "He said, 'Die, cop.'"

"Was there anything that stood out to you about
the voice? Anything that made it unique?" Terry
asked. He nodded at Madison when she looked at him,
acknowledging that the two of them had discussed this
aspect with Gardener at the gas station. He obviously
wanted to hear it firsthand.

Hines shook her head. "Nothing. Just that it was a
man's."

"How old?" Terry kept the questions rolling.

"I wouldn't know. I didn't see him."

Terry's jaw tightened. He flicked a sideway glance
to Madison. "Just in general, then. Did his voice sound
older, younger?"

"He sounded young, I guess."

"Adult or teen?"

Hines's face contorted, taking on sharp lines, and she
pressed her fingertips to her brows. "I'm not sure. Maybe
a teenager? Maybe in his early twenties?"

Street gangs recruited young men, and usually required
that they prove themselves with some sort of criminal
act, most often a violent one. Killing a cop, sadly, would

buy them a lot of respect on the streets.

"You're sure it was a younger man?" Madison pressed.

"Pretty sure, yeah."

Madison jumped to her feet and rushed to the front door. She heard Terry tell Hines that they'd be in touch again soon, and then his steps pounded after Madison. She knew they hadn't broached the subject of the missing person from pump two or asked if Hines had heard squealing tires, but all that seemed inconsequential in light of what Hines had just given them.

Madison pulled her cell and dialed Winston. "Sarge," she said when he answered, "I think Weir was targeted for a gang-initiation ritual."

CHAPTER 11

SERGEANT WINSTON AND SOME OTHER detectives, including Sovereign and Stanford, were already in the squad room when Madison and Terry arrived. The district attorney, Amos Buchanan, was there, too. Winston must have invited him to the briefing. Buchanan may have had the appearance of a grandfather figure with his gray hair, ruddy cheeks, toothy smile, and deeply set dimples, but he was definitely a man who was all business.

Troy was also in the room, looking like a caged animal planning his escape. He wasn't making eye contact with her, but that didn't stop her from walking over to him.

"Hey," was all he said when she got closer to him.

"Hi," she said with a frown. Grief really had a way of transforming loved ones into strangers. She wanted him to know she was there for him, but she sensed she had to watch how she communicated that. She wanted to take his hand or touch his arm, but she couldn't do that there.

"How are you making out with Barry's reports?" she asked instead. She could have smacked herself in the forehead, it was so cold and impersonal. So *safe*.

Troy jutted his head toward Winston. "I'm going to update everyone all at once. Not that there's anything to offer, really." Disappointment and hopelessness coated each of his words.

She wished she could hug him and take his pain away. She had to focus on the business aspect of the investigation again, though, to get her mind off the emotional toll this was all taking. "Where's Andrea?"

"From what I know, she's over with Joni—helping her, sorting out arrangements." His voice was gruff. It was obvious he was taking the loss of Barry very hard, but something told her they had been closer than she'd realized.

"What aren't you telling me?" The question came out of its own volition.

Troy looked away, his jaw stiffened. "It's not the time."

"It's not the—" His attitude was making her earlobes heat with anger. She was just showing concern and he was shutting her out. Maybe she'd been a fool to think she might have actually found the one. But as she thought it, she began to cool. It could have been Troy who'd lost his life. Maybe instead of abandoning a relationship at the first sign of a hull breach, there was something to be said for hanging on—even if she went down with the ship.

"Knight." Winston was signaling for her to come over to him.

She flicked a quick look at Troy before complying with the sergeant's request.

"Knight has some news," Winston announced to those in the room. "And so does Marsh."

Madison glanced at the detective from the guns and drugs unit, who formerly had been with Gangs.

"You go first, Knight," Winston went on as a means of preamble.

"Terry and I just got back from speaking with the eyewitness from the gas station, Janet Hines," Madison began. "She's confirmed that the shooter's voice belonged to a young male. That, combined with what the voice shouted, leads me to believe there's a gang out there making new members shoot a cop in order to get in with them."

There were a few seconds of silence, followed by some whispering.

She scanned the room and met Sovereign's gaze.

"But there haven't been any other shootings involving an officer in this area," he said.

"There's always a first," she defended.

"My CI has come through for us," Marsh jumped in. He apparently wasn't going to wait any longer to share his update. He stepped toward Winston, who moved back to let him take the floor.

The door opened then, and Andrea entered. She tucked herself to the side of the room near her brother, but Troy didn't acknowledge her. Andrea bobbed her head at Madison, and Madison reciprocated. Even though Andrea was the police chief, Madison found it hard to think of the woman as anything other than *Andrea*. It might have had something to do with the fact that she was sleeping with Andrea's brother.

Her hair, which was normally styled flawlessly, had a few wandering strands. She was wearing makeup, but if she had put on lipstick, it was gone now. Andrea Fletcher wasn't a girlie girl, but she took pride in her appearance. Madison couldn't remember ever seeing her without lipstick, not even on a Sunday morning when Madison and Troy went to her house for brunch.

Marsh clasped his hands. "The word on the street is that a gang *is* claiming responsibility for the shooting."

Madison's stomach tightened. It was one thing to lean toward Barry's murder being the work of a gang but another to hear it come back at her.

"Now, we don't know which one. It's rumor at this point. And whether Weir was targeted specifically or this was just a gang initiation can't be confirmed yet."

"Is your informant in with a gang?" Madison asked.

Marsh nodded. "The Hellions."

Madison recognized the name. They were one of the larger gangs in the city with at least a hundred members. Street gangs tended to fashion themselves after the Crips and the Bloods, the original LA gangs. The Hellions, however, were organized somewhere between a hierarchy and the mafia, with a head guy and drug runners.

Marsh went on. "My informant has made it clear that the act is garnering a lot of talk and respect on the streets and within the Hellions."

"We can't afford to just wait around for another cop to be shot. If we don't put a stop to this, we'll have copycats." Troy's voice was loud as it bounced off the walls of the room.

Andrea put a hand on his arm briefly, but he shrugged her off and headed to where Winston stood, and reached him in a few long strides.

Buchanan remained poker-faced, seeming to take everything in.

"Other detectives are still on the streets trying to see where they can get with their informants," Marsh stated calmly.

"And we're standing around talking," Troy blurted out.

"I recommend that you stand down," Winston warned.

The two men were locked in eye contact, but they may as well have been rams locking horns. Which one would weaken his position first?

"The longer we stand around, wait it out, we're risking

lives." Troy's gruffness had softened somewhat. "I say that we start digging into the history of the Hellions."

Winston squinted. "And why's that?"

Troy pointed toward Marsh. "His informant heard this 'rumor'"—he attributed air quotes to the word—"but none of the other detectives have gleaned this from their informants? I think it's likely that the shooter is part of the Hellions gang."

Winston gave a cursory glance over at Buchanan, who shook his head before speaking. "We don't have enough to—"

"Let my team get started on the paperwork," Troy interrupted. "We'll work with the gangs unit. They'll likely be able to provide an overview of the Hellions' hierarchy and a layout of their hideout. We'll pull full backgrounds on the men at the top. After that, we'll get started on the preliminary operation plan."

Winston rubbed his chin and slid his jaw askew. "Hold off on that for a bit."

"What are we waiting for?" Madison had never seen Troy in such a hurry to rush into something. "We'd want to strike at midnight."

Madison was familiar with the fact that when a search was being executed after ten at night, it required a special warrant. Standard warrants permitted search and seizure during the hours of seven in the morning until ten at night. With the target being a gang hideout, acting later at night would mean more gang members would be there.

"Tonight? Don't you think that's rushing things along?" Winston balked. "More than likely we'll have enough information to make a move *tomorrow*, not today."

"Tomorrow?" Troy's temper was rising again; she could hear it in his voice.

Winston made eye contact with him again and remained silent for a few seconds. "Have you or Benson found anything that stood out in Weir's reports from his final shift?"

Troy looked away from the sergeant, and Benson answered. "No one stands out as having strong motivation to go after Weir. And no one appears to be connected with any of the local gangs, either."

Winston slid a glance to Troy. "Keep looking."

Troy appeared as if he were going to explode as red touched his cheeks.

"Now, if there's not anything else…" Winston looked over the room. No one held up a hand or started to say anything. "Get out there, and let's find the bastards who did this."

Chairs scraped against the floor as the detectives got up to leave. Troy beelined for the door. She'd never seen him lose his temper quite like that before. She knew he had one, but he was usually better at keeping it under control. She just wished that he'd open up to her and let her be there for him right now. Didn't talking about one's feelings go part and parcel with the words *I love you*?

Terry came up to her as she was almost to the door. "Just give me a minute," she said.

"Sure."

She left the room, looking down the hall to see if she could catch Troy, but he wasn't there.

"What's going on?" Terry said, coming up behind her.

She continued silently staring down the corridor. Her heart was beating fast, and it felt like it was breaking.

"Maddy?" The voice behind her belonged to Andrea this time.

"Yeah?" Madison turned around to face Troy's sister.

Andrea was in the doorway of the squad room and crooked a finger for Madison to go inside with her.

"One minute, Terry." Madison entered and said, "What's up?" Nonchalant, chummy, indifferent. Anything to hide her hurt over Troy.

"Losing Barry's been really hard on him," Andrea stated softly, as if she'd read Madison's mind—and the situation—perfectly.

"I've noticed." Madison rubbed her arms. Usually she was comfortable with Andrea, but given the topic of their conversation… "He's not good at discussing his feelings, is he?"

"That's an understatement." Andrea smirked, trying to add some levity to the conversation.

"I know that he was friends with Barry, but so was I and—"

Andrea's eyes teared, and she shook her head. "He hasn't told you."

"Told me what?"

"I was afraid of this."

Coolness blanketed the back of Madison's neck. "What?"

"Troy and Barry have been friends since childhood— they went to the same college, went through the academy together, were each other's best man at their weddings."

Madison sought out a wall for support and leaned against it. Troy taking Barry's death so hard was making more sense now.

"He's even the godfather to Barry's girls," Andrea continued.

Madison tried to ride out the wave of emotion as it washed over her. Her heart ached, not so much for her as it did for Troy. Though she wouldn't claim that it didn't hurt that he'd kept so much from her.

"Just give him a little space…but please don't give up on him. I know men can be a pain in the ass with all the macho we-don't-talk-about-our-feelings shit."

Madison forced a small smile. "Troy said you've been over at Joni's helping her? How is she?"

"She's having a rough time, as to be expected. I ended up seeing the girls, too, and I don't really think it's hit them yet."

"And Emily has her birthday tomorrow."

Andrea nodded and blew out a deep breath. "I'd suggest doing something for her, but they were going to have a party for her and Joni had us cancel it."

Madison's heart went out to little Emily. It would be her first birthday without her father. And fathers held a special place in their daughter's lives. Madison loved how her own father would listen and not jump to conclusions the way her mother did.

Maybe she should just pick up the phone and call her parents. She might even get lucky and her dad would answer. Of course, it was still best to prepare for the conversation she'd always have with her mother, which circled around to when she was going to settle down and leave her job.

"What if we just do something very low-key for her? Joni said she loved ponies," Andrea suggested.

Madison took a few steps toward her. "What are you thinking?"

Andrea shrugged her shoulders. "We could just get her a couple gifts and have them dropped off to the house. That way she knows people are thinking of her and that she's not alone. That she still matters."

Madison was nodding. "I think that's a terrific idea."

"Both Joni's and Barry's parents are staying at the house," Andrea said. "I waited until they all arrived before I left."

That brought up another sad spot for Madison—the fact that Barry's parents had lost their son. She didn't need to have children to know it wasn't right when they went first.

TOMORROW? A cop was already dead, and someone on the streets was claiming responsibility, quite possibly someone right inside the Hellions. Were they waiting for someone else to get shot before they took action?

Troy was pacing the halls of the station, wandering one direction, then backtracking. If someone saw him, they'd think he'd lost his mind. And in a way, he had. It was then that he heard footsteps coming toward him. He found himself hoping it wasn't Madison.

He took a few deep breaths, prepping himself to face a barrage of questions. And if he heard *How are you doing?* one more time, he might really lose his temper.

Barry had been dead for only a few hours. How exactly could anyone just shake that off?

"It got pretty heated in there." His sister caught up to him and jacked a thumb over her shoulder toward the squad room, even though he was already around the corner and down another hallway.

"Don't start."

"Don't start what exactly, Troy?" Andrea was resigning to her eldest sister voice, the one that rang through with an air of maturity and sense of being in charge.

"Anything, all right?" He turned his back on her and started to walk away.

"Have you even been over to see Joni and the girls

yet?"

He stopped walking and took a deep breath. He didn't bother to face her. "Don't mother me, Andrea."

"You can't make this better. You can't bring him back."

Anger swelled in his chest and he was on the verge of tears, and he freaking hated it. This unraveling person he was becoming wasn't who he really was. He was always put together. Reserved. In control. He took another breath and faced his sister. Her eyes were full of tears, and her facial features softened under his gaze.

Damn it! He didn't need her pity. He'd be fine…on his own.

"Maybe you should sit this investigation out," she said.

"Is that your sisterly advice?"

She lifted her chin, and her gaze flicked away.

"Andrea, don't do this." A heaviness sat on his chest, squeezing his heart and lungs as if they were in a vise.

"As the police chief, I have to look at the larger picture. Your emotional state isn't the most conducive—"

"Fu—" He pointed a finger in her face and dropped it. "You know what? Do whatever the hell you have to. But you know that I'm the best person to have on this case. I won't stop until Barry's killer is behind bars."

Silence stretched out between them. She was scanning his eyes, trying to read them.

"I'm probably making a big mistake here," she started, pausing only to give him further scrutiny.

He wasn't going to say another word. Why give her fodder? He was at her mercy. All he knew was if he tried to justify his abilities any more he'd officially be off the case. Still, it was hard to resist saying anything. He was about to say her name, ignore his gut telling him to keep quiet and plead his case, when she spoke.

"I'll let you stay on the case." Her gaze was laser-focused on him. "But you have to promise me something."

He felt like his lungs could expand again. "Anything."

"If you find it's too much—" she put her hand up to stave off his defensiveness "—you promise to remove yourself from the investigation."

He shook his head. "That's not going to happen."

Her eyebrows shot downward.

"As in, I've got this. And I pro—"

Another officer walked past them. Once he was out of earshot, Andrea put a hand on Troy's shoulder and said, "Okay, but get over to see Joni."

His heart sank in his chest. What was he supposed to say to Joni? Pile on more condolences, bury her so deep that she choked on the inevitable truth that her husband was gone?

"I'm sure she'd love to see you. Okay?"

Andrea was trying to make him accountable, but he had so much to do, didn't he? He should at least get started with his men on gathering intel on the Hellions and pulling prior criminal history.

"Troy?"

His thoughts had gotten so carried away with the job, he'd almost forgotten her question. He met her eyes. "You've given me a second chance, and I'm not going to blow it."

She tilted her head. "So when are you going to go over to see her?"

"There's a lot to do." Troy made a show of looking at his watch. "And time's moving quickly. I'm of better use to Joni here—finding her husband's killer."

I'm not ready to be strong for her yet...

"All right, fine." She sighed.

Fine was never fine for a woman, but he was just going to pretend it was and run with it. He waved to her as he headed for his desk.

CHAPTER 12

WHILE THEY WERE WAITING FOR the camera footage to come in, Madison and Terry pulled the backgrounds for Janet Hines, Melody Ford, and Rico Beck.

Janet Hines's record was just as Gardener had said; nothing of interest stood out. No criminal record, and she was single. Add this to how shaken up she was over what had happened and it released Madison's suspicions of Hines's involvement.

Ford's background was clean, too, but showed she was married. Her husband's record was also clean.

"Rico Beck, owner of the gas station, is fifty-three," Terry read to her from his computer monitor. "No prior offenses. He's married and has one kid. Lives in the north end of the city."

"What about Rico's wife?" Madison asked.

"One minute." Terry clicked his mouse a few times. "Nancy Beck was charged with reckless driving when she was in her late teens. Nothing else stands out about her."

"How old is their kid?" Madison's mind was now on gangs and how they tended to attract youths searching for a sense of belonging and family. She didn't know what home life was like for the Becks yet, but if they had teenagers, she'd be finding that out.

"Their son, Scott, is fourteen."

"He's at a vulnerable age."

Terry met her eyes, assessing her. "Are you wondering if this kid is involved somehow?"

She shrugged. "I think it's worth visiting the Beck family and talking to him. I know that Hines said Barry filled up at different times during his shift, but she also mentioned he was often there in the morning. If the kid is involved with a gang, he could have offered up that information. Of course, we'd have to prove that he even knew when Barry would be there."

Terry exhaled audibly. "Orchestrating the shooting of a cop at his own dad's gas station? Bold."

"Or smart. He might think he'd be the least likely suspect," she considered aloud. "We need to find out where he was early this morning."

"My Scott's a good boy, and besides, he's not home right now." Nancy Beck crossed her arms, standing in her doorway as if she were a heavyweight bouncer when she likely only weighed a hundred pounds. Her blond pixie cut would make people perceive her as cute and timid, but the scowl on her face would prove first impressions wrong.

All they'd asked was if they could speak to her son and Nancy had bristled.

"How long has he been gone?" Madison asked.

Nancy narrowed her eyes. "An hour, tops. He's out with a friend, if you must know."

"All right, and where was he at five this morning?"

"He's a fourteen-year-old boy. Where do you think he was?"

Madison held her ground. "I don't know. That's why I asked."

Through gritted teeth, Nancy said, "He was in bed sleeping. Oh...now I'm getting it." Nancy paled. "You think my son was involved with the shooting?" She tightened her crossed arms. "Nope, there is no way."

"Going back to five this morning... You can verify that he was in his room at that time?" Madison cocked her head. She wasn't going to take grief from anyone on any given day on any case, let alone this one.

Nancy puffed her cheeks out as she exhaled. "Of course not, but I know—"

"How?"

"I just do, all right."

"So there is no way that Scott could have climbed out a window in his room?" Madison looked past Nancy into the house, implying that she wanted inside.

Nancy's gaze was fiery as she stepped to the side to let Madison and Terry in. "Living room is on the left. Sit wherever you'd like."

Madison and Terry both took a seat on a sofa. The home was what one would expect of a family with a teenager—clean but definitely lived in. There were a few pairs of socks on the floor, a couple of dirty glasses around the room, and an assortment of magazines on an end table.

Nancy came into the room behind them but remained standing. "I'm sorry about what happened to that cop," she said, her earlier bark gone. "But my son would never be involved with something like that." She licked her lips.

"His name was Officer Barry Weir," Madison said. "He's left behind three daughters and a wife." Since this information had already hit the media, she wasn't disclosing anything confidential.

"It's sad, and I feel for them, I really do. I just know

Scott. He's a good kid," Nancy repeated in maternal defense.

"Does he do well in school?" Terry asked.

"He's a teenage boy. He's skipped a few classes here and there, but he's a good kid."

"As you said." Madison let her eyes trace over Nancy. "Where did he go when he skipped school?" Madison realized that even if the kid did tell his mother, it could just as easily be a lie.

"He's friends with these two…" Nancy jutted out her chin. "I don't really care for either kids' parents."

"The parents of both kids?" Madison asked to clarify.

"Yeah. They work part-time jobs, but it seems like they are looking for employment all the time. If you can believe it, the one boy's father even tried to use the relationship Scott had with his son to get a job at the gas station."

Trying to put food on the table? Yes, absolutely detestable…

Based on the rings that adorned Nancy's fingers and the size of the house, the Becks were used to the finer things and probably saw themselves as having higher standards than other people. Or rather, *above* other people.

"Where does Scott go when he ditches class?" Madison repeated her question, not giving any attention to what Nancy was going on about.

Nancy's jaw sprung open. Shut. Her eyes narrowed. Apparently she wanted Madison to weigh in on the parents of her son's friends. Madison wasn't getting pulled into it. "They like to go to the mall. Innocent kid stuff. Not shooting cops."

"And these friends of Scott's, were they new in his

life?" Madison inquired.

"No, they've been friends since preschool."

Madison nodded.

"And how are his grades?" Terry asked, circling back to his first question. Terry approached the inquiry in a calm, interested manner, as if they were just two parents talking. There was nothing confrontational about his tone.

"He does fine. Bs and Cs."

"Has Scott ever smoked or taken drugs that you know of?" Madison asked, switching focus.

Nancy's gaze shot to Madison. Her eyes showed absolute insult to have her son come under further questioning.

"We could go to his school and see what the principal has to say," Madison ground out.

"He smelled like cigarette smoke *once*. But Rico and I put an end to that awfully quick."

"How's that?" Terry leaned forward, elbows on his knees, hands clasped.

Nancy pulled her eyes from Madison and looked at Terry. "We took away his cell phone and his video games for a month. He never stunk of the filthy habit again."

A few seconds passed without anyone saying anything.

"I know you are both just doing your job, but if you're looking at my son, you're looking in the wrong place. He wouldn't shoot anyone. He wouldn't even know how to pull the trigger let alone... Where would he get a gun?" She was wringing her hands. "But his friends." She glanced quickly at Madison but didn't hold eye contact. "They might be the kind to get involved with gangs."

Madison shrugged. "We never said anything about gangs."

"No, but it's what you're getting at." Nancy pointed a finger at Madison, drew it to Terry, and then dropped her hand.

Madison remained quiet, using her silence to encourage Nancy to keep speaking. Terry didn't say anything, either.

"Melody called. She heard that it was a drive-by. That sounds like a gang to me. And you thought you'd come by to see if he's happy and cared for, well-adjusted... I assure you he is. His largest issues are who to take to school dances and pimples." Nancy rolled her eyes. "Pimples might as well be the end of the world. He gets so worked up over them, you'd think he was a girl."

If Nancy honestly thought dances and pimples were Scott's biggest issues, she was living in a fantasy world. High school was wrought with societal struggles, bullying, peer pressure, substance abuse. Today's youth faced more trials by the age of fifteen than previous generations may have ever encountered in a lifetime.

An attentive mother would know all of this, though. So either Nancy was naive or she wasn't that attentive. But being a less than a perfect mother hardly made her son a gang member. And given the way she was defending him, she believed in him and would give her life for him. That spoke to her being a loving mother. From what Madison saw in front of her—the home, the woman—Scott didn't seem like the ideal recruit for a gang. But looks could be deceiving...

"Before we leave, could we please see his room?" Madison phrased it as a question, hoping Nancy would receive the request favorably.

"Sure. I'm telling you, he's not involved, though." Nancy gestured for them to follow her and led them up the staircase and down a hallway. Outside the second room on the right, she pointed to a closed door.

Scott didn't have any posters facing the hallway or signs saying to "keep out" like many others his age often did. Madison opened the door, and the smell of perspiration and stinky feet immediately hit her nose. A gym bag was on the floor with clothes spilling out of it, and stained socks dotted the floor. In fact, clothes were strewn everywhere—the floor, the bed, a study desk in one corner, the chair in front of it. She turned to Nancy, who held up her hands.

"Hey, he's fourteen. He takes care of his own room. I do his laundry."

Obviously, the dirty laundry's not making it out of the room...

Madison's eyes scanned the space again. There was a fish tank against the one wall. Green slime was built up on the sides of the glass, and the water was murky. Three goldfish swam around but didn't seem to do so with much gusto. Madison was surprised they were even alive.

"He wanted a pet. Rico said he could have fish." Nancy obviously wasn't impressed by her husband's decision given her defeated tone.

At least Rico didn't let him get a dog...

The back of the door had a full-length, colored print of an Asian model dressed in a highlighter-pink string bikini with an ocean backdrop. The walls of the room were much the same—littered with more scantily clad women and music posters.

Yeah, his greatest concerns are school dances and pimples...

Madison noticed a desktop computer at the desk. Given the money the family seemed to have, she was surprised he didn't have a laptop. But that wasn't the thing that really struck her. It was suggested that families with children keep a computer in a main living area so that parents could watch what their children were up to online, especially with the Internet and social media being such stalking grounds for pedophiles. She'd seen some photos that the cyber crime unit had to look at, and describing them as nauseating wasn't doing them justice. It was no wonder officers rotated out of that division as soon as their time requirement was up.

Terry pointed toward the monitor and addressed Nancy. "Do you track Scott's online activity?"

Nancy tilted her chin up and straightened her back. "I trust my son and wouldn't want to invade his privacy."

"Can we?" Madison asked bluntly.

Nancy seemed to hesitate but then consented with a nod.

Terry went over to the desk and turned on the computer. A screen came up asking for a password. He looked over a shoulder at Nancy. "Do you know what it is?"

Nancy was rubbing the length of her neck, her long, slender fingers striking Madison as disproportionate to her otherwise petite frame.

"Mrs. Beck?" she prompted.

"I don't know. I really don't have a clue, all right?" Her cheeks flushed, and her mouth snapped open and hinged shut, as though she contemplated saying more but was embarrassed and couldn't even defend herself.

"No, it's not all right…really," Madison said. "Your son is at the ripe age for gangs. He skips class. Who really knows where he goes…"

"He goes to the—"

"How do you know he goes to the mall?" Madison let the question sit there, and Nancy didn't touch it this time. Madison could empathize that parents didn't always know everything, but Nancy didn't seem to get too involved with her son or she'd know he had larger things to face beside pimples and school dances. "I'm sure you can finally see our concern," Madison continued. "And if your son was involved with the shooting, it would be very intelligent of him to strike at your husband's gas station."

"And he just happened to know when the officer would be there?" Nancy's skin was blotchy as she flushed.

"Your son might not even be involved," Terry said, playing good cop. "We just need to cover our bases."

Nancy seemed to cling to that hope, and she touched Terry's arm. "He's not. I know my son… How can I say I know him?" Her strength quickly crumbled. Her chin quivered, her body trembled, and tears fell down her cheeks. "I don't know all he's up to, but I know we raised him better than to become a killer or a gang member. We love him, we—"

"Sadly, sometimes none of those things matter." Terry's voice was smooth and calm. Parental. He was probably coming to realize, even in the short span of his young daughter's life, that some things were outside his control. Imagine how much more so things would become once she was a teenager and had a mind of her own.

Nancy was rubbing her arms. "I don't know the password to his computer, but—" she left the room and then tucked her head back in "—follow me."

She led them to an office and sat behind a desk. She flicked the monitor on, keyed something in, and said, "I'd almost forgotten we had this. Here." She got up.

Madison and Terry traded places with Nancy behind

the desk. Terry sat. On the screen was what looked like a forum. Messages alternated between red and black text.

"What's this?" Madison asked.

"It's called YouthSecure, all one word. It's an online monitoring system that allows parents to see their children's online activity, social media, and text messages on their phones. It even shows deleted texts."

"So when you said you didn't monitor—"

Nancy interrupted Madison. "We're not good at checking it regularly. Well, I forget about it. But please feel free to look. I'm sure it will prove he's not involved in the shooting." She went to the door, resting her hand on the frame. "Either of you want tea?"

"No, thanks," Madison responded.

Nancy left them to it, and Madison focused on the screen. She pointed to a string of messages between Scott and a girl named Eva. The wording made it clear they were sexually involved. "I'm glad I'm not Scott."

"*You* are? You're not usually terrified of anyone."

"She's feisty," Madison said at a low volume in case Nancy came back.

"How are you making out?" Nancy cleared the doorway, hugging a cup with both hands. If it was tea, it had already cooled as there was no steam.

Good thing Madison had spoken quietly.

"Nothing, right? You haven't found anything?"

Terry stood, and both he and Madison came out from behind the desk.

"The good news is, based on his messaging, your son doesn't appear to be involved with the shooting," Madison began.

"And why do I sense there is some bad news?" Nancy's eyes slid to Terry.

"He's not at the mall when he skips school," he told her.

"What? Where is he then?" The original gutsy spirit they saw in Nancy's eyes earlier came back, even if for a different reason this time. The fire was directed toward her son, not them.

Madison wondered if Nancy *ever* logged onto YouthSecure.

"Since it's really a family matter, we'll leave that to you," Terry said.

Nancy's gaze went toward the back of the monitor.

"We can see ourselves out," Madison added. Nancy nodded, and they made a quick exit.

"Guess she'll find out Scott's more grown up than she thought," Terry said as he was getting into the department car.

"Yep, there's more to his life than school dances and pimples." Madison put the car into reverse, and her phone rang. She pressed the brakes and answered on speaker.

"We've got all the footage from the city and the gas station," Cynthia said. "You guys coming in to watch?"

Madison pushed the gas. "We'll be there in ten."

CHAPTER 13

THE AROMAS OF DELI MEAT and cheese greeted Madison the moment she got off the elevator with Terry. Her stomach growled, but at the same time, she wasn't sure if she should eat. With all the drama of the day, it felt like she was walking around with the feeling of being freshly punched in the gut.

Terry got the door to the lab, and Madison walked in first. On the table was a small tray of sandwiches, plastic wrap bunched up beside it, and a small stack of paper plates. There were also cans of soda and bottled water.

Cynthia looked up from what she was doing on her computer. "Help yourself," she said, bobbing her head toward the food. "The chief had them dropped off in the cafeteria, but I just helped myself and brought some back here for us."

The woman never ceases to amaze…

"Don't mind if I do." Terry went over to the table and plucked what looked like egg salad on whole wheat from the tray.

Madison eyed a turkey and Swiss on pumpernickel loaf, trying to decide if it was worth a shot. Her stomach requested she take the chance. She expected the first bite to taste marvelous, if nothing else, but either its flavor fell flat or her taste buds weren't working. It had to be the grief.

"All right." Cynthia swiveled in her chair. "I have the surveillance ready for us to watch." She used a remote and turned the TV on that was mounted in the corner of the room. A frozen black-and-white image was on-screen. "Before we watch this, I have an update for you."

Madison swallowed another mouthful of sandwich. "What is—" The bread was dry in her throat. She grabbed a water bottle and took a swig to wash it down. "What is it?"

"Sam's been able to narrow the gun make down to six different types."

"Six?" Madison blurted out.

Cynthia held up her hand. "As she explained to me, there were no land and groove impressions, but rather there was more of a wavy rifling pattern left on the projectiles. This indicates the bullets were either fired from a Heckler & Koch, Kahar Arms, Magnum Research, Tanfoglio, CZ USA, or a Glock. And we know we're looking for a model that fires nine-millimeter rounds." Cynthia extended a sheet of paper to Madison. "This is a list of the different makes and models that could apply here."

Madison took the sheet and scanned it. "Not exactly what I was hoping for," Madison moaned.

"Finding this gun will be like looking for a needle in a haystack," Terry said with a mouthful of food, his appetite obviously not affected by recent events.

She'd normally shoot him a glare for the cliché, but it seemed so trivial in light of everything else.

"Now, I took a quick look at the footage, both from the gas station and the intersection, to get us to the timeline we're interested in," Cynthia began. "The shooter's vehicle was a BMW sedan, black, but it was an older model."

"Plate number?" Madison asked.

Cynthia shook her head. "There were no plates."

"They obviously had plans to do something illegal. We still don't know if Weir was a specific target, though, or if they would have been happy with any cop," Madison thought aloud.

"I have one feed from the gas station ready to go first. This is from the camera facing the road." Cynthia hit "play."

The BMW came to a stop next to the east entrance to Rico's station. The window was two thirds of the way down, and while the occupants of the vehicle were in shadow with the camera's angle, the driver's mouth was wide open. There was no sound to the video, but this was probably when he had screamed out, "Die, cop." Quickly following were flashes of light.

She thought of Kayla from the Bean Counter. *I saw a flash of light.*

The shooting was over in less than a minute, and the driver tore off, the nose of the car even lifting as the rear tires bit into the pavement.

"Can you pause it there?" Madison asked.

Cynthia stopped the footage.

The perps' faces were in shadow, and they were wearing dark clothing.

"That window is down more than a crack, but we still can't make out the shooter's face," Terry grumbled.

Madison nodded. "We can see the hands on the gun, though. Caucasian. And the shooter knows something about handling a weapon as they're using both hands."

Terry pressed his lips together. "That doesn't indicate a newbie to a gang."

"Firing more bullets than necessary belies real experience in firing a gun, though," Madison said, playing devil's advocate to her own theory.

"The gang could have told him how to hold the gun."

"Cyn, can you reverse a bit?" Madison asked.

Cynthia backed it up a few frames. "Where do you—"

"Right there."

Cynthia hit "play" again.

The shooter pulled the trigger, and the recoil had the gun arching upward. The process repeated four times.

Madison looked at Terry. "Not experienced after all. Look how the shooter's body posture stiffens trying to offset the recoil."

"Yeah, and four rounds."

"Did you see how the front nose of the car lifted on acceleration?" Madison added. "That means we're looking for a model with rear-wheel drive."

Terry looked over at her, then glanced at Cynthia.

"As I said at the crime scene. And, sadly, most BMWs are," Cynthia said. "We can, however, eliminate the X series as they are all four-wheel drive."

Madison gestured to the screen. "And there's no way to tell the model of this vehicle from what we have here?"

Cynthia didn't answer but brought up another video. "This is from the intersection, facing north."

The vehicle came toward them, approached Rico's, and stopped. Cynthia paused the footage and overlaid a grid pattern to the video.

"Cyn?" Madison was wondering if a view from the front could help identify the model given the grill or body line.

Cynthia held up her index finger and was clicking here and there. Seconds later, she grinned at Madison and

Terry. "We're looking for a BMW 3 series sedan, probably a 2012 to 2014."

"See if any of those have been reported stolen in the area."

Cynthia conducted a quick search. "Nope. None."

"All right," Madison said, thinking now about how the plates had been removed. "What about people who have that kind of car registered to them?"

Cynthia did another quick search. "Fifty people."

"Holy crap." All the hope that was starting to grow in Madison started to dim.

"I'll print off the names for you."

Madison nodded as the printer clicked to life and then started spitting out paper. Fifty people would take a lot of time to question—more time than Madison wanted to sacrifice. "Heaven forbid we catch a break." Madison sighed. "Let's continue with the city's video."

The footage resumed, and Cynthia slowed the playback, pausing when the BMW was closest to the camera. Both shooter and driver were wearing hoodies, heads tilted downward. The driver was taller than the passenger.

"Can you calculate their heights?" Madison asked.

Cynthia smiled at her, and then overlaid another grid pattern over the image. "Accounting for the forward curve of their heads, you're looking for a driver of approximately six four and a shooter just under six feet."

"You're a genius," Madison said, beaming at her friend. "What about weight?"

"I'm a miracle worker but not that much of one." Cynthia laughed, but it came to an abrupt halt. "Actually, if I get the riding height of the car itself and measure how low to the ground it actually is, that could give us an idea.

Granted they didn't modify the car, of course."

Another genius moment…

Madison watched as her friend did her thing.

"All right, the way the car's riding, it indicates an added total weight of approximately three hundred and fifty pounds."

Madison was smiling.

"But remember, that's an estimate," Cynthia began. "The trunk could be full of crap, who knows."

Madison pegged the driver as 180 to 200 pounds and the shooter at 150 to 170. She thought back to the other video, how the shooter's body was angled toward the window, two hands on the gun. They would have to be small enough to turn their entire body in the passenger seat to face out the window.

"Now, was any gas station camera facing west toward pump two?" Madison asked.

"One thing at a time, Maddy. Let's watch another video first. This was taken from the one mounted on the storefront, facing the lanes of pumps. But before I start it, I'm going to warn you, this one will be harder to watch."

Madison's chest tightened and her breathing slowed down as her stomach fluttered. Cynthia pressed a button and another feed began.

The vehicle pulled up, there was the burst of light, and Barry went down. The small bit of sandwich Madison had eaten swirled in her gut.

"Unfortunately, none of the shots will work for running facial recognition. As you can see, it's quite dark, and with the poor quality of the cameras… Well, it's not helpful."

Madison took in the shadowed face of the killer, then the body of the car. Her eyes stopped on the back fender.

It was round and looked like a sticker. She hadn't noticed it before. It must have been blocked from the other angles.

"Cyn, zoom in there." She pointed toward it.

Cynthia focused in. It was definitely a decal. It was hard to make out the image, but it looked like a pentagram with a goat head in the center and what resembled the rebel flag.

"Is that what I think it is?" Terry stepped closer to the monitor and then turned to Madison and Cynthia.

Madison raised her eyebrows. "What do you think it is?"

"Except for the rebel flag, this is the sign of the Devil."

"Ah, just great." Madison glanced toward the ceiling. "We're hunting someone involved with a gang that uses the Devil's symbol as their call sign?"

Terry opened his palms. "Not necessarily. It could just be a sticker."

Madison was about to ask Cynthia to run the decal through the system, but Cynthia was already on it.

Minutes later, Cynthia was shaking her head. She glanced at Terry but settled her gaze on Madison. "It's not in the system, and as much as I hate to say it, maybe Terry's right and it doesn't really factor into the shooting."

Madison considered what that might mean. Was there a new gang in town they didn't know about yet? She'd have to ask the gangs unit if they'd come across the symbol before.

"And for the record, I'm right more often than I'm given credit for." Terry shot both women a glare.

"Aw, hug him, Maddy."

Madison smirked and rolled her eyes. "He's a big boy. Hit 'play,' please."

The few seconds of lighthearted banter died as they

watched Barry fall to the ground again. Madison's eyes skipped to the left of the screen, to pump two. The mystery driver and the Chevy SS. But one thing at a time.

A common admonition that kept coming up with this case...

She had Cynthia replay the gunfire at super slow motion and counted the flashes of light until Barry went down. "He was hit with the third bullet."

Madison walked over to the screen and pressed a finger to the image of the driver of the Chevy, who was pumping gas. The driver was a woman. She calmly put the nozzle back in its cradle and left the station from the south exit as Kayla had said she had. After the fourth bullet had fired.

"Can you replay the part just before the mystery woman gets in her car?" Madison asked, and Cynthia did as she requested.

When the fourth round fired, the woman's shoulder appeared to be pushed backward. She was already working to get the nozzle back into the pump when she was hit. Her face registered a few seconds of shock, but otherwise, she seemed pretty put together. It had to have been the adrenaline.

"Right there." Madison pointed to the screen again. "She was hit with the fourth bullet."

"I'd like to know why she leaves her car door open while she's pumping gas," Terry said.

Madison shrugged, having noticed the same thing but not thinking anything of it. "It could just be how she pumps her gas."

"Or she could have left her door open so she could make a quick getaway."

"That would lead to another question. If she was

involved, why run at all? She could have just stayed on scene, been treated for her injury, questioned, and released. She wouldn't even seem suspicious."

"Who knows what people think most of the time," Terry said on a sigh.

"True enough," Madison conceded. "When we catch up with her, we'll ask. But there haven't been any reports of single GSWs that have come in…"

"She could be receiving treatment at a clinic," Cynthia offered. "Sometimes they are slower about reporting these types of things."

"What about the plate on the Chevy? Can you get a closer look?" Terry asked.

"Let's see." A second later, they were zoomed right in on it and they had a partial.

Madison and Terry hurried to Cynthia's side as she punched in the digits they had and cross-referenced it to vehicle type.

A DMV photo came up showing a brunette with a rather forgettable face. Were they looking at a spooked eyewitness or an accessory? And if she was the latter, was she connected with a gang? Even if she wasn't involved in the shooting, she was an eyewitness who had failed to come forward.

"The car is registered to an Erica Snyder of Stiles. She's twenty-one, single, holds an office job. No criminal record."

"Her address?"

Cynthia rattled it off as Madison wrote it down.

"Perfect." Madison pointed to Snyder's address on the monitor. "We'll be there if you need us."

"Hey, wait a second," Cynthia said, bringing up another piece of footage. "There's one more. This is from inside the store."

Cynthia played it, and they watched as Hines dropped to the floor, and then she reversed the footage until Snyder appeared as she was paying cash.

"I'll print this off. It shows you a close-up of what she was wearing this morning. Maybe the sarge will issue a media statement saying she's wanted for questioning."

"Doubt that," Madison said. Sergeant Winston never rushed into those for fear of tarnishing a person's reputation, but there was something she could do. They could get a BOLO out on Snyder's car.

CHAPTER 14

MADISON AND TERRY GOT THE call that a hit came back on the BOLO issued for Snyder's Chevy SS when they were on the way to Snyder's house. The car was found in the parking lot of a strip mall. It consisted of a grocery chain, a pharmacy, a dollar store, an office-supply store, and an urgent care clinic, which was located on the north end of the strip mall.

Madison nodded toward the clinic. "How much do you want to bet she's in there?"

"The regular amount?"

She glanced over at her partner. They tended to make a bet—or two—over the course of most investigations, but usually their bets had more to do with the innocence of suspects. "I meant it as a figure of speech this time."

Terry shrugged his shoulders and looked out the passenger window.

She was thinking of Snyder as she scanned the lot and spotted officers standing next to the Chevy. But there was no Erica Snyder in sight. Were they *trying* to spook her?

"Did both these guys get their badges yesterday?" Madison rolled the department sedan into the spot beside the officers and put her window down. "Get the hell away from the car."

The smile that had been on one of the officers' faces

melted away.

Without waiting for him to say anything, she pulled out of the spot and drove off the lot. A few minutes later, she reentered from a side exit and parked closer to the clinic. She just hoped that Snyder hadn't seen the officers and fled the area. She could have called a cab or gotten on a city bus. And if she was on the run, she'd avoid going home.

Madison got out of the car and looked at the strip mall. She was thinking that she'd hit the clinic first, even though she knew privacy laws would protect Snyder if she was in there. But there had to be something she and Terry could do. She glanced at Terry, who was now standing next to her, and observed all the cruisers coming into the area. There were cars posted near the exits of all the stores now. It would make it harder for Snyder if she did try to run now.

"The front lot is covered. I'm going around the back side of the clinic," Madison said.

"And me?"

"You stay up front, near the clinic's main door."

"Got it." Terry hung next to the building, the door to the clinic still in his direct line of sight, and Madison made her way around back.

She had just reached the clinic's back door when it cracked open.

Erica Snyder was looking straight at Madison and seemed frozen for a few seconds. Then she was gone, retreating into the building again.

Madison lunged for the door handle and turned it before Snyder could lock it.

Madison entered the clinic, pursuing Snyder down a hallway. "Stop! Stiles P—" Madison crashed right into a nurse who was exiting a room.

The nurse put a hand to her chest. "What are you—You can't be back here. Someone call the police!"

Madison held up her badge. "I *am* the police. I need to take that woman"—she pointed to Snyder's form disappearing down the hallway—"in for questioning."

"You need a warrant to be back here," the nurse spat out, her eyes defiant.

Madison was pursuing someone reasonably believed to be involved in a serious crime, and that outweighed the need for a warrant at this point. She tore off after Snyder, ignoring the nurse.

At least there was only one way for Snyder to go, and that was out the front door where Terry and other officers were waiting.

The nurse was still yelling about privacy and ethics when Madison reached the front door and burst outside.

Terry had Snyder by one of her arms and her shoulder. There was a white bandage wrapped around her upper arm—the same arm that had been pushed back after the gunfire. "Put your hands behind your back," he said.

Snyder complied, likely wanting as little damage done to her arm as possible. "I didn't do anything."

People stopped to watch, their mundane activities suspended for the time being.

"You fled the scene where a police officer was shot and killed," Terry spat out as he snapped the cuffs on Snyder's wrists.

"And you just ran from me," Madison added.

Snyder stopped moving, her legs buckling beneath her. *Great. All I need is someone else passing out.*

Terry managed to keep Snyder upright. She looked at Madison. "He died?"

Madison wasn't about to repeat what Terry had just said. "You're going to tell us everything you saw and why you left a crime scene." Madison's heartbeat was in her ears.

"What about my car?" Snyder's voice rose with each word, straining.

"Oh, don't you worry about that. We'll be taking it in." Madison yanked on the woman's uninjured arm, directing her to the closest cruiser.

All resistance stopped, and Snyder's eyes were suddenly wet. "I had nothing to do with the shooting."

"Then I guess you'll have no problem talking to us."

CHAPTER 15

ERICA SNYDER WAS SET UP inside an interrogation room, and Madison and Terry were watching her through the two-way mirror. They were about to leave and join Snyder when Winston entered. Based on the man's scowl, news had traveled fast.

"Knight, we need to talk," he barked, passing a look to Terry that told him to get out.

She wanted to ask why he was being shy now. He'd reamed her out in front of Terry before. But it was best she not play stupid because it would drag everything out for too long and she wanted to talk to Snyder. She had a feeling what this might be about… "Did someone from the urgent care clinic call you?"

"What were you thinking?" he ground out. "Or weren't you?"

"I was pursuing a lead in the case, that's all. I didn't violate any privacy laws."

"You entered through the back door of a medical clinic without a warrant."

"Because that's where the subject went. She was running away from me." Madison heard the stress enter her voice and took a deep breath before continuing. "Listen, I'm not sure what you were told, but I'm thinking it was an exaggeration of the truth. Snyder was already treated and released, and was trying to leave out the back door. I simply followed her back inside."

His facial expression softened marginally, telling Madison her assumption had been correct.

"Let's get the focus off me, Sarge, and back on Snyder. She was at the clinic getting treatment. The video shows that she was struck by the fourth bullet from our killer's gun. Did the clinic bother to report they were treating a GSW?"

"That's not the point here, Knight."

"Hmm? I thought it was a good one." She cocked her head. "Maybe we should look into why they didn't? Is the doctor involved—"

"You know what—" he held up his hand "—I'm done here."

In her head, a crowd cheered. That meant she'd be able to get back to work.

His footsteps tapped against the floor as he walked away, and she turned to look at Snyder again in the interrogation room.

Snyder was slouched in the chair, her eyes staring at the two-way mirror, and she was biting her nails... *Chewing* might be a more apt description based on the way she was going at them, one after the other.

Terry was already heading down the hall, and he entered the interview room before Madison could catch up. He took his regular position, leaning up against the back wall.

Snyder straightened and put her hands underneath her legs. Madison dropped into the chair across the table from her.

"I know my rights." Her words were more poignant than her delivery. Her voice wavered and her eye contact was unsteady.

"We've been over this. You left the scene—"

"I was going to come forward."

Madison glanced at Terry and pressed her lips together. She didn't say a word, but it should have been apparent to Snyder that neither of them believed her.

"Honestly. I…I…"

Madison looked back to Snyder. "You weren't going to come forward. That's the real truth, isn't it?"

Snyder's eyes dipped to the table. "I was afraid. I'd just been shot. Bullets were—" She pulled her hands out from under her legs, flailing her uninjured arm wildly beside her head. "It was crazy. Like I was in a movie. At least until I felt the burning…" She delicately touched the bandage on her arm.

Terry started jingling the change in his pocket. He often did this to play with people's minds.

Snyder spun around to look at him. "Is that necessary?"

Fastest reaction to that yet…

"Why did you flee?" Madison asked, ignoring Snyder's question.

"I didn't *flee*. But a guy was firing a gun in my direction. I'm lucky I was just grazed." She touched her injured arm again.

"Yeah, you are," Terry said. His words hung in the air, carrying the heavy implication that an officer hadn't been so lucky.

"The faster you start talking to us, the sooner you can leave. Why did you drive off?" Madison understood fight or flight, but she wasn't convinced it was that simple when it came to Snyder. "Maybe you were involved somehow," she stated nonchalantly.

Snyder shifted in her chair and leaned forward. "I'm

not. I swear."

"So you left…*why*?"

The woman started squirming.

They couldn't make out the shooter's face given shadows and camera angles, but maybe Snyder had. "Did you get a look at the shooter?"

A huge sigh. "Maybe."

"Maybe?" Madison raised her voice. "This person killed a police officer, and if you don't start talking, we'll throw you in jail as an accessory after the fact." Madison was trying to read Snyder's eyes to detect if she knew more than she was saying. Given the flicker that flashed over her gaze, Madison would wager Snyder had, in fact, gotten a look at the shooter.

Terry pushed off the wall and stopped jingling his change. He stood next to Snyder. "Talk to us. Now."

Snyder cut a sideway glance to Terry and held eye contact with him briefly. But she didn't say anything.

Terry leaned on the table, turning so he was face-to-face with Snyder. "What did the shooter look like?"

She rubbed her forearm. "I live in a bad neighborhood. I can't just be flapping my lips."

Madison leaned across the table. "So you know the shooter?"

"I never said that."

"If you don't, what are you so worried about?" Terry raised his brows.

"There are a few questionable characters in my neighborhood. I don't even like taking walks anymore. There are always needles in the park. When I'd come across anyone and dare to look at them, most of the time their eyes were…you know…just gone. No one home. The way everything happened this morning was like,

like—" Snyder rolled her hand "—like on TV when gangs do drive-bys. Well, almost, except they actually stopped."

Madison had made the same observation, but she latched on to something else. Street gangs identified themselves with anything from style and color of dress to tattoos, mannerisms, symbols, and graffiti tags. All they could see from the video were the subjects' black hoodies, and members of pretty much any gang could wear that. Maybe Snyder was worried because she saw something else that connected the shooter to the people she'd encountered on her walks. Madison would have to look into what gang was located in Snyder's neighborhood.

Madison pulled out a photo of the decal as Terry returned to standing against the wall behind Snyder. "Do you recognize that?"

She seemed to study the photo for a minute, then met Madison's gaze. "No."

"You're sure?" There was a niggling in her gut that told her otherwise. People were quick to look away when they either hadn't seen something before or were trying to hide the fact that they had seen it. The fact that Snyder had looked at the image for so long made Madison think she had seen it before and was trying to remember where.

"Yes, I'm sure."

Madison held eye contact awhile longer before putting the photo back in a folder. She'd let the matter of the decal go for now and focus on getting a description of the shooter's face. "We're going to need you to sit with a sketch artist—"

"It was rather dark." Snyder paused, her gaze going from Madison to Terry and back to Madison before she continued. "He was wearing a hoodie, but he had a big nose. It almost seemed too large for his face. That much

I could see."

Madison sat back in her chair, doing her best to give Snyder the impression that her observation hadn't made much impact. But inside, Madison's heart was racing. "What nationality?"

"He was white."

That coincided with the camera footage. "Would you be able to identify him in a lineup?"

Not that they had any suspects yet…

Snyder let out a deep breath that seemed to deflate her. "I'm not sure."

That wasn't what Madison wanted to hear.

With Snyder's hesitancy over sitting with an artist, Madison thought it best to take a detour. If she kept pressing Snyder about the shooter, she'd clam up completely. And Madison didn't need that. Hearing about a crime from a witness firsthand was the ideal way to pluck vital information. "Run us through everything from the time the car showed up to when you left."

"I was getting gas."

"Why so early? You work in the office at—" Madison looked down at Snyder's background check "—Water Depot. It's Saturday. The earliest they'd open would be eight thirty."

"You really think I was involved? You do remember that I was shot?" Anger flashed in Snyder's eyes, but it was quickly doused by fear. Her shoulders lowered.

Madison curled her lips. "It's not uncommon for criminals to inflict injuries on themselves to throw an investigation off course."

"Wha—" Snyder turned to Terry, then faced Madison again, but Madison caught Terry's eyes before looking at Snyder. His gaze contained a warning not to push too hard. Madison rarely followed directions, though.

"You still haven't answered my question," she went on. "Why were you getting gas so early?"

"Is that a crime now?" Snyder crossed her arms. "I have a key to the place, and on Saturdays I go in early. As long as I put in six hours, I can go home. I like to be gone from there about noon or so. You can check with my boss if you'd like."

Madison made a mental note to do just that. "All right, so you were pumping gas…"

"Yeah. Then I heard a bang. At first I didn't realize it was a gun. I'd never heard one fired…at least not that close."

"Where had you heard one fired before?" Madison asked.

"My neighborhood? But off in the distance. Maybe a block or two over, but never right where I was."

"Okay. Then what?"

"I was going to duck, but I obviously wasn't quick enough." Snyder touched her injured arm again.

The video didn't show Snyder about to duck, but she could have just thought about it before getting struck.

"Was the officer already down when you were shot?" Madison asked, even though she knew the answer from watching the video.

"I don't know. I'm sorry. I think so…?" She briefly looked at the ceiling. "Yeah, yeah, he was. Everything happened so quickly, but in slow motion somehow. I was hit and I looked over to where the police car was, but I didn't see the cop so he must have been down already. Then I got into my car."

"Speaking of your car, do you always leave your door open when you get gas?" Terry asked, still caught up on that detail.

Her brow furrowed. "Uh, yeah."

"Why?" Terry didn't sound convinced.

Madison suppressed her smirk. She was the one tagged with the nickname *Bulldog*, but her partner could be just as stubborn when he had his mind made up about something.

"I don't know. I just always have." Snyder slid her gaze to Madison.

"How many bullets were fired?" Madison asked.

Snyder closed her eyes for a few seconds. "Four, I believe."

"All right—" Madison went to stand up "—we'll be sending in a sketch artist to work with—"

Her face was pale. "I said I couldn't ID him."

Madison sat back down. "But you did see him. You told us he had a dominant nose. You work with an artist, and he'll know the right questions to ask to spark more from your memory."

"No."

"No? An officer was murdered."

"If those people find out that I ratted on them, they'll come after me. They have a way of knowing things like this…"

Adrenaline swirled within Madison, warming and then cooling her, cooling and then warming her. She was sure now that Snyder had recognized the decal and just wouldn't admit to it, but maybe Madison could pull that information out of her another way. It would involve a little white lie. Madison would look at it as an unverified conclusion. "That decal belongs to a gang."

Snyder's eyes snapped to Madison's. "If they find out I said anything—" She looked away, her body shaking slightly.

Some cops would assure Snyder of her safety, make a bold claim to that effect, but Madison wasn't going to make a false promise. With everyone tied up in hunting down Barry's killer, there simply wasn't the manpower to watch over Snyder. But there were options. "I can get you set up in a safe house." Even if that ended up being a motel room, Snyder would be safer than at home. "But only if you speak with a sketch artist."

Snyder took a staggered breath. "What happens after I leave, though? You can't protect me forever."

Madison wasn't getting into the fact that Snyder might not see full freedom for a while. She was a material witness and might be called upon to testify. If things escalated to that point, full-blown witness protection might even be necessary. "We'll protect you as long as you need protecting." She stood. "I'll call for the artist, but you might have a bit of a wait before he gets here, so get comfortable."

CHAPTER 16

MADISON AND TERRY STEPPED OUTSIDE the interrogation room. She wasn't looking forward to speaking with Winston about a safe house for Snyder, but Madison didn't have much choice if she wanted the woman to speak. And if Winston wouldn't play along, she'd go directly to the chief. Letting Snyder go home and have something happen to her wasn't an option. Madison had been in that position before, and that person had been murdered.

She just hoped that she hadn't caught Snyder's paranoia. And while Snyder claimed she wasn't able to identify the shooter, Madison was quite certain the same didn't go for the decal. While the decal wasn't connected to one of the gangs in the database, it would be a good idea to ask someone in Gangs which one ruled the streets in Snyder's neighborhood. But before she could allow herself to buy into Snyder's innocence, they needed more evidence in order to believe her.

"Can you quickly call Water Depot and confirm Snyder's working arrangement for Saturdays?" she asked Terry. "I'm going to contact Gangs."

"Sure." Terry pulled out his phone, found the number online, and dialed. Madison made her call at the same time.

About five minutes later, both of them were finished.

"Well, the owner of Water Depot told me he was prepared to fire Snyder next time he saw her," Terry began. "Apparently, he's been trying to reach her all day."

"Well, she's had a good reason for not answering."

"He confirmed what Snyder told us, though. What did you find out from Gangs?"

"The gang in Snyder's area is called YJS, which stands for the Yellow Jackets…like the bees. They wear yellow above the waist but only wear black from there down."

"So they aren't behind the shooting, then."

Madison shook her head. "I was just hoping they'd recently adopted the decal, but they wouldn't be in black hoodies." Madison consulted the clock on the wall in the bullpen. *6:30.* It had been over twelve hours since Barry had been shot. Time stopped for no one.

"Let's go talk to Winston," she said.

She led the way to their boss's office and knocked on the doorframe. Winston didn't say anything, just motioned for her and Terry to enter.

"We have questioned Snyder, the eyewitness from pump two," Madison stated.

"The one who fled the scene?"

Madison wasn't going to touch the fact that he'd said *fled* the scene. "She'll be working with a sketch artist."

"She saw the shooter?" Hope filled Winston's voice.

Madison nodded. "Yeah, not a good look, though, from the sound of it. I'm cautiously optimistic, though."

"Let's grip onto any hope we're offered."

Madison and Terry were silent, and the sergeant looked at each of them. "What else?"

"She's fearing for her life," Madison said.

Winston straightened up. "She knows them?"

"Not that she's admitted to, but I have a feeling her fear is connected to the decal on the BMW."

"The decal never tied back to the Hellions or any other gang."

"It didn't tie back to a *known* gang." Madison made solid eye contact with her superior. "She's going to work with a sketch artist, and I've offered her protection. At least a safe house."

"Hmph." Winston swiveled his chair side to side.

Anything that could be an uphill battle became such with him…

"She's a material witness, Sarge," Terry said.

Winston looked at Terry. "It takes time to get these things sorted out—"

"That's why we came straight here." Madison made a beeline for the door. "Thanks," she said over a shoulder, and she heard Winston mumble something.

She spotted Troy walking down a side hallway, and her thoughts went to what Andrea had told her. Childhood friends, godfather… Why hadn't he told her? They should be coming together at a time like this, but she felt him slipping away. She turned to Terry. "Can you give me a minute?"

"Yep…"

Madison jogged down the hall and caught up with Troy outside. He was headed toward his Ford Expedition.

"Troy," she called after him.

He stopped walking but didn't turn around right away. He waited for at least ten to fifteen seconds, but it felt more like sixty. When he did face her, his eyes were cold and distant.

"We need to talk," she said.

He gestured with opened arms as if to say, *By all means.*

How could he be so nonchalant with her? Her heartache was quickly turning to anger. She'd done nothing to him, and this was how he was going to treat her? Not acceptable.

"Have you even bothered to consider how I might be feeling? I lost someone that I cared about, too." She scanned his eyes, but they had hardened even more. "What are we doing, Troy? Are we just going through the motions?"

"Going through the…motions?" He was angry now, too, but he had no right to be.

"The truth hurts sometimes, doesn't it?" Witnessing the callousness in his gaze, her heart was putting back up its defensive wall.

"Madison."

"If you really loved me, you wouldn't be shutting me out." She paused, hoping that he would interject, say something to smooth out her words, remedy the situation.

He remained silent.

"We both have had crappy pasts." She offered this as if it were some sort of reconciliation or explanation for his inclination to deal with Barry's death on his own.

"This has nothing to do with that." He reached for her hand, but she pulled back.

"Your wife cheated on you, my fiancé—"

"Why are you bringing all—"

"I'm bringing it up because it's there for us every day, whether we like it or not."

"We've worked through all that."

"I thought so, too, but apparently, we haven't. If we were really moving forward, you would trust me enough to talk to me." Her heart felt like it was splintering.

"If that's how you really feel," he said slowly, darkly, "maybe we should take a break."

She swallowed the emotion that welled up in her throat, pushing back the tears, and gazed into his eyes. He'd told her that she wouldn't get rid of him easily like she had previous boyfriends and that unless she did something to really piss him off, they'd always remain a couple. Had she messed up?

She shook her head, but it was in response to her own question, not his suggestion. She had to stick up for herself. She'd always been good at that, she'd always known when to back out before it was too late. Maybe she'd gotten sucked in too far, well past the breaking point, and had just failed to see it until now. But this was her opportunity—he was giving it to her—to make a clean break.

"I think that's a good idea." The words barely cut from her throat, but she held her ground and raised her chin.

"Fine." He sliced his arms through the air and turned and stalked away.

As she watched him leave her, she could barely breathe. She rubbed her arms and headed to the bathroom where she could find privacy to cry.

But somewhere amid the tears, her mind went to Joni and the pain she was suffering. Madison felt the need to go visit her, and she wasn't going to allow Troy to stop her from helping her friend. This was just another relationship, she told herself. She'd survived breakups in the past, and she'd survive this one. Her breath hitched as she hiccupped another series of soft sobs.

She stared at the hook on the back of the bathroom door, getting her breath to slow down, and after a few deep inhales and exhales, she was ready to leave. She'd have to learn to live with the pain in her chest.

Madison found Terry at his desk. He looked at her, and she could tell by the way his gaze probed her eyes that he knew she'd been crying. She wasn't giving into the drama of heartbreak, though. Forget it. Forget Troy.

"You want to come with me to see Joni?" she asked, even managing to muster a brief smile.

"Sure." Terry turned his monitor off and got up.

"Actually, before we head over, let's go to the lab." She hurried toward the elevator. "Maybe they'll have something for us, but I really want to get the card from Barry's cruiser to give to Joni."

Terry touched her shoulder, and she was afraid he was going to ask her if she was okay. If he did, she'd fall apart right in front of him. But he didn't say a word. She pushed the button to go up.

Inside the lab, Cynthia was looking at a slew of photographs that were spread out on the table in a grid pattern. She didn't look up when they entered the room.

"Hey, Cyn," Madison said.

Cynthia jumped back and put a hand to her chest. "I never even heard you come in…"

Madison and Terry moved closer to the table. The pictures were of the decal, the shooter, and driver.

"I just wish I could get their faces," Cynthia said. "I've been staring at these practically nonstop since you left." Cynthia looked at the two of them. "How did you make out with Erica Snyder?"

"She's working with a sketch artist right now," Madison said, trying to muster the confidence that something useful would come from it but not getting too attached to the idea.

Cynthia's tone was light and hopeful, though. "She saw

the shooter?"

"She did."

"Wonderful." There was a bit of a smile curving Cynthia's mouth.

"Well, don't get too excited yet. She saw that he was Caucasian and that he had a dominant nose."

"That could be enough. We've been led to the bad guy going on less before."

Madison nodded, admiring her friend's optimism and wishing she were infused with more of it herself. "How did Sam make out with Snyder's car?"

"There was a nine-millimeter bullet embedded in the ceiling of the Chevy. It entered there through the top of the car's doorframe. Samantha is comparing it to the other three to confirm that all four bullets came from same gun."

Madison knew it wasn't because they had reason to suspect a second weapon, but it was a matter of being thorough. "Terry and I are going to go visit Joni. You wouldn't have that card close by, would you?"

Cynthia left them standing at the table and went over to her desk, where she retrieved the card, returned, and extended it to Madison.

Madison took the card, not daring to take another peek at it. If she did she'd likely lose it and start crying again. She felt as if she were loosely taped together as it was.

"I haven't been by to see her yet, but please send my love and give her and the girls a hug for me." Cynthia gestured over the table. "I need to stay here."

Madison nodded and took a step toward the door, Terry behind her.

"Guys," Cynthia began, and they both turned around.

"Do you think we're just looking at a one-off thing here?"

She must not have heard that a gang was claiming responsibility. Madison shared the intel with her.

"And we don't know which one?" Cynthia leaned back against the table. "So it was an initiation killing? I'm going to be sick."

"It's too early to say." Madison tried to sound convincing, but based on the way Cynthia cocked her head, she wasn't very successful. And the truth was, things could get a lot worse before they got better.

Chapter 17

WHAT THE HELL HAD HE JUST DONE? He obviously wasn't thinking straight, and given the way his body hurt all over, Troy would swear the cause of the pain was actually physical exertion, not an emotional overload. But if Madison couldn't just give him some space so he could deal with his loss in peace, maybe it was better that they were taking a break. Maybe they weren't as perfect together as he'd thought.

He walked into his home office and opened one of his desk drawers. His eyes fell to the small box with a bow. He'd had it all figured out—how he was going to ask her—and was ready to defend his proposal, but none of that mattered now.

He slammed the drawer shut, the *thud* hitting his temples and drilling home the start of a migraine. But he'd been weak already. And he had to take a break and try to get some rest. He'd worked seven full shifts before being called in today, which was supposed to be his day off. All of this was just adding to the toll of losing Barry... and now Madison.

Troy had driven around the city for half an hour before building up the courage to go past Barry's house. But he couldn't bring himself to stop the car and get out. Words were failing him, and Joni needed to be surrounded by people who were strong enough to comfort her. He was failing even himself in that regard.

A single tear fell, and he swiped at it. "Why?" he cried out toward the ceiling, but even though he was alone, he quickly felt foolish for doing so. His mind churned, bringing up his other hurt. "Damn it, Maddy."

He went into the living room and dropped onto the sofa.

What was happening to him? He'd always prided himself on having control of his emotions, a key aspect that made him good at what he did. As a SWAT team leader, logic had to dominate hunches. Basing decisions on feelings most certainly would get someone killed. And yes, he'd lost men before. Yet even though those losses weren't his fault, each time he was sucked into this sort of abyss where he'd question everything in life from his career choice to his relationships. But it had never affected his personal life this severely before—or had it? Maybe that's what had torn his marriage apart, what had driven Lauren to cheat, what had given him his cool detachment and his steel focus on the job.

His eyes drifted to the floor and then to the few dog toys that were tossed into a corner of the room. Madison had pretty much moved in. At least, it felt as though Hershey had. Maybe Troy had rushed things and jumped into this relationship too soon. But it hadn't been compulsive. He'd harbored an affection for Madison long before he had acted on it. He'd been logical about it.

But somehow, in this moment, love didn't seem logical in any sense. It opened one up to pain and suffering, either through a breakup or with one person dying. Very rarely was the brushstroke of fate fair enough to take lovers together.

Yes, maybe it was best he and Madison were taking a break. Some pain now could spare him more down the road. He knew he was thinking like a cynical old man, but his thoughts were forming rapidly. And God, did it hurt.

He leaned back on the sofa and shut his eyes.

His doorbell rang then, and his breath caught. *Madison?*

But she wouldn't ring the bell. She'd likely let herself in and be yelling at him when she did. The bell rang a second time.

"Hang on!" he called as he got up and headed for the door. He looked out the window next to the door and let out the lungful of breath he'd been holding when he saw his visitor. While he was somewhat relieved, he was also disappointed that it wasn't Madison.

He opened the door. "What are you doing here?"

Andrea stepped inside and handed him a bag of Chinese takeout. "I came bearing dinner and that's the response I get?"

"You came to check up on me?" She might not be here to force him off the investigation, but he wouldn't put it past his sister to be checking on his welfare. "I'm a grown man."

She was slipping out of her coat and shoes. "You are my baby brother so I do have that right, you know."

He rolled his eyes, a habit he'd picked up from Madison, and a splinter shot through his heart.

"I just thought you might like some company," Andrea said.

"How did you know I'd be here?" He walked back to the kitchen with the food, his sister following.

"Winston told me you had stepped out for a break."

She opened a cupboard and pulled out two plates.

He pulled out forks and knives. Neither of them used chopsticks.

"And—" Andrea put her hand on his "—I thought you could use someone to talk to."

He pulled his hand free. "I'm fine."

Hands on her hips, she stared at him.

He hated when she did this. Madison told him he had a way of prying into her thoughts, and apparently, it was a family trait he'd inherited from his sister. "I *will* be fine."

Andrea hugged him faster than he could even consider getting away.

He gave himself over to the embrace, even finding comfort in it.

Easily a minute passed. He tapped her shoulder. "I'm good."

Andrea released him and smiled subtly. "You've never been good at talking about your feelings."

"I take it you and Robert chat about each other's feelings a lot?" He held eye contact with her, and again found that she was falling back into reading his mind.

"How is the investigation coming along from your standpoint?" she asked, going off the script he'd expected her to stick to.

"It's going." He opened the lid on a container and found it full of chicken fried rice. He dished some onto his plate.

"Just be careful."

"Of the rice?" he teased.

"You know what I'm talking about. On the job."

"Always."

She pressed her lips into a firm line. "I don't even want to—"

"No, no, no. Don't get started down that path."

"You're out there every day, risking your life."

"Are you forgetting that you used to be an officer on the streets?"

"*Used to be* being the point there."

"I take precautions." Not that any of that would have helped Barry…

She was looking him in the eye again and nodded a few seconds later.

They ate their food in front of the TV, and Andrea left soon afterward.

With her gone, his mind drifted back to the investigation, this time to the perps' license plates.

Had the car had any in the first place, or had they been removed just for the shooting?

Troy pinched the bridge of his nose. When he opened his eyes, he was staring at the far wall, but he had his answer.

He would assume that they hadn't driven very far without the plates—otherwise they'd risk getting pulled over—and while they drew attention to themselves by yelling out and squealing their tires, they wouldn't want to be pulled over before or after they'd carried out the crime. The car could have been stolen, of course, and if so, from anywhere, but the plates were likely removed near Rico's. What if Barry had a history with someone in that area who wanted payback?

CHAPTER 18

NOTHING ABOUT VISITING JONI WAS going to be easy. Even as a seasoned detective who faced death on a regular basis, Madison was a conflicted mess. The cop part of her told her to detach—even though this loss struck close to home—and to accept that people's lives sometimes came to an unfair and tragic end. The human side of her, though, found it hard to let go and surrender.

It was odd how time passed in the aftermath of tragedy—lightning quick yet also so slow. The shooting had only taken place this morning, but it already seemed forever ago. Maybe it only felt that long because she had a promise to fulfill. It was the *why* and *what-ifs* that were the large questions that, even when answered, never seemed to satisfy.

Why did this happen? Why did someone kill Barry? Why were a mother and children left without a husband and father? What if Barry hadn't been filling his tank at that time? What if he hadn't gone in for his shift? These were the types of questions that could bury one faster than quicksand. And just as with the sand, if one obsessed over the "why," lives would be lost to obsession and insanity.

And she'd lost more today than a friend and fellow officer, too. She'd lost a lover, the man she was starting to consider to be even more than that. But love was an illusion. It had to be, with the way it kept slipping through her fingers. Yet despite her heartbreak, she found herself worrying about Troy. Had he even been by to see Joni yet?

She took a deep breath, supposing it wasn't her problem, and pulled into Joni's driveway. Nerves tied her stomach in knots.

A cruiser was at the curb, and the driveway had two vehicles in it with another parked on the road behind the cruiser. One would have been Joni's, and the other two likely belonged to her parents and Barry's parents.

Madison parked the department sedan in front of the cruiser, and the officer waved at them as she and Terry turned to walk toward the house.

"Are you ready?" Terry was standing on the patch of grass between the public sidewalk and the curb. She was just standing by the car.

She had to admit that despite her desire to see Joni, her legs weren't cooperating. In fact, it seemed like her entire body just slowed down. But she would be strong. For her partner. For Joni. And for Barry and Joni's daughters.

"Let's do this." She tugged down on her jacket and led the way to the front door. Her coat was zipped up, the card tucked carefully inside.

She had her hand to the doorbell when the door opened. An older woman with gray hair was looking at them, assessing them. Her cornflower-blue eyes were wet, and she was holding a bunched-up tissue in one hand.

Madison pressed a palm to her chest. "I'm Madison Knight, and this is my partner, Terry Grant. We're both friends of Joni and Barry's. We both work for the Stiles PD in the major crimes division."

"Very well." She turned away, leaving the door open for them to come inside.

That wasn't exactly the reception Madison had expected, and by the shocked expression on Terry's face, she'd say he felt the same way.

"Be sure to take your shoes off," the woman stated gruffly.

They removed them as well as their coats, draping those over their arms.

"She's in here," the older woman said, pointing a finger to the right toward the living room.

Madison took a deep breath, steadying herself, before she breached the doorway.

Joni was sitting in the reclining chair. Tissues were piled up in a trash can next to her, but she wasn't crying at this particular moment. Two older men were seated on the couch, and the woman who had answered the door dropped into another chair.

Joni shot to her feet and hurried toward Madison when she saw her.

It took all of Madison's strength not to cry. But despite her internal coaxing to stand strong, a few tears fell after a moment. Joni threw her arms around Madison, and Madison hugged her with her free arm.

"I'm so sorry, Joni," she said. Joni was still holding on to her tightly, probably not realizing that the embrace was also soothing Madison.

A few seconds later, Joni's grip grew weaker and she pulled back. Her eyes were now red and full of tears. "I don't know how I'm supposed to live without him."

"I'm here for you. We're all here for you." It sounded like such a pathetic offering.

"If it weren't for the likes of you in the first place, my

daughter would still have her husband," said the woman who had answered the door.

Now it was very clear why they'd received such a cold reception. This woman was like Madison's mother— against the job because of the sacrifices it required. *The blood sacrifices,* as her mother had put it once.

"Mother, stop that!" Joni barked. "Barry was happy being a cop, and we've been through this."

Here Madison was thinking *her* family was dysfunctional, yet even in the face of such a devastating loss, this one insisted on pointing fingers.

"I told you from the beginning. Being a cop is no job for a husband and father." The older woman's face had turned a bright red by this point.

Madison sensed Terry shrinking behind her, either wishing to get out of here quickly or doing his best to steady his own temper. Not long ago, Terry had fought with the same issues. His wife had wanted a baby, and he had been worried about having a family due to the nature of the job.

"You're not married, are you." It was a statement, not a question, as the woman maneuvered to see Madison's ring finger. Madison did her the favor of holding up her hand.

"Good. See, that's who the job is meant for."

Ouch...

"Mother, stop it right now. Madison is a friend of mine, and she was—"

"A friend of Barry's? He's gone—"

"Moth—" Joni's word froze there, and tears fell down her face.

"Now look at what you've done, Gail." This came from one of the older men. He had a full head of gray hair and deep creases etched into his face. Madison assumed he was Joni's father.

"Well, I'm sorry, I'm just saying what I feel," Gail said, her hands flailing.

"We all know how you feel." The man sliced a cold glare at his wife.

Joni dabbed her nose with a tissue she must have pulled from a pocket when Madison hadn't been looking. "If you haven't guessed already, these are my parents, Gail and Albert." Then she gestured toward a man with dark hair and pleasant hazel eyes. They seemed vacant, though, as if touched so deeply by grief that his soul had withdrawn. "And this is Barry's dad, Myron," Joni added, but then paused for a moment.

Madison could only guess what she was thinking. It would be hard to know what tense to say that in. Technically, the man would always be Barry's dad.

"And everyone," Joni continued, "this is Madison and Terry."

Terry held up a hand to the room, and the three older people dipped their heads in acknowledgment.

"All of you worked with my son?" Myron asked.

"We did," Terry responded. "He was a wonderful man."

"You don't have to tell me." Myron seemed to attempt a smile, but it fell short.

"No, I suppose I didn't… But I wanted to."

Madison wondered where Barry's mother was, but just as the thought entered her mind, she turned in the direction of the sound of feet padding toward her along the wood floor. A woman who looked like the female version of Barry was standing next to Madison now, carrying a mug with a tea bag string dangling over the edge. Her eyes were clear. Of the four parents, this woman seemed the most composed. Madison would wager she was still in denial over her son's death.

"Mom, this is Madison and Terry," Joni said to the woman.

Both her hands were cupping the mug, disclosing her discomfort. "I'm Elise."

"We're sorry for your loss," Terry offered.

Elise made eye contact with him. "Thank you. You two should hang up your coats and stay awhile." She then entered the room and squeezed onto the couch between the two men.

Madison supposed this was a good time to do what else she'd come here to do. She glanced at Terry, and he nodded, having received Madison's silent communication.

"Barry had such a great sense of humor," Terry began as he took steps toward the parents. "This one time…" He left Madison standing alone with Joni in the doorway to the living room.

Madison touched Joni's arm. "Can we go somewhere to talk in private?"

"Uh, yeah, sure. I'd love some fresh air. Do you want to go for a walk?"

As tempting as that sounded, Madison thought it best to stay near the house, or even better, on the property. "We could."

"I sense you want to stay around here for some reason?"

Madison nodded. "If you don't mind."

Joni signaled for Madison to follow her toward the door to the back patio. Out of earshot of her parents, she said, "I've started smoking again, and I'm dying for a cigarette." Her face fell. "Horrible choice of words… Let's step out into the yard."

That was a suitable alternative to a walk. It would get Joni the fresh air she desired and provide privacy for their conversation. Madison wasn't even going to focus on the irony of fresh air combined with smoking. "Let's do that."

Madison grabbed her shoes from the front mat and carried them to the back door.

"Hey, Maddy." Allison, the Weir's eldest daughter, came to Madison and wrapped her arms around her.

Madison held her tight. When Allison pulled back, Madison ran a hand over her hair and kissed her forehead.

"Where's Troy?" the girl asked.

The question had Madison stumbling backward. He still hadn't come by? Allison's blue eyes were peering into Madison's. "I'm sure he'll be around as soon as he can." It took all her willpower to keep it together. She was angry that she'd been placed in a position to make him look good, especially when he wasn't looking so good to her right now.

"Let him know I'd like to see him."

If I'm talking to him…

"I will, sweetie."

Allison bit her bottom lip and headed for her bedroom. The other two girls must've been in their rooms already.

By the time Madison turned to Joni, she'd already gotten herself into a jacket and a pair of oversize shoes.

Joni followed Madison's gaze down to them. "They were Barry's."

"That explains it." Madison smiled, confident the expression showed based on the reciprocated flicker in Joni's eyes.

Joni slid the patio door open and led the way into the yard and around the side of the house. She took out a pack of cigarettes and a lighter. "You want one?"

Madison held up a hand. "No, thanks. I gave that habit up a week after I started."

"When was that?"

"I think I was sixteen." The smoking phase of her life was just that, brief. It was the cool thing to do in high school. Everyone who was anyone hung out at the back of the school, puffing away and gossiping about everyone else who didn't smoke. Madison had taken the plunge and actually found she'd liked the way it made her feel. She'd even liked the smell in mild doses, truth be told. She didn't like the nicotine-yellowed windows and walls, though, and butts built up in ashtrays, and bars that allowed smoking on their patios where everyone reeked of cigarettes.

Joni slid one out from her pack and lit up. She took a puff. "I feel like a teenager again"—she motioned with the cigarette, creating small arcs with the orange glow—"like I need to hide this from them."

"I take it your mom especially wouldn't be happy."

Joni rolled her eyes. "Isn't she a piece of work?"

I'm not going to touch that...

"She thinks she can still control my life and I'm thirty-eight years old, for crying out loud." Joni took another inhale, followed by a long exhale.

Just watching Joni smoke was melting away Madison's tension. Maybe one drag wouldn't hurt... When Joni put the cigarette to her lips again, it took all of Madison's willpower not to reach out for it.

"Are you close to knowing who did this?" Joni looked over at Madison, her eyes full of sorrow. No doubt they would remain that way for a long time before life came back into them.

"We have some leads."

"Better than nothing, I guess." Joni had gone back to looking straight ahead, leaving Madison to view her profile.

"It is," Madison consented. "But I promise you I'll find who did this to Barry."

"You did promise me." Joni made eye contact with her.

"I did, and I will make good on it," Madison said again, her heart beating off rhythm. All those at the Stiles PD were essentially *her*, were they not? If any of them solved Barry's murder, that, by extension, meant she had kept her promise. But she'd love to be the one who personally took the bastard down.

Joni's cigarette was almost gone, the amber glow not far from reaching her fingertips now. "What did you want to talk about?"

Madison stood in front of Joni. She swallowed the emotion that welled up in her throat.

This isn't going to be easy...

Should she say something in an effort to prepare Joni for what was coming next or just present the card? She reached into her coat and pulled it out. It was no longer in a plastic evidence bag but inside the white envelope that would have come with it.

Joni eyed the envelope skeptically, flicked the cigarette to the ground and extinguished it with a twist of her shoe. "What is that?" she asked.

Madison nudged it toward Joni until she seemed obliged to reach for it. "This was found on the passenger seat of Barry's cruiser."

Joni glanced at Madison, and then she slid a finger under the edge and opened it.

Madison pointed to the deck stairs. The wood would be a little cool to sit on, but Joni probably should be seated when she read the note from Barry. "Actually..." Madison put her hand over Joni's. "Why don't you look at it later? Maybe when you're alone?"

Joni's eyes grew wet with tears as she scanned Madison's face. "This is from Barry, isn't it?" She said it in such a way that she didn't need an actual answer.

"It is."

Joni stopped pulling out the card and pushed it back inside the envelope. She sniffled. "We should probably get back."

Madison waited a few seconds and nodded.

"Thank you." Joni touched Madison's wrist, and with the contact, Madison absorbed the woman's heartbreak. There would be no bringing back the man she loved, even if his killer was found. She'd have to move forward without Barry, comforted only by the memories and the love they had shared.

Madison wished, as she had many times before for the families of murder victims, that she had the power to resurrect them or somehow reverse time and circumstance. But instead, she had to surrender and tackle what she was capable of doing: finding their killers.

CHAPTER 19

MADISON STORMED INTO THE POLICE STATION. Terry was next to her, keeping up with her strides now. Her drive had been reignited from their visit to the Weirs' house. A part of her would love to punch Troy in the nose for not going over there yet, but another part knew he was hurting too much to realize just how selfish he was being. Maybe it was this pain that blinded him to how he was treating her, but she found that thinking harder to accept.

She headed straight for the room where Erica Snyder would be consulting with the sketch artist, assuming she wasn't finished. Two hours had already passed.

"I better check in at home after this," Terry said.

Madison glanced over at him. She wondered how much Gail's comment about being a cop and a husband and father had affected him. "Why don't you give Annabelle a call?"

"I did that when you went after Troy."

It was there in the tone of his voice. He knew something had happened between them. If her partner were a woman, this would likely turn into a big ordeal. Women tended to dig deeper, cull out underlying feelings more than men. It wasn't sexist; it was nature. She'd have observed a change in Madison's attitude, sensed her heartbreak, and poked and prodded until Madison burst into tears. Thankfully, Terry was letting her off without giving her too much trouble. He was still a detective, though, and she could tell he'd figured something was wrong, but he was smart enough—or just male enough—not to dig into it, and she took advantage of the pass.

Madison opened the door to the room, and the artist looked up at her. He was bent over, putting his things away in his satchel. "Detectives—" he came to a full seated position "—we've actually just finished up here." He held up a tablet, and on the screen was the sketch of a young adult, Caucasian male wearing a hoodie. His nose was bulbous and wide, and his eyes were shadowed.

Madison looked over at Snyder. She was sitting back in her chair, one hand holding a soda can.

"You meant what you said, right? I'm safe?" Snyder asked.

"It's being worked out."

Snyder sat straight up, panic lacing her features. "What do you mean 'worked out'?"

"Just that." Madison turned to address the artist. "Make sure a copy of that gets out to everyone."

"You're kidding me," Snyder sulked.

The sketch artist spoke over her, to Madison. "This isn't my first rodeo." He got up, gathered his bag, and put the strap over a shoulder. "You both probably already have the e-mail with the photo on your phones."

Terry pulled his out, seemingly to see if that was the case, but the artist left the room before her partner could confirm.

Madison focused on Erica Snyder. "You'll be staying in a safe house."

Snyder's shoulders seemed to relax.

"But there's something that isn't sitting well with me,"

Madison said. "You told us that you didn't recognize the shooter."

Snyder stared into her eyes. "I didn't."

"But you're absolutely terrified to go home." Madison sat down in her chair. "Here's what I'm thinking. You do know the people behind the shooting. You saw either them or people similar to them in your neighborhood before."

Snyder glanced away.

"Street gangs adopt symbols that represent them." Madison paused, waiting for Snyder to react. "Do you get where I'm going with this?"

"You think I've seen the decal you showed me." Stated without emotion.

"That's right."

"I might have seen it before…in my neighborhood."

"Where exactly did you see it?"

"No, no." Panic flashed in Snyder's eyes, and she started shaking. "You're going to go there and somehow they are going to know that I snitched on them."

Madison balled a fist under the table but managed to keep her tone calm. "You do know these people."

"No."

"A cop is dead. He was my friend. My brother." Emotion was turning her voice gravelly, and Madison gestured to Terry. "His friend. His brother." She made a circle with her arm to indicate the entire police department. She took a deep breath. "We need your help. Tell us where you saw the decal."

"It might not even mean anything."

"We'll determine that. Now where was it?"

"The next street over from where I live. Chestnut. It's a beige-sided house, two stories. It was on the side of a jalopy that was parked in the yard, up on blocks, but I could see it from the sidewalk."

"And you're absolutely certain this was the decal you saw?" Madison pulled the photo up on her phone.

Snyder looked at the screen. "I swear to you."

"When did you see it?"

"Last week." She glanced at Terry, then back to Madison, and she hitched her shoulders. "I braved a walk."

"And that's all. You've only seen it the one time, and it was last week?" Terry asked incredulously.

"That's right."

Madison narrowed her eyes at Snyder. For some reason, she believed the woman. And if the woman was telling the truth, they just had their first real lead.

Troy was at his desk working through Weir's arrest history, on the lookout for any addresses in the vicinity of Rico's and so far not striking any gold for his troubles. Someone tapped him on the shoulder, and he turned around to find Sergeant Winston staring down at him.

"What are you doing?" Winston asked, his tone hard.

"I'm working." Troy went back to his scrolling.

"I thought you excused yourself to get some rest."

"I did. And now I'm rested." Troy let go of the mouse and sat back, clasping his hands in his lap. "I'm good."

"No one asked if you were, but I'm glad you are…"

Troy ran his hands down his face. He was exhausted. His eyes caught the clock on the wall. Eight going on midnight… He just hated the holding pattern he was currently stuck in.

Winston pointed at the screen. "What are you looking for?"

"The shooter's car didn't have plates."

"Not a new revelation."

"Well, I don't think they'd drive too far without plates and risk being stopped. I think they either came from a neighborhood near Rico's or removed them in that area. I'm looking to see if Weir's history pointed to anyone in that vicinity."

"Unless Weir wasn't their target." Winston raised his eyebrows. "They could have been happy with any cop they came across."

Troy hated to admit to that possibility. It would make narrowing things down near impossible.

After a few seconds, Winston consented. "I'll play along. Say Weir *was* the target… Still, maybe the car never had plates to start with. They might not have cared about that risk."

Troy nodded. "I thought of that, too."

"Did you try looking into BMWs registered in close proximity to Rico's?"

"First thing I did, and no luck."

"Well, I might as well tell you now. We've got Gangs officers listening in on a few gangs' hideouts, including the Hellions."

"Are they using a parabolic mic?"

"Yeah."

"For the Hellions', where are they positioning themselves?" If the officers were set up in such a place that they picked up on members outside, it was considered public.

"A neighboring property that backs up against the yard for the Hellions' hideout." Winston checked his watch. "They'll be in position now."

"Keep me posted." Troy looked back to his screen. One

benefit to the varied approaches on this investigation meant a wider net, making it more likely they'd catch the driver and the shooter sooner rather than later.

CHAPTER 20

"DID YOU WANT TO STOP by and see Annabelle first?" Madison fastened her belt as Terry settled into the passenger seat. They were headed to Chestnut Street in search of the beige-sided house with a decaled jalopy.

"Since when are you so concerned about Annabelle?"

"I guess it's just everything that's happened today… We can never know what's going to happen."

"No, we can't."

Silence fell in the car for a while, and then Terry broke it. "I'm probably going to be in for a butt-kicking when I get home, though."

Butt-kicking. Only Terry wouldn't call it an *ass-kicking*. Him and his aversion to anything close to swearing.

"That's if I get home," Terry added with a small grin. "We're headed to Satan's house."

Only her partner would say something like that and toss in a smile.

She put the car in gear, and twenty minutes later, they were on Chestnut. The house was easy to spot and one of the least cared-for properties in the area. Just as Snyder had described, part of the backyard was visible from the road, and there was a rust bucket up on cinder blocks. From this vantage point, Madison couldn't see the decal. Maybe once she got out of the car and onto the sidewalk… But first things first.

She plugged the address into the laptop and searched for information on the history of the house and its current residents. The good news was the Stiles PD hadn't been called out to the house before. She brought up the residents' names and turned the monitor so Terry could see the results.

Terry leaned over to read the information, his eyes only a few inches from the screen. "Three names, all males, early to midtwenties."

"Do you need glasses?"

He straightened up. "No, I—"

"The way you've got your nose to the screen, I'd say you do."

"I can see it perfectly from here." He held eye contact for a bit longer before glancing back to the laptop. But doing so was straining his eyes if the vein popping in his forehead and the skin pinching in the corners of his eyes were any indication.

"Uh-huh. I can see that."

He rolled his eyes, and she smiled. Usually she was the one shooting him a narrow-eyed glare or rolling her eyes.

Terry pressed a finger to the screen. "Their names are Clark Cousins, Travis Sommer, and Mike Godfrey." He clicked on Cousins's record. It showed a misdemeanor charge a few years back. Next was Sommer, and his record was clean. Godfrey's record showed he was in and out of foster homes as a kid and spent some time in juvie, but he hadn't been behind bars as an adult. "No BMWs or weapons registered to any of them," Terry added.

"All right, let's go meet the Three Stooges."

"Ha-ha."

Madison shrugged a shoulder and got out of the car.

"It doesn't look like anyone is home," Terry said, obviously noting, as she had, the drawn "curtains" that were really bedsheets.

"Guess we'll find out."

They walked up the drive, and with the light from the moon and the back porch, Madison made out the sticker on the rear quarter panel of the jalopy before she got too far. She pointed at the decal. "There it is."

A shiver raced down her spine, and she talked herself into calming down. It was an image, nothing more. It couldn't reach out and bite her. Despite not being raised in a religious household that drummed the concepts of heaven and hell into her head, she still had a respect for good and evil, light and dark. And if these people knew what they had put on that car—if they were aware of its symbolism—they were potentially dangerous. She was ready to draw her gun if the need arose, but she wasn't going to put her hand anywhere close to her holster so as not to possibly provoke anyone watching through a crack.

Her heart was pounding as she headed to the front door with Terry. She banged on the wooden door and then rang the bell. "Stiles PD! Open up!"

Terry was gaping at her. "You think you could go about things a little less—"

The door flung open. A man in his twenties, about six foot two, appeared. Smug arrogance had his face scrunched up, his lips curled in disgust. His eyes were sharp and focused. "What do you want? None of us here have done anything wrong."

"It's funny how your mind instantly goes into defensive mode," Madison snapped.

"What do you 'spect? Cops show up at my door, nearly

banging it down."

She lifted her badge, which was on a chain in a holder around her neck. "What's your name?" She let the badge fall back against her chest.

"Hey, you came to my house, you should know."

"Three men live here. Your name?" This time Madison's tone didn't allow for wiggle room or avoidance.

"I'm CC. Now it's your turn."

Clark Cousins, she presumed.

He hooked his thumbs into the waist of his jeans, which were already riding low on his hips and appeared to have seen better days. But then again, tattered jeans were *a thing*.

"Detectives Knight and Grant. Why don't you tell us about the decal on that piece of crap car out there?"

"How 'bout I don't?"

She cocked her head and leveled her gaze on him. "How about you do and we don't lock your ass in jail?"

He pressed his tongue to his cheek, pushing it out. "What's it to you?"

If she told him a cop had been shot and that the decal had been seen on the shooter's car, he'd probably be the type to find it amusing, and then she'd have a really hard time not busting his face. Or if he was involved, things could turn dark fast.

"The same decal was seen on a car at a crime scene this morning."

Cousins laughed. "As you can see for yourself, that car hasn't gone anywhere."

"I never said it was *that* car. I said it was the same decal. What does it mean, and where did you get it?"

"You'd have to ask Sommer. The POS out back is his. So is the decal."

"Did he design it?" Madison asked.

Cousins shrugged.

"Where is Mr. Sommer now?"

"*Mister?* All formal. I like it." He leaned against the doorframe and ogled her from her shoes upward. His eyes paused at breast level. Eventually, his gaze came up to meet hers. The invitation in them was all too obvious and instantly nauseating.

"Hey, Casanova." Terry snapped his fingers. "Travis Sommer—where is he?"

Cousins curled his lips and gave one more fleeting look at Madison before trudging down a hallway.

"Where are you going?" she called out.

"To get T."

When Cousins was out of earshot, Madison turned to Terry. "CC, T… What the heck? Hey, you could be T, too."

About a minute later, the sound of a back door swinging open caught their attention.

"He's making a run for it," Terry said, leaping off the front stoop and rounding the side of the house.

"Ah, son of a bitch!" Madison grumbled.

She followed Terry, but she hated running pursuits. *Detested* might not even be a strong enough word to accurately describe her feelings.

The west end of the backyard was mostly covered by a crooked, run-down garage. That left the north and east sides of the property. Chain-link fences lined both those sides, but at only four feet high they weren't much of a challenge for a motivated suspect to hop over.

Madison saw a man running north. It wasn't Cousins, so she guessed it was Sommer. So much for his clean record. Only the guilty and/or the terrified fled. Either way, it meant he had something to offer the investigation.

"Stop!" she called out as she kept moving. Since she'd been with Troy, she'd started exercising more, taking Hershey for daily walks, but still… Running was the Devil's pastime. "Shit!" Her ankle twisted slightly on the hard, uneven ground. She somehow caught her balance and stayed upright.

"Stiles PD!" Terry yelled from ahead of her. "Stop where you are!" Then, as if he had nitros attached to his ass, he really kicked his speed into high gear. He jumped over the fence, clearing it by at least six inches.

Maybe she could just stand back and catch her breath… Terry had this under control.

But despite her weak body trying to control her mind and willpower, she pushed through. She sized up the fence and pictured herself jumping over it and clearing it in the same way Terry just had.

She amped up her speed. The exertion of her muscles was actually feeling good and feeding her energy. She was ten feet from the fence, five, two— Her legs ground to a halt, but her upper body didn't get the message in time, and she slammed against the fence.

Her heart was pounding fiercely. All she could keep picturing was a broken arm or leg and blood. She swallowed the bile that rose simply from the image in her head of not clearing the fence and looked in the direction Terry had headed.

Terry tackled Sommer, and both men crashed to the ground. Sommer was aiming blows at Terry's head, but Terry jerked out of the way each time and rolled so that he was on top of Sommer. With the guy pinned beneath him, Terry managed to flip Sommer facedown and yank his arms back to cuff him.

And now it's on.

CHAPTER 21

"WHY DID YOU RUN, TRAVIS?" Madison was pacing the interrogation room while Terry had assumed his spot against the back wall. He hadn't yet started jingling his change, but he would soon enough.

Travis Sommer was seated at the table, his arms on the surface, hands no longer cuffed but clasped in front of him. His eyes followed her every step as she, too, watched him.

"I ran because cops were there to see me." Derision licked every evenly paced word.

"Not a good enough answer, Travis."

"Why do you keep saying my name?"

"As you said, it's your name. Should I call you something else?" She stared at him blankly.

Sommer expelled a heavy breath. "Travis is fine."

"Do cops come to see you often?"

Sommer remained silent.

She addressed Terry. "He's hiding something."

"I don't—" Sommer ran a hand down his face. "You know who I live with, right? CC and Godfrey. They're both criminals, not me."

"Wow, friend of the year," Madison said.

"I'm just telling you how it is, and it's probably not anything you don't already know. I don't have a record of any kind."

Madison slipped into the chair across from him. "That doesn't really mean anything. Maybe you just haven't been caught."

He leveled her with a stare. "Are you serious?"

She solidified her stance. "What do you think?"

"Well, I'm not guilty of anything."

"You ran from police officers," she stated. "You must have something to hide."

"What do you want?"

She placed a photo of the decal on the table in front of him. "What does it mean, and where did you get it?"

"That's why you want to talk to me? Because of a sticker on a piece of junk? That car isn't even roadworthy."

Madison slapped down a photograph of Barry in uniform. She remained silent for a few seconds. But it wasn't for dramatic effect and it wasn't to further impact Sommer; it was because she needed to steady her emotions.

"That is Officer Weir. He was killed this morning. Shot while he was pumping gas into his cruiser," she said sharply.

"Well I didn't do it."

"This decal—" she pressed her fingertip to the photo "—was seen at the crime scene on the shooter's vehicle. So you need to start talking."

Sommer blinked rapidly. "I had nothing to do with that."

Madison leaned across the table. "Talk."

Terry started jingling the change in his pockets.

"I, uh, I got the decal a long time ago."

Do I need to hold his hand the entire way?

"We're listening…"

Sommer went pale except for splotches of red in his cheeks and on his neck. "You were right about not getting caught... I did some things in my life, things I'm not proud of, but I'm a changed man."

"As evidenced by the company you keep." She couldn't force the skepticism from her voice.

His eyes fired to hers, but he didn't hold the gaze. "Judge them however you like. Anyway, I got involved with some questionable people." He looked down at the photo of the decal. "That star and the goat—it's the Devil's sign. They thought it was cool to toy around with that crap. They performed ceremonies... They hurt animals."

Liquid heat made its way from Madison's stomach and up her spine, the rage pulsing beneath her skin. "You hurt them, too?" She could barely get the words out through her clenched jaw.

"No! I couldn't bring myself to. It's part of why I was kicked out."

Even to hear that Sommer himself didn't get involved in animal cruelty and torture did little to dampen the fire that had started inside Madison just at his mention of it. She worked to defend human lives that were snuffed out, but she felt just as strongly about standing up for animals who looked to humankind for nurturing. Anyone who raised a hand to—or neglected—an animal didn't deserve to be called human. Her mind slipped to the K-9 unit and the law under review that would approach the killing of these fine animals in the same way as taking down an officer. Her vote would be cast in favor thereof.

She pulled out the sketch artist's drawing of the shooter. "Do you recognize this man?"

Sommer studied the image for a while before responding. "I wish I could say yes."

"Who else was involved with this gang you were in?"

"A gang?" Sommer's lips twitched, and his eyes brightened. Was that pride?

Technically, the law considered any group of three people joined together for the purpose of participating in criminal activity a "gang."

"How many of you were there?" she asked.

Sommer stared her in the eye. He wasn't going to answer.

She'd let that question go. *For now.* "Did they ever torture or kill people?"

Sommer leaned back in the chair and crossed his arms. "Maybe I need a lawyer."

"The only reason you'd need a lawyer is if you were directly involved with those crimes. Were you?"

Now Sommer wouldn't look her in the eye.

"Were you?" she repeated.

"No," he spat. "But I feel guilty about it every day. I didn't do anything to help. I—"

"You feel guilty but you weren't involved?"

"I witnessed things…"

"Murders?"

No answer.

"Human or animal?"

Still no response.

"Did you witness what they did with the bodies?"

Sommer crossed his arms.

"Did you—"

"Yes, yes, all right!" His eyes widened, and he banged the table with the side of his fist.

She put a lined notepad in front of him with a pen and pointed at the office supplies. "Their names. Now."

Sommer picked up the pen, holding it lengthwise and

pinching an end with each hand, and stared at it as if it would provide him answers. "They will kill me if they find out. I'm surprised they've even let me live as long as I have."

"Would these people kill a cop?"

Sommer let go of the pen. "I don't know. But I want to see a lawyer."

"I DON'T KNOW!" Out in the hallway, Madison spun to face Terry. "I can't believe this. He knows where bodies are buried, he knows what these people are capable of, but he's demanding a lawyer? Barry is dead, and Sommer's so-called friends from years ago might even be behind this. How can we just stand by while the clock is ticking?"

Terry's face was stoic.

"How can you be so calm about this?"

"We don't know that these people were involved in Barry's death. All we have is a sticker, Maddy."

"All we have is a sticker? Are you being serious? Do you hear yourself right now? The word on the street is that a gang is claiming responsibility—"

"The decal doesn't tie back to any gang."

"That we know of," she pointed out. "And how are we supposed to just close our eyes to these other violent crimes Sommer mentioned? How do we know that Sommer isn't connected in some way to the Hellions now?"

Terry was quiet for a second. "Let's take things one step at a time."

"Again, how can you be so calm, Terry? Barry's killers are out there and…" She saw the pain in her partner's eyes. "You know that."

"Like you said, they're out there. We need to keep

ourselves together and focused. For Barry. We don't have enough to hold Sommer." He held eye contact with her, and she found the adrenaline cooling in her system.

"Sommer mentioned fearing for his safety. What if we offered up a safe house to him like we did for Snyder? In exchange, he'd have to give us information on the gang he was in."

"It's worth a try, I suppose," she said and led the way back to the interrogation room.

Sommer lifted his head when they walked in. "I'm free to go?"

"You have information we want," Madison stated.

Sommer looked away. "I asked for a lawyer."

"What if we made you a deal?"

Sommer shrugged and made eye contact with her.

"You're afraid for your safety. You talk, and we'll ensure that safety."

Sommer burst out laughing.

She formed fists with both hands. Maybe it was a good time to take up boxing. She had a little experience with it from physical training at the start of her career and hadn't really loved it, but the idea of slamming blows into a punching bag sounded good right about now.

Madison stormed from the room and threw her arms in the air.

Terry came out after her. "We can't make him talk, Maddy. And we don't really have enough to hold him."

She felt a coolness blanket her now. Did he think she didn't know that already? It was just so frustrating. "Well, he told us something." She aligned her gaze with her partner's. "He's not that afraid, is he?"

"I'd say no."

"It honestly wouldn't surprise me if he was still

involved with his previous friends. Did you see how he looked when I referred to them as a gang?"

Terry nodded. "I did. He almost seemed proud."

"So we need to figure out how he and this little gang factor into Barry's shooting…"

"Yes, Maddy, but it's not happening tonight. I'm headed home for some sleep. I'm going to hug both my girls and kiss my wife. You go home and get some rest, too."

She nodded, and while she was happy for him, loneliness suffocated her. She'd be going home to an empty apartment, an empty bed. It was a feeling she hadn't felt in a long time, and its eerie familiarity definitely wasn't welcome.

CHAPTER 22

MADISON PLANNED TO PUT OFF going home as long as she could, and she figured she may as well try to accomplish something during that time. She started with reviewing Snyder's file. For someone who claimed to be afraid to talk, Snyder had done a lot of it, but they'd had to work to get information out of her. What if she was still holding back? What if she wasn't afraid because she simply recognized the shooter, or even because she recognized the decal? What if she actually knew the group—or gang—behind it?

If she did, Madison had to get her to talk. She signed out a department sedan and drove to the safe house where Snyder had been set up.

The place was a two-story, redbrick, turn-of-the-century house in a middle-income neighborhood. Madison showed her badge and was directed to Snyder's room. She knocked, and Snyder answered wearing a cotton robe over a pair of plaid pajamas. Somehow seeing her like this made Madison view her more as *Erica* than *Snyder*.

"What are you doing here?" Erica asked. "I thought you got everything you needed from me."

"Can I come in?"

"Do I have a choice?" Erica stepped back, and Madison

squeezed between her and the doorframe. She didn't understand why Erica was giving her attitude. She'd followed through and had gotten Erica the protection she'd wanted.

The room was on the claustrophobic side, even though the furnishings were minimal. There was a twin-size mattress and a night table, a desk with a chair, and a table with a hot plate and a kettle. There wasn't any running water in the small room, and Erica had to share a communal bathroom.

Erica sat on the end of the bed.

Madison remained standing and closed the door behind her. "I'd like to talk to you more about that decal you saw."

Erica took a heavy breath. "What about it?"

"Do you know what it stands for?"

Erica licked her lips and bit down on the bottom one.

Madison let the silence ride out until Erica broke it.

"A rebel flag and a goat's head in a star?"

Madison stared at her and remained quiet. Erica's eyes were giving her away.

"Fine. I know what it is and what it stands for."

Why was everything with this woman like peeling away layers of an onion?

Erica continued. "The goat head in the star on its own stands for the sign of the Devil. This imagery, along with the rebel flag, was adopted by the Devil's Rebels."

"A gang?"

"As far as I'm concerned."

"Do you know how many members they have?" Madison would ask Gangs about them, too, but she wasn't hopeful.

"I couldn't know for sure," Erica answered.

Madison scanned her eyes. "But you have an idea."

Erica shrugged. "They're small. Maybe ten guys."

"If people wanted to get in with them, is there some sort of initiation?" Madison asked even though they didn't exactly seem to be the recruiting kind. Their circle seemed tight-knit, a handful of friends.

"Don't know."

"So do you know a Travis Sommer?" Madison tossed it out there as bait to see if Erica would nibble.

Erica's eyes snapped to Madison's. "Trav?"

To refer to him by abbreviating his name, they must have been close. "Do you have a romantic relationship with him?"

"No," Erica punched out. "But I did years ago."

Madison's ears heated with rage. Trying to extract information from this woman was beyond frustrating. Madison could shake her.

"He's the one I'm afraid of," Erica told her then.

"Why didn't you tell us this from the start? Did you know it was his place on Chestnut?"

"No, but I wondered… Trav has a way of finding things out. He'll have me killed for talking. I've seen what he's capable of."

The information was coming fast now. For Travis Sommer to have her killed, it would mean he was a top player in the Devil's Rebels. It would explain the pride in his eyes when Madison referred to the group as a gang. Maybe if Madison squeezed harder, got more out of Erica, she'd be able to gather the evidence that would get a criminal charge to stick to Sommer. But how did this tie into Barry's murder? The sketch of the shooter didn't resemble Sommer, and there was no connection between him and a BMW—at least not yet. But it could belong to another Devil's Rebel…

She needed names, but she was after something else first.

"What did you see him do exactly?" Madison asked.

"I got to Trav's place early one night."

"When was this?" Madison interrupted.

"About two years ago."

"Where did he live then? Still on Chestnut?"

"No. The other end of town." Erica provided the street name and number. "We lost touch."

"So you arrived at his place early…" Madison prompted.

"Uh-huh. A couple of his friends were there."

"Names."

"I only know one name."

So much for getting a list out of her…

"Mike," she said.

"Mike Godfrey?" Madison confirmed.

It couldn't be this easy, could it?

"I only remember his first name."

Madison recalled Godfrey's DMV photo but appreciated that his characteristics could have changed from the time Erica knew him until now. "Dark hair to his collarbones, skinny, sunken cheeks?" she tried anyway.

Erica nodded. "Sounds like him."

"What were they doing?"

"Well, there was yelling inside. I let myself in the back door and… I can't get the images out of my head. Travis and the other two were beating on some guy. There was so much blood on the kitchen floor they were having a hard time finding traction, but it didn't stop them from kicking him in the ribs and the head." Tears fell down her cheeks.

"Were the police called?"

"I don't know."

Madison would look into the history of the property. "Did they kill him?"

Erica's eyes were glazed over, and Madison snapped her fingers. She repeated her question.

"I…I don't know. Trav told me I should never have seen what I had. He also said the guy was bad, ya know…" Erica was chewing on her bottom lip vigorously, and Madison wouldn't be surprised if she made it bleed. Erica ran a hand down one arm, then the other. "The Devil's Rebels have connections in the drug world. The guy they were beating was a dealer and had stolen from them."

"You say you don't know if they killed him, but they were still beating him when you left?"

Erica was shaking. "Travis shuffled me out the back door, and we went on a date."

What the hell was wrong with some people? A guy was bleeding all over a kitchen floor, possibly barely hanging on to his life, and it was time for a steak and a movie?

"And you just went with him after what you saw?"

Erica wiped away a fresh batch of tears. "What else could I do? I was afraid. He told me to forget about what I had seen and if I ever talked about it…"

"He'd kill you?"

"Exactly."

"Would you be willing to testify to what you had seen? If it came down to that."

"You're kidding, right? It's one thing telling you, and another—"

"We'd get you into WITSEC. New identity, new place—"

"So essentially I'd be dead anyway," Erica interrupted.

Madison could empathize with Erica's frustration. She wouldn't take to flipping her world upside down, either. But there was a larger picture to consider. "You haven't exactly been forthcoming with us. If my sergeant realized this, I'm not sure he would have approved this." Madison gestured around the room, implying the safe house as a whole.

"I don't need this place." Erica jutted out her chin. "I just wanted some protection. I feel like I'm in prison. Can't you just assign officers to watch over me in my home?"

So that explained Erica's prickly demeanor when she showed up…

Madison scanned Erica's eyes, not sure what to make of her. She was scared for her life, but she was picky about how she was protected. She'd admitted to a previous relationship with Travis Sommer, but what if it wasn't all in the past? It might not be a bad idea to give Snyder her way, get a detail to watch over her for a while and see what they could find out. She'd run it past Winston.

"Let me see what I can do."

Chapter 23

Madison was back at the station and brought up the history on the address Erica had provided for Sommer from two years back. The results were disheartening. And nonexistent. But she still had this feeling in her gut that the Devil's Rebels required more attention, and she saw Snyder being released from the safe house as the perfect bait to find out just how much she knew and if she was still close to them.

She found Winston at his desk, stationed behind a barricade of paperwork—basically something that was synonymous with the man. He'd already been looking at the doorway when Madison had rounded the frame. His eyes were bloodshot, and bags shadowed them. His complexion was pale, too.

"Why are you still here?" Winston peered at Madison. "I guess I should know better."

"Do you remember Erica Snyder?"

"The woman who provided the sketch for the shooter and who I put in a safe house?"

"That would be the one. And I actually need to talk to you about that safe house."

Winston's eyes narrowed skeptically. "What about it?"

Maybe it was best she bring him up-to-date on Sommer and the Devil's Rebels and then broach the subject of pulling officers from investigating Barry's murder in order to babysit Snyder. "The decal on the shooter's car is affiliated with a gang known as the Devil's Rebels."

"Where's this information coming from?"

"Snyder. She thinks there are probably about ten members."

"Why is this my first time hearing about them, then?"

"They must be good at not getting caught. Snyder has provided me the names of a few members, and she has told me that she witnessed a man being brutally beaten."

Winston seemed interested now. His elbows were on the desk, and he leaned toward her. "Did this man die?"

"I don't know. She doesn't know. I ran a background on the address where the assault supposedly took place, but it shows nothing. Oh, and Sommer is involved in her allegations. From what Snyder told me, he's pretty high up the totem pole, though according to him, he left the gang a long time ago. But that's not all… Snyder admits to a romantic relationship with Sommer and claims that it ended, but I have my suspicions."

"Ah, I think I see where you're going with this." Winston steepled his fingers. "If we get her pulled from the safe house, we can put surveillance on her and see if Sommer comes around."

"Correct."

"So you believe they might be the gang behind the shooting?"

"It's possible. I find it hard to ignore that their symbol was on the shooter's car."

Winston looked away, and there was something in his energy that told Madison he already had something in the works.

"What is it?"

Winston made eye contact with her, and the way he was studying her eyes conveyed he was impressed by her ability to read him. "Well it has nothing to do with these Devil Rebels, but we've got people in place listening to well-known gangs around the city."

"Meaning?"

"Parabolic mics."

"Has the name of a gang claiming responsibility come back, then?" Anger was growing in her belly, the thought of being left out of the loop gnawing on her.

"Not yet."

"All right, well, do you really see a gang using another's symbol? Because I don't."

"The BMW could have been stolen."

"So? They'd have taken the decal off. Running with the seeming fact that a gang was behind this, they'd want to earn respect on the streets for the murder." She picked up on how she'd really gotten into detective mode, detaching herself from the fact the man murdered had been her friend. "Besides, I'm not so certain the BMW used in the shooting was stolen. None were reported stol—" There was something there beneath the surface of her words, a clue… "Wait! While the shooter and driver didn't seem too concerned about getting caught, they aren't entirely stupid, either. They did take the plates off…" She made sure to look Winston in the eye when she continued. "If they stole the car, they wouldn't have even worried about the plates. Why not let it tie back to the owner?"

"What are you thinking, Knight?"

"The car wasn't reported stolen, so they must know the person who owns the car."

"They stole it from a friend?"

"Or borrowed it. They could have used a friend's or

relative's car—with or without their knowledge." She might not have a list of Devil's Rebels members yet, but she could start with the names she had—Sommer and Godfrey. For good measure, she could look deeper into Cousins's family and Snyder's, too. Then she could compare any of their relatives' names and see if they matched up with any of the fifty people who owned the model of BMW they were after.

Winston seemed to literally gnaw on her hypothesis as he chewed the inside of his cheek. "I'll get Snyder back home and put uniforms on her."

"Thanks, Sarge."

Winston looked at the clock, and Madison followed his gaze. It was almost midnight.

"Now why don't you go home and get some sleep. Tomorrow will be another long day."

She nodded and went toward the door, acting as if she were going to comply with his advice when she certainly wasn't planning to go home yet only to be alone.

CHAPTER 24

MADISON DROVE AROUND THE CITY, dreading the thought of going home to her apartment. Without Hershey there, and knowing that the man she woke up next to this morning was no longer a part of her life, left her with such a coldness in her chest that it was hard to breathe. And something about the darkness of night only made it worse.

She dabbed the tears that fell down her cheeks with a fingertip and found that more were coming faster than she could wipe them all away. She gave up and let them fall.

The traffic light ahead just turned orange, and she pressed the brake. As she waited for the green, she cried, her chest heaving as her lungs hungered for oxygen. Barry's loss washed over her, as did her separation from Troy. She cursed herself for her vulnerability. Maybe her initial instincts in that area had been correct: if she exposed herself, all that would come of it was a broken heart.

The light changed, and she accelerated, realizing that she was in her sister's neighborhood. She glanced at the dash. One in the morning.

Madison shook her head. It was absurd that she was even thinking about dropping in. Chelsea, her brother-in-law, and her nieces would be fast asleep.

"Go home." She said the words to herself, but they rang empty in the car, and she found herself turning into their driveway.

She turned off the car and stared at the house. Maybe she could just sleep in her Mazda tonight...or this morning. It wouldn't be long before the sun would be coming up anyhow. Five, maybe six hours.

She tilted the driver's seat back, put her arms under her head, and closed her eyes. Thoughts about what she'd say to her sister in the morning were overpowered by pure exhaustion. The tears had dried up and left her feeling empty.

A knock on the driver's-side window had her bolting upright. Her heart was thumping so hard her ribs were taking a beating.

What the—

It was Chelsea standing next to the car in pajamas.

Madison turned the key in the ignition and lowered the window.

Chelsea cocked her head to the side. "You're not even going to get out of your car?"

Her sister wasn't like other people. Other people would have asked her what she was doing there first.

"Yeah...uh, sure." She put the window up and turned the car off. The grogginess in her head and the stiffness in her neck and back told her she must have drifted off for a while. The clock on the dash confirmed that she'd been out for a couple of hours.

Madison unlocked the door and Chelsea had it open before Madison found the handle.

Whoa. A bad hangover had nothing over the way she was feeling right now. Her head was spinning. It had to be from sitting up so quickly, or maybe she'd pinched a nerve in her neck from the way she'd been resting.

Chelsea reached for her and drew Madison into an embrace. She kissed Madison's cheek. "Come on inside."

Madison waved a hand. "It's all right. I'll go." She glanced at the house, which was no longer in complete darkness as the front porch light was on. So was the one inside the entry.

"Nonsense. Get inside." Chelsea reached around Madison and pushed the car door shut. Her sister was as hardheaded as she was.

"I didn't want to wake you up," Madison said.

"Well, it's too late for that now, isn't it?"

"I guess it is." Madison took a few steps with her sister, Chelsea's arm around her. "Oh, wait." She hurried back to the car for her keys and locked it by using the button on the door so as not to inadvertently double-click on her key fob and cause the horn to honk.

"You can sleep in the spare room. It's not made up, but there are sheets and a comforter in the closet." Chelsea entered her house first and held the door for Madison. Once Madison was inside, she locked the dead bolt.

"It's okay. I should go, Chels."

"Seriously?" It was phrased with the arch of a question but wasn't really intended as one. It came out more like a chastisement than anything, probably for getting her out of bed. Her sister was a stay-at-home mom, and that would be Chelsea's only saving grace come six AM. Although she'd still have to cart the girls off to school before eight.

"I don't need to sleep. I'll be fine." Guilt for waking her sister was snaking through Madison. "Jim still—"

Chelsea was nodding. "He'd sleep through a hurricane."

"How did you know I was in the driveway?"

"I saw you pull in around one. The lights shone into the bedroom."

"Sorry." Madison cringed and wondered why her sister hadn't come out then if she'd woken up.

"I wanted to let you be for a while. I figured if you wanted to come in, you would," Chelsea explained herself as if she read Madison's mind. "I drifted off but woke up realizing I'd have to go get you."

"What were you doing up at one?"

"I'm a light sleeper, you know that. It stinks, but it is what it is. I'm surprised you can sleep at all given what you see every day."

Maybe it hadn't been a good idea to come here. Had all their mother's incessant yapping about her career choice finally affected Chelsea? Madison wasn't sure exactly where Chelsea was headed with her comment, but it was probably best to leave that one untouched.

Madison slipped out of her shoes and headed up the stairs in the direction of the spare room. Her body was so exhausted that each step was a struggle. She'd made it up about five of the stairs when her sister spoke.

"That's it? You're not going to tell me why you're here in the middle of the night?"

Madison turned around and found Chelsea still at the base of the staircase. God, she didn't want to tell her all about Troy and her broken heart and her empty apartment…her empty life.

"Tea?" her sister offered, seemingly picking up on how lost Madison was feeling.

"Fine." Madison headed back down to the main level, but there would be no need to bring up her failed romance. Comparing herself to her sister, knowing she had a husband who loved her and three beautiful daughters sleeping above them, just drove in what a disaster Madison was when it came to her personal life. "Decaf," she added as she trailed behind Chelsea. With any luck, they'd talk for a short time and Madison would still get some shut-eye.

Minutes later, the water had boiled and the tea had steeped. Madison sat across from her sister at the kitchen table, cradling her mug, drawing its warmth to her and hoping it would comfort her and lift her spirits. She took small sips, careful to blow on the hot liquid first.

"Tell me about the cop who was shot." She was staring in Madison's eyes.

"His death is still hard to talk about. Talking about him—" She swallowed roughly, the ache in her chest cinching her heart.

Chelsea nodded. "Of course, it would be. Sorry." She took a drink of her tea, lowered her mug, and sat back in her chair. "Mom called today. She'd heard about the shooting and wanted to know how you were."

Hearing this was like another stab to her heart. The woman had found time to call Chelsea but not her? She swallowed the emotion that welled up in her throat, refusing to give in to the urge to cry.

"If she wanted to know that, then she should have called me." The words rushed out of her, propelled by complex emotions hinged on anger and seeded in betrayal. Chelsea was the golden child; it was amazing Madison and Chelsea even got along given the wedge their mother could have easily put between them.

Chelsea glanced away. Madison knew she hated to be put in the middle, but their mother tended to do that to her all the time. Chelsea looked at Madison when she said, "I really wish you two would work things out."

"That's not happening anytime soon." Madison felt her defenses hardening, the shell becoming fortified to protect her heart. She'd had enough of being vulnerable. She'd been a fool to think it was a positive thing on any level.

"I told her you were doing fine. That's what you told me when we spoke."

"And let me guess, she got into how much better off I'd be if I just quit being a cop."

Chelsea was shaking her head. "Nope, not this time."

Madison studied her sister. "Really?"

"She was really worried about you, how you were taking it."

Madison lifted her chin. "Like I said, she could have called—"

"Yeah? You would have taken her call? I doubt it. Besides, when you're on a case, you shut everything and everyone out." Her sister's words were spoken with caution, presented in a delicate and loving tone, but they struck Madison like a spear nonetheless.

"I answered *your* call," she said in her defense, but her own doubt crept in. Had she been so focused on solving Barry's murder that she hadn't really made time for Troy and what he was going through? Was that why they were on a break? She pushed the doubts away. No, she'd tried to open him up, to get him to talk, and he'd refused.

"Why are you here, Maddy? Why aren't you with Troy?"

A tear escaped, and she wanted to retreat, run away, do whatever would take her out from under her sister's watchful—yet caring—eye.

Chelsea got up for a tissue box and brought it back to

the table. Instead of sitting where she had been before, she pulled out the chair beside Madison and sat down.

"He's taking all this…" The tears came on full force then, and Madison couldn't stop them. Grieving and being vulnerable absolutely sucked.

Her sister rubbed her back, but Madison pulled away. Chelsea's eyes showed hurt at the rejection, and Madison met her sister's gaze. Chelsea's expression softened as if she'd truly picked up on the extent of Madison's pain.

Madison took a few deep breaths. "He was really close to Barry. I guess their friendship goes back to childhood. Not that he told me that for himself." Madison pulled out a tissue and dabbed her nose. Chelsea didn't say anything. Apparently using silence was a family trick to getting people to open up. "I tried to let him know that I was here for him. You know, I really thought…" Was she actually going to bare all her feelings? She sighed. "I thought what we had was something special."

"I see the way he looks at you. He loves you. It's just grief—"

Madison held a hand up to her sister. "Please don't."

"What?"

"Please don't justify his behavior. Anyway, we're taking a break… What that means to him, I don't know, but I'm done. Maybe I'll become a lesbian."

Chelsea chuckled. "Yeah, like that's gonna happen."

Madison pressed her lips. "I never did give it a shot."

"I think you need to do what feels right to you. What's your heart saying?"

"About if I should become a lesbian?" Madison retorted quickly.

Chelsea angled her head. "Be serious."

Her sister wasn't going to let her leave without really

opening up. "I care about him…a lot."

Her sister was staring her down now.

"Fine, I love him. Are you happy?"

"All right, then." Chelsea sat back, still facing Madison. "Can I speak openly?"

"When haven't you?"

Chelsea bobbed her head from side to side. "You have a tendency to give up on people too quickly. You don't really give them a chance."

Madison felt herself bristle, and she shook her head. "No, I've changed."

"You were hurt by that loser—"

That loser was her sister's nickname for Toby Sovereign. Not exactly original, but it was fitting.

"—and you've let it stop you from giving your heart to someone else," Chelsea said. "But real living is from here—" she balled her hand into a fist and placed it on her chest over her heart "—and involves giving this away without thinking about the consequences and just trusting that it all will work out the way it should."

Thinking back on the last time she did that… "Huh. So Toby was meant to screw around on me?"

"Stop looking at it as so black-and-white. Okay, look at me and Jim. We've been married, what? Ten years? But every second hasn't been easy."

"Really? You guys are sickening to watch together."

"Thanks." Chelsea smiled. "Because if sickening means it's obvious we're in love, then I'll take it. But my point is, sometimes we have to fight for what we want."

"I tried, sis, but it's over."

"If it was, you wouldn't be over here in the wee hours crying in your tea."

Madison rolled her eyes, but her sister had a point. It

was far from over, but eventually it would be. She'd work through the disappointment and maybe not discount the lesbian thing entirely.

"The problem is, Maddy, that so many people are concerned about being right that they lose out because of it. But relationships are give and take. What's more important to you? Being right or making it work with Troy? If it is being right, sure, write him off and move on. But if you love him and want to be with him, being right isn't what's important."

Madison let out a small huff. "I'm just supposed to be okay with him shutting me out?"

"That's not what I'm saying at all. But at the end of the day, a relationship that's founded on tallying scores won't last. That's just my piece of advice." Her sister reached across the table for her tea and took a sip of it.

Madison's had cooled in her hands, but she didn't much feel like drinking it anyway. Maybe her baby sister had a point. Maybe she could try to find more empathy within herself for what Troy was going through. Still, when she thought about going to him, her ego took the hit.

What's more important to me? Being right or making it work with Troy?

Her heart was screaming out the answer, voting for the latter.

She shook her head. She couldn't handle this right now. Maybe after some sleep, she'd be able to think about it, but right now she just…couldn't.

CHAPTER 25

MADISON HAD LEFT CHELSEA'S AT seven and slipped home for a quick shower and change of clothes before hitting Starbucks for a venti caramel cappuccino on the way into the station. She'd need the caffeine to get through the day. She'd just sat down at her desk and Terry was walking toward her. While she'd planned on starting the request for all the family information on Sommer, Godfrey, Cousins, and Snyder, she'd fill her partner in on her visit to Snyder and what else she'd gleaned first.

"Hey," she said.

He was holding a Starbucks cup, too, and lifted it in greeting.

"I saw Snyder last night and got more out of her," she told him.

"Do tell."

She shared what she'd found out about Sommer, his history with Snyder, the alleged assault she'd witnessed, and her own suspicions that Snyder and Sommer were still involved, as well as Snyder's release from the safe house and how she was now being watched from her home.

"And nothing came back on the address she gave you?"

"Where the beating took place?" Madison shook her head. "No."

"I don't know about this girl. First, she flees the scene of the shooting and only speaks once she's cornered. Second, she offers information in bite-size pieces that we pretty much have to force out of her. She should have laid out everything when we first spoke with her. But she didn't. It's hinky."

"Hinky." Madison fought a smile. Her partner always had a way with words—if one could call it that. "But we can't prove anything yet. I'm going to request a comprehensive background report on all three roommates and Snyder, see if any relatives own a BMW 3 series sedan."

"Good idea."

"But the sergeant seems pretty certain a higher profile gang is involved." She told him about the parabolic mics. Then she looked at the clock. *8:20.* Their morning briefing was at 8:30.

"Come on," she said. "Let's get going."

MADISON STARTED OFF ON A mission to get into the squad room as quickly as she could but found that the closer she got, the more her legs wanted to stop moving. Troy would be there, and it would be the first time they'd have seen each other since they decided to take a break.

Her heart was beating slowly, but her breathing was labored—that old familiar feeling of heartbreak, one she should be used to by now. She came to a standstill outside the door, and Terry went past her.

"What are you doing?"

She looked in his eyes, and there was no way she'd be getting into her fractured love life now—or ever. So she resorted to a lie. "It feels like I have a stone in my shoe." She pulled up one leg, reached for her shoe, and Terry left her. With him out of sight, she lowered her leg. So now she was lying to her partner to protect her feelings? How low could she sink?

Her sister's words washed over her, or at least the part about living from the heart without thought to consequence. Could vulnerability really be a key ingredient to a truly magical life?

Somehow she wasn't drawing the correlation. But who was she to know? Chelsea could at least talk from the perspective of someone in a secure, lasting, loving relationship.

"Hey, Maddy."

Her breath caught at the deep voice. Troy was coming up from behind her.

She took a deep breath and steadied herself to turn around and look at him. His eyes that were usually such a striking green were stormy and dark, and the whites were bloodshot. Being right or making amends—which was more important to her?

Play it cool…

But she didn't know what to say.

"Guess we're going to find out if the gangs unit picked up on anything," he said.

She nodded like one of those stupid bobblehead dolls and felt as if she had just about as much air in her head right now.

He was peering into her eyes as if he wanted to say something else to her but wasn't certain if he should.

Maybe he would rather be right, and if so, she had to protect herself somehow. "I can come by and pick up my—"

Troy was shaking his head. "We'll sort it out later." She didn't know what to make of his tone. Was he holding out the hope of reconciliation or was he resigned to accepting that their relationship was over? Whichever it was, it wasn't the time to get into that here.

She gave him another look before stepping into the room.

Winston was at the front with Andrea. Both of them glanced at her and Troy as they entered. Madison felt the chief's continued gaze on her but wasn't going to acknowledge it right now. She spotted Terry and headed over to him.

"We have at least two solid leads at this time," Winston began. He recapped what Madison and Terry had learned about the decal. "They call themselves the Devil's Rebels, but before now, none of us were familiar with the name. There's reason to suspect they are—or at least were— involved with criminal activity, but Detectives Knight and Grant are still investigating to see if they can find any connection with the shooting of Officer Weir. But what we do know is that a member of the Hellions has started bragging about his involvement with the shooting. This fact was confirmed last night."

A hush fell over the room but no one interjected, and Winston continued. "As many of you know, officers from Gangs conducted surveillance on several gangs in the city last night, hoping to overhear or see something that might help us. Well, at the Hellions' hideout last night, they struck gold. A man named Russell Coleman—" Winston pointed to a colored photo on the whiteboard behind him of a man in his early twenties, Caucasian, with dark, scruffy facial hair and a small, almost beak-like nose. "He was boasting to his fellow Hellions that he and another friend took out 'the cop.' Why don't you fill us in?" He gestured to a detective with Gangs.

The man stepped between Andrea and the sergeant. "He's six foot four and weighs approximately two hundred pounds. These physical attributes align with CSU's estimations of the driver's body type. Coleman is a new member to the Hellions and still climbing his way up."

Coleman could just be making a false claim, trying to get in with them, seeking the approval of the top guy.

"Do we have any leads on his friend, the shooter?" Madison called out.

The Gangs detective looked at her. "None yet. And there's no direct tie to Officer Weir. However, we will be surveilling the subject today and seeing if we can find any leads that way. In light of the claim, this is enough to substantiate an arrest warrant for Coleman and a search warrant for the Hellion hideout. He doesn't have a current address on file, and it's suspected that Coleman is residing there."

The officer turned to Winston and Andrea, and they both nodded.

"And in the meantime, SWAT will be putting together an operations plan," he continued. "They'll strike the hideout tonight at midnight."

CHAPTER 26

NICK BENSON WAS ALREADY IN the planning room, positioned behind a computer with a pile of folders to his left. "Hey," he said when Troy walked in and gave a deep exhale. "Burying a brother never gets easy."

Nick could speak from experience. He'd been serving with the Stiles PD for more than ten years and had come from a smaller department where he had worked for five years. His age was starting to show in the deep grooves that ran from his nostrils to the corners of his mouth and his balding head, but his gray eyes were full of light and life, and when he smiled, it was genuine.

"It's always going to be one of the hardest things to face as a cop," Nick added. "I wish I could say you learn to deal with it, but I'd be lying."

Troy wasn't going to get pulled into a variation of the same conversation he'd been having over and over since yesterday morning. He pointed to the ream of paper. "Is that the history associated with the Hellions' hideout?"

"That it is. And backgrounds on the leaders, including everything from their addresses to dates of birth, photos, and charges previously pressed against them. Help yourself."

The stack seemed overwhelming. There was a benefit to looking at things online; somehow on a computer screen, reports didn't seem so long. "Why don't you just give me the brief breakdown to start?"

"The leader is Lonnie Hogan." Nick sorted through the folders and handed one to Troy.

Troy opened it and looked at the mug on the guy. He had dark hair, dark eyes, and a goatee with flecks of gray in it. Troy skimmed the summary page. Hogan was only twenty-seven. The set of his jaw and mouth spoke to a smug attitude. Even though the picture was a mug shot, the fire in the eyes told Troy this guy didn't fear going to jail. And from the looks of it, he had faced charges for armed burglary, but there wasn't enough evidence for the prosecution to convince a jury of his involvement.

Lonnie had probably toyed with the jury…

"Hogan's mother was a meth addict and a hooker," Nick added.

"No excuse for his lifestyle choices."

Nick held up his hand. "And I never said there was." He lowered his hand. There were a few seconds that Troy wondered if Nick had seen through him to the pain that was a constant ache in his chest since the news had come in about Barry. But if Nick had, he let the matter alone. "The deed for the Hellions' hideout belongs to Hogan. Now, Hogan's right-hand men are Saul Armstrong and Bernard Schultz."

Nick pulled out a couple more folders and handed them to Troy. Troy put Hogan's on the table and opened the one for Armstrong first. His photo was from the DMV and showed a man with a goatee and a mussed dark mane that reached his shoulders. A tattoo laced the left side of his neck.

"What about this Russell Coleman?"

Nick glanced past Troy to the clock on the wall.

"When's everyone else expected in? I'll wait and go through it once, if that's all right."

"That's fine. Everyone should be here any—" Troy stopped and gestured to Marc Copeland as he walked in the room. Right behind him was David Murphy.

Troy had worked with them and Nick for more than a decade. He'd worked with the other four members of his team less than that, but it averaged out to about five years, and Troy knew enough that he trusted any of these men with his life. Anyone who applied for SWAT had to go through rigorous physical testing, as well as grueling interviews. They also had to have a minimum of five years of service as a police officer.

"Hope we're not too late," Marc said.

"We're just getting started," Troy replied.

"Where's everyone else?" David asked.

"Hey, watch your mouth, Murphy." Jay Porter came into the room with the rest of the team. "I know you're lost when I'm not here."

"Shut it, Portly."

Jay just laughed, letting the nickname roll over him. He was all of 170 pounds and six foot three.

Each member of his team was trained in specialized weaponry, such as automatic rifles, Tasers, flashbangs, and close-quarters defensive tactics, and were repel masters, which came in handy when they had to jump from a roof and land on a balcony. The team knew how to coordinate and work with the K-9 unit, and SWAT members shot at the range weekly, with the exception of Jay, who was their sniper. He shot twice a week. While the average officer was trained to aim for center mass, members of SWAT were taught to target the triangular area that made up the eyes and nose if they had a sightline. This delivery would result in an immediate "lights out" for the subject. In addition to knowing a bit about everything, each member brought a different strength to the team.

Marc specialized in breaching, and it was fitting, as the guy was built like a tank. Nick was a trained shield operator and the front of the line when it came to entry. The backup officers would flank him, using his shield as partial cover. David was trained in explosives. Troy was particularly skilled in negotiations. The remaining four were certified in Tasers and rifles.

Jay took a seat at the table and clasped his hands. "What's the plan, boss?" He turned to Troy.

Troy nodded to Nick. "We were just discussing the leader of the Hellions and his two right-hand men."

Nick proceeded to fill them in on what they had missed.

"We were just about to discuss Russell Coleman," Troy said. "As most of you know from the briefing this morning, he's bragging about his involvement with the shooting. He's saying he was the driver." Troy looked at Nick to take over again.

"As the gangs unit informed us, Coleman's believed to be a new member of the Hellions, but it's also believed that he may live at their hideout. Surveillance will be put in place to see if they can confirm this, and we're hoping that he'll lead us to the shooter."

"In the meantime, we consider Coleman to be a high threat, armed, and dangerous," Troy summarized. "The plan is to strike the Hellions' hideout at midnight, so we've got a lot of work to do. Everyone in?"

The room came alive as each member of Troy's SWAT team confirmed their eagerness to nail the son of a bitch.

Troy turned to Nick, who connected his laptop to a

television at the front of the room to display the screen for everyone to see. It showed images of the hideout. "These pictures were taken yesterday." Troy provided his team with their approach to the house from a geographical standpoint, explaining how to get close while drawing the least attention. "You can see that the structure is two stories. There is no basement. The primary entry point is going to be the front door, and the secondary entry is the back door. The potential hazard with the front is that it's in the open, no real means for cover and concealment. But in the backyard, there are some bushes for concealment and a shed for cover." Troy pointed to the front of the house. "To clarify, this side will be referred to as A, and the backside is C." To prevent anyone outside of law enforcement from interpreting directions on scene, letters were assigned starting with the primary entry point, working clockwise. "Is everyone with me?"

Heads nodded.

"Nick, David, Charlie, Derek, and myself will take a position at point A. Marc, Jay, and Clayton, you'll be at C. You will be responsible for providing a distraction so the primary team can enter more easily and safely."

"And that distraction will be...?" Clayton asked.

Troy smiled at him. "I was just about to say. I am certain the warrant will stipulate the use of a flashbang. You'll bust in the back door and toss one in on *sighted* delivery."

Troy added the last part even though that condition should be a given for his men. Simply tossing a flashbang into a room was irresponsible and just asking for trouble. While a flashbang was considered a higher use of force, the intention of deploying one was to distract, not injure. It would emit a deafening sound of greater than 170 decibels, as well as a brilliant flash of white. Its purpose was to overcome the sight and hearing of the subjects, opening up a short window to make entry. Failure to have a sighted delivery had dire consequences. For example, one time an officer had tossed a flashbang into a window and it had landed in a crib. The baby had been badly injured, and rightfully, the department had been sued and lost.

"We'll all be wearing hearing protection and obviously our communication pieces. All right, let's talk about the outer and inner perimeters we'll need to have set up." Troy paused to look over his team. It was an honor to serve with them, and pride struck his heart. Barry had the best men hunting his killer.

CHAPTER 27

MADISON LEFT THE SQUAD ROOM, and she and Terry put in the requests for comprehensive reports on Sommer, Godfrey, Cousins, and Snyder. It would take some time for all the details to come back—at least an hour—and then they'd have a look through them and see if any of their relatives were connected to the ownership of a BMW 3 series.

While they waited for the reports, they headed out of the station for Sommer's residence. It was time to question the man himself again.

Sommer answered the door and stepped back to let them inside. Apparently his threat about needing a lawyer was just that.

The front door opened to the left of the living room, and inside, a flat-screen TV was mounted to the wall. Beneath it were a bunch of electronics—a Blu-ray player, an amp, a couple of video game consoles. One of the games was paused on-screen. The house was clearly home to three single men. When they did pick up women, they'd probably have better luck going back to the woman's place or renting a hotel room.

There was no sign of Cousins, but another man was on the couch across from the media area. Given his long, dark hair and skinny build, Madison figured he was Mike

Godfrey.

"Hey," the guy on the couch said.

Sommer gestured toward the guy. "That's Mike."

Madison nodded, her attention on Sommer. "You lied to us."

Sommer's eyes shot to her but then drifted to Terry.

"We know about your friends, about the Devil's Rebels," she continued, glancing at Godfrey, who looked away. She turned back to Sommer.

He curled his lips and shook his head. "I told you that I'm no longer with them."

There was no sign of shock or surprise that she knew about the group's name. "You're not curious where I got the name of your little gang?"

"Why should I be? You're detectives. It's not *my* gang, though."

"See, I believe otherwise."

He gave a nonchalant shrug. "People are free to believe as they wish."

Madison had to admit that Sommer was definitely calm in the face of law enforcement. She remembered how Snyder had said he'd been beating a man one instant and taking her out on a date the next.

"Well, let's talk about your friends, then." Madison headed into the living area and sat on the couch next Godfrey, looking at him while she spoke to Sommer. "You said they were a dangerous crowd."

Godfrey was avoiding eye contact.

"I'm not sure I said that," Sommer said.

Madison cocked her head. "You acted like you were going to be sick, like they'd come after you to kill you."

A thick layer of disdain washed over Sommer's face.

Madison leaned forward. "You said they hurt animals

and alluded to them killing people. There is no statute of limitations on the latter." She wished she could say the same of animal abuse.

"I've had a night to sleep on this, and I don't think I should have said anything."

Madison mocked laughter. "You need to start talking to us and providing us with something of real substance right now, because it's looking like you're involved with the shooting of an officer."

"What?" Sommer yelled, smacking a hand to his chest. "Because of a decal on an old car?"

"If you have nothing to hide, then I don't see why this is a big deal," Madison pressured. "Just tell us where you were yesterday between four thirty and five thirty in the morning."

"I was sleeping."

"And who can verify that?"

Sommer gestured to Godfrey. "Him."

Godfrey's head snapped in Sommer's direction.

"It doesn't look like he's willing to lie for you, Travis. Besides, your friend here is a fellow Devil's Rebel. Do you really think he's a good alibi?"

Godfrey looked at Madison. "I'm not—"

"Mike, come on, man," Sommer said, a desperate tone to his voice. "You know I was sleeping here."

Godfrey's eyes briefly slipped to Madison's. Just when she was thinking they'd have to talk to him away from Sommer, Godfrey shook his head.

"Man, you know I can't lie to the police," he said.

"Since when?" Sommer scoffed.

Godfrey turned to Madison. "I've made some bad choices in life, ones I'm not proud of."

"Like the Devil's Rebels." Madison stated it matter-of-factly.

Godfrey was the one of the three roommates who had been bumped from foster home to foster home and had even spent time in juvie. Life hadn't dealt him a fair hand—at least at the beginning. While his background didn't show any charges as an adult, Madison didn't put entire faith in his being a changed man, especially after what she'd learned from Snyder. And how changed could Godfrey be to live with Sommer, a man who he allegedly collaborated with in beating another man?

"Are you still with them?" she asked Godfrey.

He averted his eyes. "What does any of this have to do with anything?"

Madison sank her shoulder deeper into the couch, her torso still facing Godfrey. "A police officer was murdered, and there was a decal on the shooter's vehicle. Can you guess what it looked like?"

Godfrey smacked his lips. "Why don't you humor me?"

"A goat's head inside a pentagram with a rebel flag background." She stamped out each word slowly, almost allowing one full second for each syllable. "Do you know anyone who has a black BMW 3 series sedan?"

"No," he said quickly.

"You're positive of that?" She was always more than willing to provide the rope for suspects to hang themselves with.

"Tell them, Mike. I was here," Sommer interjected, obviously not willing to give up on his contrived alibi.

Madison didn't even acknowledge him but kept her attention on Godfrey. His eyes were blazing and looking straight ahead at the TV; he was probably anxious to get back to his video game. After a few seconds, Mike said,

"Travis might be unhinged—"

Sommer threw his arms in the air. "Seriously?"

"But a cop killer?" Godfrey continued, ignoring his roommate. "I don't see it."

Madison angled her head to the right. "So were you with him yesterday from four thirty to five thirty?"

"No." Godfrey's gaze slid to Sommer.

"Wow, thanks for your support."

"Like I said, I'm not lying to the police." Godfrey's voice was sulky.

"Where you at that time?" Madison asked.

"Now I'm a suspect? You've gotta be shitting me." Godfrey stood.

"Sit." Madison stared him down.

Terry took a step toward Godfrey, and he complied. Godfrey wasn't looking at her when he spoke again. "I was at this girl's place until around six when she kicked me out."

"What's her name and number?" Terry asked, his pen and notepad in hand, ready to write the information down.

Godfrey swiped a hand down his face. "I just met her at a club and came home on the bus. I was still plastered from the night before so I don't know where she lives, either."

"That's convenient," Madison said. "And you never saw Sommer yesterday morning between—"

Godfrey's eyes snapped to hers. "No, I told you."

"What about this guy?" Madison pulled out a photo of Russell Coleman and extended it to Godfrey. "Do you know him?"

Godfrey barely looked at it. "No."

"What about you?" Madison got up and showed the

image to Sommer.

He shook his head. "Never saw him before."

Or at least that's the story he was going with…

Chapter 28

Back in the department sedan, Madison turned to Terry. "They're involved somehow, I just feel it."

"Unfortunately, the law requires more than feelings."

She angled her head. "We still don't know who Coleman's friend is, and Sommer doesn't have an alibi."

"Neither does Godfrey, but we need more than that."

"And who knows if they're telling the truth about Coleman." Madison put the car into gear. "The reports should be back on known relatives. Maybe we'll get lucky."

Sadly, when they got back to their desks twenty minutes later, the reports still weren't ready.

"We don't know who all is involved in this Devil's Rebels gang," Madison said, tapping her fingers on her desk as she thought, "and the gangs unit hadn't heard of them. But what if there's another way to prove their existence and find out more about them?"

"What are you thinking?"

"I'm thinking about Marsh's informant."

"You really think he's going to let you talk to his CI?"

"It's worth a shot."

Madison and Terry tracked Detective Marsh down to interrogation room three, where they watched him question a meth addict. The addict's face, neck, and arms were covered with scabs—just one sad consequence of the drug's use, which caused its users to hallucinate that something was crawling under their skin and they needed to dig it out.

Marsh tapped the edge of a closed file folder against the table and headed for the door. Madison and Terry hurried down the hall to catch him.

Marsh opened the door and stepped back when he saw them standing there.

"We need to speak with your CI," Madison said.

He gestured toward her but addressed Terry. "Is she serious?"

Terry pressed his lips together and nodded.

"They talk to *me*." There was no room for negotiation in Marsh's voice.

"Well, I need information. And quick."

"Stop dancing around here, Knight. What's going on?"

"We have a new lead and believe it may tie back to Russell Coleman and Barry's murder."

Marsh slid his gaze to Terry. "What's this lead?"

"A gang that calls themselves the Devil's Rebels."

"All right, you mentioned them in the briefing, but I'd never heard of them before that."

She pressed on, knowing he'd say that. "You've seen the decal that was on the shooter's car?"

"Of course."

"Well, it's affiliated with the Devil's Rebels. We first want to confirm they are a gang, and if anyone will know, it's the people on the street."

"You just referred to them as a gang, and now you're not sure?" He barked a laugh. "And you want access to my CI to confirm whether or not they are?"

"Yeah, that's right." How did she manage not to roll her eyes?

"No."

"No? What do you mean *no*?"

"N-O."

Madison crossed her arms. "They could lead us to Barry's shooter."

"She doesn't know the word *no*, apparently." Marsh looked at Terry, and Terry wisely didn't give any impression he heard him. Marsh continued. "They're used to dealing with me. You go in there and you could mess everything up. Forget *could*. You *will*. And you do realize SWAT's planning to hit the Hellions tonight…"

"Like I said, I think these people might be connected to Coleman. And if you're not going to let us talk to your informant, you're going to have to talk to him for us."

"And I take orders from you now?"

"For Barry," she said sharply.

Marsh's expression softened, and he nodded. "Fine. You can talk to *her*, but if you mess this up—"

"Her?"

"Yep. My CI is a woman."

"Where can we find her?"

"Hold on there," he said. "I'll reach out and set up a time."

"Make it quick," Madison responded.

Marsh rolled his eyes. "You're going to have to give me some time, Knight."

"Fine," Madison grumbled.

She looked at her watch. It was only midmorning. They were at a standstill with the investigation, but there was something she and Terry could do…

"DO YOU REALLY THINK THIS is a good idea?" Terry asked her from the passenger seat.

"I don't think it's a bad one." Madison was driving them over to Joni's house. They'd stopped into a department store to pick up a couple of gifts for Emily that tied into her love for ponies. "Andrea—" She stopped there. If she wasn't with Troy anymore, she'd have to go back to addressing Andrea by her position, not by her first name. "The chief thought doing something to acknowledge her birthday would be nice for her."

"As you told me, but, man, it's gotta be rough on the kid."

"I'd think everyone forgetting about her special day would only make it worse."

Madison approached the house, and there was a horse trailer out front and a man arguing with an officer. She parked the car and went over to them. "What's going on here?" The smell of manure and fresh hay hit Madison's sinuses, and she sneezed.

"He's determined to set up here," the officer explained.

"I was paid in advance. I can't just leave," the man protested. He was in his late fifties with a round face and pleasant eyes.

"I've tried to explain to him that there's been a death—"

The man looked her square in the eye. "I offer no refunds."

Her last concern was payment, but her first priority was making the little girl happy. If people from the department were going to be stopping in throughout the day to bring Emily gifts, what would a pony hurt?

"Give me a minute." Madison left the two men and Terry behind, and headed for the front door. She was still holding her gift, and she tucked it under an arm and knocked.

Joni answered, her gaze going first to the box in Madison's arms and then beyond Madison to the trailer. "What's going on?"

"It's Emily's birthday today..."

Joni looked at her blankly as if she didn't need to be told when her daughter's birthday was.

"Did you read the card from Barry?" Madison asked the question, and dread sank in her stomach. She knew it wasn't appropriate to ask a widow something so personal.

"I..." Joni wrapped her arms around herself.

Madison touched her shoulder. "I'm sorry to ask that. It's just... In the card, Barry mentioned finding the perfect gift for Emily... She loves ponies, right?"

"Yeah." Joni's chin quivered. "He got her a pony?"

Madison nodded. "It sure looks like it."

"What am I supposed to do? She's walking around the house staring at the floor. She woke up in the middle of the night sobbing." Joni broke down now, crying and shaking.

Madison hugged her. "Barry already paid for the pony, and—" Madison made sure to soften her voice "—he wanted her to have the experience."

Joni stopped crying as if a switch had been flipped and sniffled. She nodded. "You're right. She can't have her dad, but... Let me ask her." Joni turned, likely to go get Emily, but the girl was already standing there.

"Mommy, is that a horse?" Emily pointed toward the trailer.

"Yeah, sweetheart, it is."

"I thought the party was canceled." Emily's blue eyes were wet and wide as she looked at her mother. Then she noticed the gift in Madison's arms and her jaw dropped slightly. "Is that for me?"

"It is." Madison pressed her lips together, the closest she could get to a smile at the moment, and handed her the gift.

"Thank you." Emily put the box on the floor and wrapped her arms around Madison's legs.

Joni tapped her daughter's shoulder. "Do you want to see the pony?"

"Can I ride him, Mommy?"

Joni glanced at Madison, and Madison waved at the men at the curb and caught the pony owner's eye. He nodded and worked on getting the pony from the trailer.

Joni got down on her haunches, took her daughter's hands, and said, "This gift is from your daddy, sweetheart."

Madison was having a hard time holding herself together. Oh, the tears wanted to fall... She expected Emily to cry, but instead, her face lit up into a wide smile.

"He was always the best at birthday surprises!" She squealed and went deeper in the house, galloping and whinnying.

This time Madison couldn't help but smile.

She turned to say something to Joni, and her phone buzzed in her pocket. It was Marsh.

The appointment was set for her to meet with his informant at one that afternoon. That was only a couple of hours from now. She'd better enjoy this downtime while she could.

CHAPTER 29

Marsh's CI's name was Lulu, a name that gave Madison the impression that the woman worked the streets. But she wasn't a call girl and she didn't take money in exchange for sex. However, she did have a close—and likely sexual—relationship with Lonnie Hogan. According to Marsh, the man trusted her with his life. So when two years ago, at the age of nineteen, Lulu had almost died due to a cocaine overdose but had survived to face charges in connection to an armed robbery she'd taken part in while high, she'd been given the option to go to jail or become an informant. The choice had been an easy one for her.

Madison was set to meet Lulu alone at a coffee shop. She'd dropped Terry off back at the station to get started on looking at the reports that would have come through by this point, and now she parked down the street and around the corner from Java Joint. The time on the dash read 12:55.

She entered the coffee shop and looked for a woman of Lulu's description—dark hair and dark eyes, bone thin, with a tendency to go heavy on the makeup. Madison spotted Lulu hunched in a corner booth holding a cell phone and texting with one hand, leaving the other one free to hold a cardboard cup. She'd lift it for tiny sips every few seconds. She was nervous.

She looked up at the door as if she sensed someone's eyes on her, and when she met Madison's gaze, she subtly dipped her head. Then she lifted her cup to her lips again.

Madison casually walked up to the counter and ordered a large coffee before joining Lulu at her table. "Glad we could get together today. It's been too long," she said to create the pretense of two friends meeting for coffee.

"Yeah, terrific." Lulu spoke without looking at Madison, her eyes on her cell phone, both hands cradling it now.

Madison took her own phone out, brought up an image of the decal, and held the screen for Lulu to see. "Do you recognize this?"

Lulu took her eyes from her screen but didn't seem impressed by the interruption. Her eyes were ringed with thickly applied black eyeliner, her lashes were coated in mascara, and her eyelids were painted a dark mocha.

She looked at the logo for about five seconds. "It's the symbol for a group of wannabes from the east end of the city. The Devil's Rebels."

The door chimed, and it had Lulu anxiously looking around Madison to see who had entered. Madison followed her gaze to a middle-aged woman in pajama bottoms and a coat. She made it to the counter, and as she was skimming the menu, she was chewing on a fingernail.

Madison shook her head and turned back to Lulu. "Tell me about them."

Lulu put down her phone but kept in on the table in front of her. "I'm not sure what all to tell. Do you know about the graffiti downtown on the back of the court building?"

"Yes." It was a common topic that hit local papers, how awful it was that anyone would disgrace such a prestigious building in the community. Madison thought back to the images that were showcased in color in the local paper. A true irony, as on one hand people were complaining about the graffiti, and on the other, they were gratifying it. Madison recalled the signature—a swirly circle that could be a capital *D* with an *R* in the center.

The Devil's Rebels were *responsible…*

But defacing buildings was a far cry from the crimes Sommer declared they were involved in, though. Violence against animals and people, murder… Pajama woman had moved down the counter and was closer to them now. Madison made sure her voice was low when she asked Lulu, "Do you know if they've killed anyone?"

Lulu burst out laughing so hard tears came to the corners of her eyes. "Murder?"

Madison settled against the back of the booth, letting Lulu get it all out, and took the first sip of her own coffee. She had taken a few by the time Lulu calmed down.

"There is no way that they—" Lulu covered her mouth to stifle another outburst. She shook her head and snorted. "No, they are small-time." She punched out the last two syllables. "I'd be surprised if they even knew how to fire a gun."

Pajama woman turned to them now, obviously hearing Lulu say the word *gun*. Her eyes took in Lulu and then bounced to Madison, who gave her a look that told her to mind her own business. The woman complied, but not before dishing out a cold glare of her own.

Madison waited until the woman had her coffee and was halfway to the door before she responded to Lulu.

"You know all this for sure?"

"I'm positive." The word *positive* came out in three distinct syllables. "Do you think they killed that cop?"

"I can't say."

Lulu held out her hand. Madison glanced at it, knowing that Lulu was likely looking for a payout for the information she'd provided. But as far as Madison was concerned, Lulu had already benefited. She wasn't behind bars.

Lulu held eye contact with Madison for a while before snatching her hand back. "Unbelievable."

Madison managed not to say anything as she stood up and left the coffee shop, but she couldn't help but think that what was really unbelievable was the fact that cops were forced to make deals with criminals in exchange for information.

She walked to the car, cognizant of her surroundings and making sure no one was tailing her. Confident she was on her own, she got into the car and called Terry to fill him in on what she had learned from Lulu.

"Well, I got news for you, too. We have a lead on the shooter's car."

CHAPTER 30

TERRY HAD THE PICTURE OF a man on his screen when Madison got back to the station. He was in his late thirties, had blond hair, and was cleanly shaven with brown eyes. There was nothing menacing about his appearance.

"Meet Phil Brown," Terry said. "I found him when comparing Cousins's detailed background to the list of BMW 3 series owners. He's the kid's uncle, and he has a Glock 17 registered to him."

"They fire nine-millimeter rounds."

Terry nodded. "Now Brown doesn't fit the physicality for the shooter, though, but he does the driver."

"But Coleman claimed he drove."

"*Claimed* may be the appropriate word here."

"So we have two potential drivers, but no leads on a shooter?" She moaned. "What else do you have on Brown?"

"His criminal history is clean," Terry continued. "He owns his house outright, has no debt, holds a steady job."

"Role model for the community," Madison stated sarcastically. "Except for being connected with Cousins, a guy who's roommates with two Devil's Rebels members. Even possibly a member himself."

"We need to connect either Cousins or Brown to Russell Coleman," Terry said. "Now, Brown was married but got divorced a few years ago. The record states irreconcilable differences."

"How long were they married?"

"Fifteen years."

"And it took them that long to realize they didn't work together? There had to be something more. He probably cheated on her."

Terry angled his head. "Basing that assumption off your past experience?"

"I'm over that." The conversation with Chelsea came to mind, as did Troy's cheating ex-wife. "Maybe she ran around on him," she said, retracting her initial judgment.

"Anyway, Brown's parents are deceased, died in a car accident, but he has a sister, Kara Brown, whose last known address put her three hours outside of the city. Brown's ex-wife is here in Stiles. Her name is Joy Pope. After the divorce finalized, she changed her name right away."

"So the divorce definitely ended on bad terms."

He shrugged. "As it stated, irreconcilable differences."

"We'll talk to her."

"Her opinion could be tainted," Terry suggested.

"You're right, but that might prove useful to us."

"Hold up. You just said that I'm *what*?" He pulled out his cell, swiped a finger across the screen, and held the phone toward her.

"You want to record me?" She scoffed.

"Please repeat what you just said a few seconds ago." He was showcasing a cheesy grin.

"You want to record me?"

"No, the other thing."

She narrowed her eyes at him. "Shut up, wiseass."

"That's not exactly what you said, but you did just

admit that I'm wise." He lifted his head, stretching out his neck, and tilted his nose to the ceiling, basking in his self-made compliment.

"Yeah, and a—"

"A *donkey*? That's what you were going to say? They *are* cute."

"Terry." She gave him the best *I'm warning you* look she could muster.

"Ha." He waved a finger in her face with one hand while he tucked his phone away with the other. "I got you to smile."

"No, you…" And then she couldn't help herself. She was smiling. "Cut it out."

"Hey, I didn't start all this."

"Technically, you did."

"No, you said I was a wise donkey. Hee-haw. Hee-haw."

Oh Lord. It must have been the sleep deprivation, but she found herself laughing at his impression. She cleared her throat. "Let's be serious here for a second. We talk to Pope, find out more about Brown's character, his nephew, and maybe then we'll even be able to make a connection to Russell Coleman."

"Let's go, boss," he said with a smirk, before he snuck in another soft, "Hee-haw."

CHAPTER 31

MADISON PULLED THE DEPARTMENT SEDAN into Pope's driveway. She lived in a two-story brick house in a middle-income neighborhood, and the building itself was in good condition. The front lawn needed a mowing, though.

Terry rang the bell, and Madison waited a second before she pressed it again.

"You're not making things go any faster, you know," Terry reminded her.

She narrowed her eyes at him and pressed the bell for a third time. Then footsteps were finally padding toward the door. It opened, and the smell of garlic and frying ground beef wafted from inside the house. An early dinner in the works at four thirty in the afternoon.

A woman in her midforties stood there with a baby on her hip. She was bouncing the kid up and down and holding a pacifier to its mouth. The baby's cheeks were tear-streaked.

The woman eyed them critically, her gaze going over them in a rushed fashion. "What is it?"

Madison held up her badge, and Terry followed suit.

"We're detectives with the Stiles PD," Madison began. "Are you Joy Pope?"

"Yeah."

"We have some questions about your ex-husband."

"Oh Lord." Pope rolled her eyes and gritted her teeth. "What has he done now?"

"Can we come in?" Madison asked.

Pope watched Madison a little longer before stepping back inside the house. She left the door open as an invitation for Madison and Terry to enter. Terry closed the door behind them.

"Oh, could you just take her for a second?" Pope passed the baby off to Madison before she could refuse.

The baby's huge blue eyes looked up at her, and Madison didn't like the way they made her feel. Children weren't in her life plan. Not now. Not five years out. Not ever. She was testing her limits having a chocolate lab. What did she know about raising a child? She'd watched her sister tackle the feat seemingly effortlessly, as if she were born with the mother gene. Madison was pretty certain she wasn't given one. But the longer this baby peered into her eyes, the more she felt her defenses melting. The baby did fit on her hip as if she were meant to be perched there. Usually there was a sense of awkwardness that came with holding a child, but something may have changed.

That scared her more than the kid.

"Here." She handed the baby off to Terry.

Pope returned a couple of minutes later. "I'm just cooking dinner and prefer that it doesn't burn." Pope's eyes went from Madison to Terry, who was now holding her baby, and then settled her gaze on Madison. She smiled. "You're not a mom, I take it."

"No. Would you have someplace we could sit down?"

"Kids aren't all that scary, you know." Pope either didn't pick up on Madison's cue or didn't care. "They're fun actually."

Yes, a riot…

They were an enormous responsibility, and the last thing she wanted was to be accountable for another human being. She had enough on her plate without adding to it. Besides, she was married to her job, and the cases could be her children. Yeah, that analogy worked, and that's all she needed. She hated that a thought of Troy fired through her mind then, quick but nonetheless potent in its message. What was Troy's opinion on children? They'd never discussed it, but she supposed that didn't really matter anymore.

Madison glanced over when she felt eyes on her, but they weren't Terry's. They were the baby's. She popped the pacifier out of her mouth, and it fell to the floor. Her attention was still on Madison, and the baby smiled.

"A place to sit?" Madison repeated her request as she bent over to pick up the pacifier. She handed it off to Pope. "Or we can talk right here."

Pope smiled, and Madison noted the physical similarities between mother and daughter. There was a tug on Madison's heart, but she'd ignore it until any inclination toward motherhood dissipated. Such an unfamiliar—and unwelcome—feeling.

Pope stuffed the pacifier into a pocket and took her baby from Terry. "Her name's Ember, like a burning ember. I wanted to give her a powerful name. Now no matter how low or bad things may seem, there will always be a spark to get the fire started again."

Madison was beginning to feel as if she were being sucked into an emotional vacuum. It certainly wasn't of her free will that she was standing here thinking about… children? Really?

"Come this way." Pope led them toward the kitchen.

The smells in there were even more aromatic than they'd been in the foyer, and they had Madison's stomach growling.

Pope placed Ember in a high chair and pointed to other chairs around a table. "If you want to take a seat, I'll be right there." She went to the stove and turned the burner off under the meat.

Madison sat across from Ember, thinking it best to get as far away from the baby as possible. What she hadn't thought through was the fact that now Ember could look straight at her. And Ember wasn't interested in the animal crackers sprinkled over the tray of her chair. She was fascinated by Madison.

Madison glanced at Terry, and he was smiling at her. Did nothing escape her partner's notice?

No, Madison mouthed to him, and he laughed softly.

Pope continued finishing up her meal, draining the pasta water and then dumping a bottle of tomato sauce into the pot, followed by the meat, garlic, and onions. She stirred it up, put the lid on the pot, and came to the table.

"We won't take up much of your time," Madison began. She most certainly couldn't afford to be here too long. That baby was starting to get to her whether she liked it or not. "We just want to know what kind of a man Phil Brown is."

"Huh." Pope sat in the chair next to her daughter. "I'm not married to him anymore, if that tells you anything. It's not that he's a bad guy… He's just sometimes misguided."

Yet her first reaction to their presence had indicated otherwise. *Oh Lord. What has he done now?*

"In what way?" Terry asked.

"He likes to see the best in people. A fault, if you ask me."

And here Madison thought that would have been a good trait to have…

"If he's in trouble, which I assume he must be, it's got to be because of someone else."

"Why did you break up?" Madison asked, hoping the reason might shed some light on Brown's character.

Pope's eyes went to Ember, who was still staring at Madison. "She really likes you."

Madison didn't say anything. She wasn't going to encourage Pope.

Pope took a deep, heaving breath. "I loved him. I still do."

"Why the divorce and the name change, then?"

"I didn't do any of those things because I don't love him. Actually, the opposite."

Madison leaned forward. Now she may have officially heard it all. "You divorced him because you love him?"

"Yeah." Pope reached for her daughter's chubby little hand and played with her fingers. "We got married young. Too young to be getting married anyhow. We weren't thinking about the future. We just figured we'd make life up as we went along. But when I got to the point that I really wanted children, I found out that he didn't. And he wasn't going to budge on it." She paused there for a few seconds. "He can be so stubborn."

It was more in the way Pope said it than in the words themselves, but there was an underlying implication that stubbornness applied to Brown in numerous ways. But Madison was going to let her continue to talk for the moment.

"Ember's not his, which you've probably figured out by this point. I left Phil and used a sperm bank. It took most of my savings, but it was worth it. Even my broken heart over Phil was worth it for her." Pope bent over to tap a kiss on Ember's head. "I changed my name right after the divorce because I wanted Ember to have my last name, not Phil's. He had no claim to her at all."

"You said that if Phil's in trouble, it would be because of someone else? Anyone specifically?" Madison asked. Pope's earlier words were just sinking in now.

"Phil's nephew is bad news, but Phil refuses to see it."

"Clark Cousins?" Terry asked.

"That's him. God, he's so blind when it comes to that kid. He stole a few video games—or at least he tried to. He was caught and sent to jail. Phil still protests his innocence. We never fought except for when Clark came up."

Madison nodded. "Why do you think he's such bad news?"

"If you met his friends Mike and Travis you'd understand. They aren't exactly living on the right side of the law. And when Clark did go to jail, it wasn't exactly his first offense. When he was a teenager, he was picked up by Walmart security for stealing. Because of his age he didn't serve time. He did have to pay a fine, though. He was banned from Walmart for some time, too. I don't remember how long."

"Why was Phil so defensive of Clark?" Terry asked, leaving out that they had, in fact, met Mike and Travis.

"He said that his nephew was just like him and that he would never steal. 'He's a good kid,' he'd say." Pope scoffed. "Yeah, all good kids go to jail."

"Is he still close with his nephew?"

"I imagine so, but I haven't exactly spoken with Phil in a while. A couple of years actually, so I can't say for sure."

"Have you ever heard of the Devil's Rebels?" Madison

asked.

Pope's face paled, and she nodded. "I wish I could say no."

"What do you know about them?"

"I just heard of them. I remember them coming up regarding Clark. Why?"

Madison took out a photo of Russell Coleman and handed it to Pope. "Do you know this man?"

Pope glanced at the picture and shook her head. "He's involved with these Devil's Rebels?"

"That's what we're trying to find out," Madison responded.

Terry leaned on the table. "What about the name Russell Coleman? Does that sound familiar?"

"I do remember Phil mentioning a Russ. Do you think that's the guy?" Pope pointed to the photo.

Madison's heart was thumping hard. "What did Phil say about him?"

"He said that Clark was innocent, but that one of his friends was trouble. That friend being Russ. Phil figured it was Russ who was actually the thief."

Madison rose from the table, as did Terry. She handed Pope a business card. "If you think of anything else we might want to know, call me."

"I don't even know what exactly this is about."

"And it's probably better that you don't. Thank you for your time, and I'm sorry we interrupted your dinner."

Ember cooed in the high chair and banged one of her arms against the tray.

I've gotta get out of here.

CHAPTER 32

CLARK COUSINS'S CONNECTION TO RUSSELL COLEMAN was enough to start the arrest warrant for him. Officers were dispatched to watch over the Chestnut residence and verify he was there. Madison insisted that she and Terry be the ones to bring Cousins in, too, but in the meantime, they would be apprehending Phil Brown.

Madison and Terry were positioned outside Phil Brown's residence armed with an arrest warrant for him and a search warrant for his property. Combining Brown's close relationship with his nephew, Cousins's supposed affiliation with the Devil's Rebels, and Brown's ownership of a Glock 17 and a black BMW 3 series sedan had provided enough provocation to act. While Brown fit the physicality of the driver, as did Coleman, this was a discrepancy cast aside in light of those other factors. The fact that Pope had mentioned Brown didn't like Coleman was also discarded, because his opinion of the guy could have changed.

Plainclothes officers had posed as utility providers and already confirmed Brown was home.

Brown's house was in a new neighborhood with cookie-cutter houses whose garages were their dominant features. There was no BMW in the drive, but it could be in said garage.

Police had cordoned off the block surrounding Brown's house, and Troy's team was there to ensure that things stayed under control. There were still several hours before the raid on the Hellions' hideout, but with Brown being a suspect in Barry's shooting, no one at the Stiles PD was taking any chances.

Three members of SWAT—including Troy and Nick—were in front of the door. Madison and Terry stood well behind them, prepared to present the warrants. She was aware of her Kevlar vest and the few pounds it added to her frame as she walked to the door. Adrenaline pumped through her system. She was aware the vest was for protection, but it could fail her. A head shot, the random positioning of a bullet like in Barry's case.

Troy knocked, and a few seconds later, a frightened-looking Phil Brown answered the door.

Madison analyzed what she could see of Brown past the SWAT team. Nothing about his physical appearance was really noteworthy except for his height and slender frame. His eyes were a flat brown but wide and panicked, and his lips were small in proportion to the rest of his face.

"Put your hands in the air," Troy demanded.

Nick moved in and patted him down. "He's clear."

The third SWAT guy—who Madison could never remember the name of—walked past them. The situation was seemingly under complete control.

Nick handed Brown off to Terry, and he and Troy headed toward the SWAT vehicle. Madison's gaze met Troy's, and he nodded at her, a slight curve to his mouth. That was the closest thing to a smile she was going to get from him.

Terry pulled Brown's arms behind his back and cuffed

him. "You're under arrest for your involvement with shooting a police officer."

"Whoa! I never killed anyone!"

Madison got in Brown's face then, her nose mere inches from his. She just wanted to look into his eyes, but he wasn't revealing anything. He did, however, smell like cigarettes. The manager of the Bean Counter's testimony came to mind. Kayla had said the driver had been smoking the entire time.

Two patrol officers came up the walkway to take Brown to the station.

She turned to Brown, who was still standing there flanked by two officers, each holding him by an arm. "Where will we find your Glock?"

Brown's eyes moved from her to Terry and back. "In its gun box."

"And where is that?" Madison asked.

"In my nightstand."

"Is it locked?" She was ready to scream.

Brown looked away.

Madison took that as a no. Did Brown not realize he was in trouble for a lot more than not locking up his gun?

"Do you have ammunition?" Terry asked.

Brown nodded, pale-faced. "Bullets are in my bedroom closet on the shelf."

Madison looked past Brown to where the SWAT vehicle was leaving the premises.

Madison entered the house and scanned the main level as she headed for the garage access off the kitchen. Terry was right behind her. She opened the door, and her eyes fell on the empty bay.

"Son of a bitch." She stormed back to Brown, who was still being held at the front door. "Where's your BMW?"

"I sold it." It was spoken with no emotion and deadpan body language.

"You sold it?" she asked incredulously. This guy must have thought they were idiots. The stupidity of criminals never ceased to amaze her. At least he didn't claim it was stolen and not reported yet. "When?"

"Uh, four days ago."

She put her hands on her hips. "There's no record of its sale."

"I don't know what to say. I've got my plates. They're in the basement."

Upon transferring ownership of the vehicle, Brown would be responsible for his plates, but she didn't think Brown was telling the truth. There was no sale. Not only was there no record of a title transfer but his body language was closed when he said he had sold it.

"We're going to get your Glock and bullets now. Are we going to find them, or did you sell them, too?" Madison raised her brows.

"Last I knew they were where I told you."

Madison glanced at Terry and nodded. He went into the house while Madison kept an eye on Brown. Liars were usually motivated by self-preservation. Brown was involved with Barry's shooting, she had no doubt. She still wondered why, though, and if it had something to do with his love for his nephew. And did Brown really hate Coleman as much as Pope made it sound? How was Brown directly connected to Coleman, and why did both men fit the physicality of the driver?

Terry returned with a gun case, a box of bullets, and the license plates.

"See, I told you." Brown was getting excited and nudged his head toward the plates. "I sold the car."

"They don't prove anything." Madison regarded Brown with irritation.

Terry spoke to her as if Brown weren't there. "The bullets are the same caliber as those used in the shooting." Terry opened the ammunition box. "And seventeen rounds are missing."

That was enough to fill the magazine. Madison glanced at Brown, who was now looking peaked.

Terry passed the ammo box to her and opened the gun case. She leaned over to look inside and felt her skin heat as she fired a glare at Brown. "And you said your gun was where?"

CHAPTER 33

BROWN DESERVED TO BE SUBJECTED to hours of solitary in an interrogation room, but time wasn't something they had a lot of. Madison entered the room first, Terry behind her.

He slammed the door, and Brown jumped.

She took a photo out of a folder she was carrying and slapped it on the table.

Brown's eyes shot to hers.

"Officer Weir was a husband and father." She pointed to the photo of Barry dressed in uniform, taken at a charity benefit. She retrieved another picture and put it on top of that one. It was a picture of the pavement next to Barry's cruiser where there was an evidence marker and a pool of blood. She wasn't going to give Brown the satisfaction of seeing the body of the man he killed.

"Your car—" she looked up, certain to make eye contact with Brown "—was involved in the shooting." She stretched the truth, knowing that without the actual vehicle on hand, it would be nearly impossible to prove her claim.

"I…" Brown's eyes widened. "I sold—"

"You didn't sell it. There's no record of you selling it." She let the accusation sit there, the still and quiet in the room creating a pregnant pause.

"I donated it to charity."

Madison glanced at Terry. This guy was unbelievable. "You sold it to charity?"

"Selling would be a tax write-off, but no, I gave it to them."

Even fully donated, he'd get a receipt for a tax write-off, and there would be a title transfer.

Madison walked around the table and stopped next to Brown. She leaned over. "I don't believe you."

Terry jingled his change. Brown didn't even seem to notice.

Brown's breathing became heavier and beads of sweat popped out on his forehead.

"You also match the description of the driver." She walked back to opposite side of the table. "You own the right vehicle."

"I told you that I gave it away."

"After you told us you sold it. Can you see why I'm having a hard time believing anything you say?"

Brown remained quiet, and a shot of color appeared in his cheeks. He looked as if he was going to vomit. It wasn't going to stop Madison.

"Or maybe you were the shooter?" She glanced at Terry. "An eyewitness could have gotten the description wrong."

"No, God, I swear to you that I had nothing to do with his murder."

She wasn't buying his stupid act. She'd seen it more times than she could possibly count. A suspect under fire only withered under pressure and claimed, *It wasn't me.* Their hands could be dripping with blood and they'd still say someone else wielded the blade.

Madison glanced past Brown to Terry.

Terry closed the distance between himself and Brown and pulled back on his shoulder, gripping his shirt, and then shuffled around in front of him. "You aided and abetted a cop killer. That makes you just as guilty."

"What's the shooter's name?" Madison ground out.

Brown's face was now bright red, and he held up a hand in surrender. "Please, listen to me."

Madison bobbed her head at Terry to have him release Brown. Terry bunched the fabric of Brown's shirt tighter before letting go.

Brown stared after Terry and then let his gaze land on Madison. "I never shot a cop. I never drove anyone who did, either."

"Explain why your car was used in the crime, then," she said, again running with a slight stretch on the truth. "And why you have a Glock 17—the same gun as the murder weapon—but it's missing." She embellished again as the exact make and model of gun wouldn't be known until they had the weapon in hand to compare with the fired bullets. "And then let's not forget the missing ammunition… I wonder if your gun will match up with the bullets we found…" She punched out each item, watching Brown's body language as she did so. He seemed to physically shrink more with each statement.

"I can't explain any of that." His voice was shallow.

"But you're going to have to." She sat down and pointed to the photo of the crime scene, this time realizing how she had managed to detach herself from the fact that it not only belonged to a friend but was also blood to start with. Adrenaline was a powerful tool. "An officer, a husband, a father is *dead*."

"If I could help you, I would. I don't know why my car was seen. I was home from the time I got in from work

Friday night at five thirty."

"Can anyone testify to that fact?"

Brown's cheeks paled. "Only Chloe, but—"

"We'll need her last name and a way to contact her," Madison said.

"Unless she learns how to talk, I'm not sure how much help she'll be."

Madison glared at him.

"Chloe's my cat."

She smacked the table. "Do you really think now is the time for you to get smart with me?"

"I'm—"

"I don't care how you're feeling, Mr. Brown. Not one iota." She could tell by the pathetic contortions his face was taking on that he was experiencing a mix of feelings—panic, fear, nervousness. And no matter what he said, she wouldn't feel sorry for him. How could she? He'd been involved in the shooting and murder of her friend. She realized that even murderers were entitled to human rights, that they were to be assumed innocent before presumed guilty, but real life greatly differed from that high peg of idealism. Hardened detectives such as herself were inclined to view subjects from the opposite direction.

"What charity?" she asked, the question somewhat cryptic. She got the reaction she was after when Brown's eyes widened and his chest heaved. "No charity, either, is there?"

A flicker passed through Brown's gaze. What was he hiding or who was he protecting?

"And your gun? It's magically gone, as well?" Terry asked.

Brown took a deep breath and hitched his shoulders.

"I don't kno—"

"Listen," she interrupted, "if you weren't involved in the shooting, I have a feeling you know who was, and you need to start talking to us. Was it your nephew?"

Brown lifted his chin and crossed his arms. "I want a lawyer."

Madison left the room without another word, Terry behind her, but she was the one to slam the door shut. They went out into the hall and then into the observation room. She pointed toward the interrogation room. "He's a lying sack of shit, Terry." Her partner's face screwed up at the swear word, but she continued. "You know it, I know it. There's too much pointing toward his involvement."

Sergeant Winston entered the observation room. "Do we have the shooter's name yet?"

She just stared her superior in the eye. Her frustration was beyond her ability to verbalize.

"He's lawyered up," Terry said.

"You didn't get anything out of him?"

She heard the skepticism in the sergeant's voice and knew that he had turned from looking at Terry back to her, but she wasn't going to meet his gaze.

"We pushed him, and all we got were lies. We do know that his BMW, gun, and ammunition are missing," Terry stated.

"And if it talks like a duck…" Winston said.

Madison glanced at Terry. What if they really struck Brown where it hurt? Maybe she could get him to talk then.

She started down the hall for the interrogation room.

"Where are you going?" Terry trailed her, and she spun on him.

"I just *mentioned* his nephew, and he clammed up and

requested a lawyer. I am going to appeal to Brown's weak spot."

"His nephew. But you just said—"

She cracked the door to the interrogation room.

"—he clammed up." Terry finished his sentence in a mumble.

"I requested a lawyer," Brown spat out the second she entered the room.

Terry went to the back of the room, and she sat across from Brown. "We're concerned about your nephew, Clark Cousins." She spoke kindly and softly, hoping to elicit worry for his welfare.

Brown's eyes left Madison, and he turned to look over his shoulder at Terry. "What about him? Is he okay?"

Madison relaxed her shoulders, clasped her hands on the table. "You told us that you don't know where your car is—" She held up her hand. His mouth that had been gaping open now snapped shut. "This isn't about you, Mr. Brown. But did your nephew have access to your car?"

"What are you saying?" Brown swallowed audibly. "Was he in a car accident?"

She smirked at him. "So he had access to your car, then." She looked to Terry for a moment. "He probably still has it somewhere."

Brown glared at her. "I requested a lawyer."

"As you keep reminding me."

"So what? Clark takes my car sometimes. You think he's involved with the shooting? I have the plates, remember?"

Madison stared blankly at him. "That doesn't mean anything."

Brown was shaking his head rapidly. "Nope, he's not involved with any shooting. He's an innocent kid. He was too young to know what he was doing when he tried to steal those video games."

"The judge didn't seem to think so."

Brown laid one of his hands flat on the table and then scraped at the surface with his index fingernail. His gaze went from his hand to her. "And he paid for his crime."

"True," Madison agreed. "But from what I understand, Clark has some unsavory friends... Like a Russell Coleman."

Brown's eyes snapped to hers. "He's the reason Clark even has a record."

The defensive fire for his nephew was alive and well. And so much for Brown no longer harboring ill will toward Coleman. Madison should have started from this angle. "Russell does have an affiliation with a local gang."

Brown crossed his arms. "That doesn't surprise me."

It wouldn't serve their purpose to bring up the Devil's Rebels and the Hellions. "Does Clark still hang out with Russell?"

Brown met her gaze, peering into her eyes silently, as if debating whether to answer her or not. "I'm done talking, Detective. Again."

Madison got up and left the room, Terry behind her. Back in the observation room, she turned toward the glass but spoke to Terry, who had come up beside her. "He's covering for his nephew. I feel it," she said. "And if Cousins has access to Brown's BMW, how much do you want to bet that he had access to his gun and bullets, too? Cousins and Russell Coleman have to be behind the shooting."

"You don't know that Brown's covering, though."

Madison drew her gaze from Brown, who was rubbing his jaw, to face her partner. "Really? He's a liar, and he thought that Cousins was hurt in a car accident. That tells me the guy has Brown's car. And if Brown doesn't have anything to hide, why lie about where his car is?"

Terry rubbed the back of his neck. "All right. What's his motive?"

"And why are you stuck on that all of a sudden?" So often cases were closed without getting all the answers as to why people had done what they'd done. Just because you got the bad guy behind bars didn't necessarily mean there was full closure.

"Forget I said anything." Terry sounded exasperated, but she let it roll off her. "The arrest warrant for Cousins should be ready now." The last sentence came out calmly.

"We'll also need to get a search warrant." She shrugged. "He might have Brown's gun and bullets." She met his eyes and found reassurance there. They would catch Barry's killer, but it still wasn't going to be fast enough for her liking.

Chapter 34

THE SEARCH WARRANT FOR THE house on Chestnut Street was signed, as was an arrest warrant for Cousins. With the Glock and at least thirteen bullets still missing, SWAT came with them again. Lou Stanford and Toby Sovereign were also there to help with the search.

Troy's team was in position at the front door. Troy, rifle in hand, kicked the door. "Stiles PD! Open up!"

He waited a few seconds and tried again. It was met with more silence.

Troy adjusted his hands to ensure a good grip on his rifle and nodded his head. Marc rammed the door, and Nick led the way inside with a shield and pistol.

This was followed by a bunch of yelling.

"We're not armed!" The voice sounded like Godfrey's.

Not long later, they were hauling Sommer and Godfrey onto the front lawn.

"There's no sign of Cousins," Troy said.

Rage propelled her down the front walk to the officers who were supposed to watching over the house until the warrant had come through, the same ones who had said Cousins was home. "Where did he go?"

The officers looked at each other. "Nowhere," one of them said. "He was inside. We saw him go in."

"Well, apparently you never saw him go out." She

balled her fist at her hip. "We've got to find him." They just stood there. "What are you waiting for? Go!"

They left, and she turned her attention to Sommer and Godfrey. "Where is Clark Cousins?"

"Uh, I dunno," Sommer said.

"Neither do I." Godfrey wouldn't look at her.

"Take them downtown. I'll deal with them later," she growled.

"What? Wait," Sommer protested. "You can't do that!"

"You bet your ass I can." She turned her back on them and said to Terry, "Maybe we'll get lucky and find the gun."

Inside the house, it looked like a cyclone had struck... and that was before the Stiles PD touched anything. It was definitely messier than it had been yesterday.

Empty beer bottles littered every flat surface in the space. Video game controllers were haphazardly left about the room. One was on the couch. The screen showed a first-person shooter game in split screen, and from the looks of it, one of their characters had just died.

Terry went to the right, where there was a dining room with some shelving units against the wall. He began poking around on a bookshelf, knocking empty beer bottles to the floor in his wake. Stanford and Sovereign were at the back of house rummaging through cupboards and drawers.

Madison turned her attention back to the entertainment unit and searched it. Then she went to the couch and carefully parted the cushions from the frame, looking for the gun. She preferred to find the bullets safely in the weapon rather than in *her*—or someone else.

But nothing was there except for crumbs. She continued working methodically around the room, and after about twenty minutes, she'd cleared the space. Terry had finished the dining room in about the same amount of time.

She met his gaze and shook her head; he did the same.

Stanford and Sovereign were still looking through the back rooms of the house, and that left the bathrooms and three bedrooms to search.

She was exhausted at the mere thought. The amount of focused effort—and time—required meant it would take them a couple of hours. It was around ten thirty now, and it would probably be midnight by the time they finished up here. She let out a yawn before she got a shot to curb it.

Troy happened through doorway and stood in front of her. "Someone needs sleep."

She looked in his eyes, took in how hot he was dressed in his body armor, weapons draping off him…

"I'll sleep once we catch Barry's killer." Her words came out harsher than she'd intended, but she'd never operated well on little sleep. It seemed like it was finally catching up to her, and she hated it. The job still wasn't done, the promise she made to Joni still not fulfilled. "I can handle it." She wasn't about to ask how he was holding up as he didn't seem to appreciate any of her previous attempts at showing concern. Even her earlier thought about reconciling sunk to a deep recess within her. She made eye contact with him. Those green eyes…damn him. He was likely seeing right through her.

"I have no doubt you can—" he brushed past her and whispered in her ear "—Bulldog."

What was he trying to do to her? If he was intending to confuse her, mission accomplished. Maybe she should say something to him now, as she might not have another chance before the warrant service on the Hellions' hideout. He was probably in here to say he and his team were taking off. She opened her mouth—

"Maddy?"

It was Sovereign, and based on the arch he'd added to her name and the volume of his voice, he'd called out for her at least once before.

She glanced at Troy, hoping that he read her eyes now, knew that she wanted him to be safe.

"What is it?" she asked Sovereign.

"Lou and I cleared the kitchen, a laundry area, and started on a bedroom. No gun, but we found a bunch of spray paint. There's graffiti-type art all over the bedroom walls and it looks like it belongs to Sommer."

Madison looked at Terry. It might not be a murder charge, but it would give her enough to hold Sommer and Godfrey for a while.

She was losing hope that they'd find the gun here, though. It was likely with the car or Cousins...wherever that was.

CHAPTER 35

THE SEARCH ENDED CLOSE TO midnight and Madison hated that she was right about two things: one, that it would take that long to search the place, and two, that they wouldn't find the Glock. What she regretted was not telling Troy to be safe. His men would be in position outside the Hellions' hideout.

She was driving back to the station with Terry in the passenger seat. Her eyes were burning and gritty, and she couldn't talk without yawning.

Terry pulled on his seat belt. "I'm thinking we should call it a day."

"Call it a day? We don't even know where Cousins is."

"And we might not find him tonight. Besides, you're not even awake."

She didn't look over at her partner, not because she was upset that he'd made the observation of her apparent weakness, and not because he was right and she hated it. She didn't look at him because she dared not take her eyes from the road for fear of veering off onto the sidewalk.

"I'm awake, Ter—" She fought another yawn.

"We'll manage this better in the morning." He yawned then.

"Ah, so it's not about me—*you're* tired."

"Yes, I am. At least I can admit to it."

She could probably sleep for a week, but that didn't mean she should. She had to keep going; stopping wasn't an option. There was always something to do, and with Cousins running around out there, how was she supposed to sleep anyway? She pulled the department car into the police lot, and she and Terry got out.

"We have Sommer and Godfrey to press about their roommate's whereabouts," she said.

"They said they didn't know."

She looked over at him, angling her head downward. "Yes, because everyone is so honest."

"Fine, but let's make this quick."

"You got it." She picked up her pace on the way into the station, and they had Sommer and Godfrey brought to interrogation rooms. They spoke to Godfrey first.

He was pacing the room like a drug addict in need of his next fix. "I didn't do anything. I don't know why I'm here."

"Sit." Madison didn't waver in eye contact with him when she gave the order.

Godfrey sat. "What do you want? I told you I hooked up with some chick and was at her place when the shooting happened."

"Yet you can't prove that." Madison crossed her arms. "Where's Clark?"

"I told you. I don't know."

She peered into his eyes. None of the telltale signs of lying were there, but some people had it down to an art. "All right. What about places he likes to go or things he likes to do? Does he have a girlfriend?"

Godfrey glanced back at Terry.

"Answer her questions," Terry said.

"He doesn't have a steady girl. He sleeps around.

He could be sleeping on a street corner for all I know." Godfrey wiped his face against a shoulder. "Let me go. You've got nothing to hold me."

She didn't say a word to him when she headed for the door. Terry followed her out of the room.

"What do you think?" she asked.

"Unless I'm losing my touch, I'd say the guy is telling the truth, but given the people we've talked to in this investigation, I'm wondering if they even hear themselves speak."

Madison nodded. It's not as if one could even conclude guilt based on lying. Some people were chronic liars even if the truth hurt no one, including themselves.

"Let's try Sommer," she said and led the way to the next interrogation room.

"What do you want from me? Should I get a lawyer down here?" Sommer splayed his hands on his chest.

Madison was too tired to deal with the machismo front. "Where's Clark?"

Sommer rolled his eyes so hard, Madison was staring at the whites of his eyes for a few seconds.

"We're not going away, you know that, right?" Madison sat in the chair across from him.

"I. Don't. Know. Where. He. Is."

Madison thought of the spray paint, the practice runs on his bedroom walls. "You tell us where he is, and we'll see what we can do about the vandalism charges."

Sommer's eyes calmly went to Madison's.

"Yep, we found your paint, got a good look at your bedroom walls. They look an awful lot like the graffiti on the courthouse. And the tag *D R* that you used won't help you out much, either."

Sommer's facial features hardened. "You can't prove it

was me," he said, calling her bluff.

Madison got up. "Forget the offer, then."

She and Terry reached the door when Sommer called out. "Fine. I know where he might be."

"I'M SLEEPING ON…my…feet here, Maddy," Terry said, his sentence fragmented by a yawn.

She followed suit and cursed the fact that yawns were so contagious.

"You know why you're yawning now?" Terry asked, almost as if he were reading her mind.

"Okay, I admit it. I'm tired."

"No. It's because you have a bond with me." He was grinning, and for some reason, the lift in his cheeks made the red rims of his eyes more noticeable. "It's monkeys."

"It's what?" She chuckled.

"They did a study on monkeys." He waved a dismissive hand. "When the leader of the group yawns, the rest know it's time to go to sleep."

"Okay…" Terry must have been sent to test her patience.

"Now," Terry continued, "if a monkey from another group yawns in front of a monkey who isn't part of his circle, the second monkey will not yawn. So, you yawned because we have a bond."

"You flatter yourself." About the bond or the fact that he essentially called himself a monkey, she'd let him decide.

"How long are you going to let yourself believe you're rough and tough, Madison Knight?"

"I am." The lie sank in her gut. A flashback of Troy talking to her at Cousins's and him leaving without a good-bye had her eyes going wet.

Terry cocked his head to the side. "This is me you're talking to. I know about your attachment to murder victims, how you always need to refer to them by name. I know that you hate the sight of blood."

She waved him off. "Now you're just making stuff up."

"And I know something's up between you and Troy."

She glanced away and bit her bottom lip.

"Yep, I'm right."

"Never mind my relationship, Terry. You said you were going home? So 'night."

Terry scanned her eyes. "'Night." He took a few steps away from her, then looked back. "Troy will be fine tonight. Get some sleep."

Get some sleep. Yeah, right.

CHAPTER 36

TROY AND HIS TEAM WERE in position. His watch read 11:55. Five minutes until go time. And yet he was calm inside, peaceful even. He'd been able to use his experience and coax himself into this state of mind. His breathing was paced and even, his heartbeat slow and steady.

Nick was in front of Troy, David, Derek, and Charlie at the primary entry point. They'd confirmed Marc, Jay, and Clayton were in position at the secondary. The inner perimeter had been established that saw the street cordoned, and the outer perimeter kept people out for a few blocks.

While it would be ideal to vacant all residents from nearby houses, it would greatly tip the Hellions off that something was up. Troy hated that clearing the neighborhood wasn't possible. Certain types of bullets could penetrate brick and mortar, and when it came to gangs, one could usually expect a fight. Gang members weren't exactly of the flight mentality.

Troy glanced at David on his right and then at Charlie and Derek. Nick kept his attention forward. David was armed with a battering ram.

"Secondary, confirm in position at B/C," Troy said over the comms. That referred to where the back of the house met with the left side.

"Confirmed," Jay responded.

One more soothing exhale and then it was time to move in. "Go! Go now!" Troy ordered.

He heard the back door break as Marc would have torn through the wood to breach the house. Then Troy heard the detonation of the flashbang.

Go time!

David rammed through the front door, and Nick led the way with his shield and pistol, providing some cover for his team members following behind them as planned. Troy and the rest filtered in, MP5s raised and ready.

Screams resonated in the home, and Troy and his team swarmed in the direction of the sound, to a living room with seven gang members gripping their ears and covering their eyes with one hand and clinging to a weapon with the other.

"Secondary heading up now," Jay said over the comms.

They'd spread out, go to the second story, and disarm and apprehend any Hellions found up there.

Nick led the way into the living room, Troy and the other primaries following behind. Three targets were seated on a couch, and four others were standing around the room. Lonnie Hogan was one of the men on the couch, yelling directions on what his men were to do. But there was so much confusion among them. The ones standing were unsteady on their feet, still knocked off-balance by the flashbang.

Hogan was the first to pull his trigger. Nick managed his shield, providing the most coverage for Troy and the rest of the men with him. The trajectory of the bullet went wide, but more followed.

Troy's senses were at high alert, even above the gunfire. He could pick up everything—movement, sounds, smells.

Jay called out over the comms and confirmed that the members upstairs had surrendered without a fight. Obviously they were smart enough to realize this encounter wasn't worth their lives. Maybe the situation was already reaching a lull in the action, except they still had to get control of the main level.

Down here, guns were still being fired. Troy and his men were seeking cover behind Nick's shield in the hallway now.

"Put down your weapons!" Troy yelled, trying to project his voice over the gunfire.

The Hellions didn't desist.

Troy turned to Charlie. "FB in five seconds!" *Flashbang.*

The secondary team would hear this request over the comms and know to put their protective earpieces in place again.

Charlie waited the five seconds and tossed a flashbang into the room. He, Troy, and the rest of SWAT shielded their eyes, and once the flash had disappeared, they scurried around the room, disarming gang members quickly. Derek had Lonnie in seconds.

Troy approached the last one, a young man of about twenty, if that. His eyes were vacant and he held his gun, its muzzle still smoking, seemingly steady, pointed at Troy's chest. His face looked familiar. *Russell Coleman?*

Troy now had the chance to get even for what he had done to Barry, but he didn't want that. He wanted Coleman to live with what he had done. But Troy had to make the call. More lives were at stake. His men were still in the room, as were other Hellions. His mind ran through the assessment in a fraction of a second.

Troy was about to pull his trigger when there was a

loud crack, and red bloomed from the kid's forehead before he fell to the ground.

He turned around and saw Nick still holding his gun aimed at Coleman.

In that moment, it was like the world stood still. Troy never relished taking a life—or even being witness to it. No good cop did. This, however, wasn't a shady moment of choosing whether someone lived or died. It was black-and-white. Nick's shot had been a good one, but that didn't mean that the kid's eyes wouldn't haunt him from beyond the grave.

Everything quieted down around Troy. He heard his men clearing out the Hellions, guiding them by cuffs that secured their wrists at their lower back. The situation had been neutralized.

Still, Troy stood there looking down on the young man who had also made his choices in life and, sadly, had just paid for them.

He pulled his eyes from the body to look at Nick. "It was a good shoot," he said.

And despite knowing that was the truth, that there was nothing to have done differently, he still felt the sickly drape of death threatening to suffocate him.

CHAPTER 37

TROY STAYED WITH NICK AS he was minimally debriefed and escorted back to the station, where they took his rifle, which was standard protocol for when an officer was involved in a shooting. Nick was then sent home for the night, although it was really morning by this point seeing as it was 2:00 AM. Troy went home, too. Gangs would handle interviewing the Hellions.

He kicked a tire on his Ford Expedition before getting in. He hated casualties on any given mission, on any given day, and they had a way of sticking to him like the humidity of summer. But why, of all the gang members, did it have to be Russell Coleman who was taken out? He didn't deserve a bullet, an easy way out. He should have had to face a judge, serve a life sentence, and live with what he'd done to Barry.

And with Coleman dead, they were also left without a solid lead in regard to the shooter's identity.

But even if Coleman hadn't been the driver as he'd claimed he'd been, a man's life was over. A good cop couldn't just shake that off. Troy was so close with Nick that he may as well have pulled the trigger himself. Weaker cops turned to the bottle, and Troy was tempted. But it would only make matters worse. He knew this from experience, from kissing the bottom of countless whiskey bottles after he found out about his wife cheating with his best friend.

Besides, there was no time for losing his head. The shooting would be reviewed by Internal Affairs—a bittersweet necessity because some cops weren't above playing both sides of the law. He and his men would be asked to testify to the situation, and with each retelling, Nick would be forced to relive the moment. Troy would go through it along with his man. He'd seen the defiance in Coleman's eyes, the hatred that lived there, and then he'd watched as that light went out, not fade with a flickering brightness but absolutely extinguish, as if someone had simply flipped a switch.

Time-wise, it would all likely be over rather quickly, but it would still mean that Troy would lose Nick to some administrative duty that would likely bore him and have him stuck at the station, unable to help actively with the investigation or interact with the public in an official capacity. He'd be proclaimed a hero by his teammates and fellow officers for acting swiftly and saving their lives, but to Nick, the reassignment would feel like punishment. Troy knew the man well enough to know that, at least.

Troy drove home, and the house felt so empty without Madison or Hershey there. With nothing else to distract him, his mind relived the shooting—first Coleman's death and then Barry's murder. How fast life could change…

Troy gave in to the voice in his head that taunted him to have a drink. He poured himself an Irish whiskey, too lazy and not really caring enough to add ice, and dropped onto his couch. He took a long sip and let the liquid warm him up, but it also stole his defenses.

The glass shook in his hands and he cried. He had nothing left. He'd had an amazing friend, and now he was gone. He'd had an amazing woman, and now she was gone. God, he was messed up right now. He drank the rest of his whiskey in big, eager gulps and put the empty glass on the end table.

He couldn't bring Barry back to life, although he'd give anything for that power. But he could get Madison back, or least make a valiant effort to do so. She didn't deserve the way he'd been treating her. All she'd tried to do was be there for him, show that she cared, and he'd brushed her off as a nuisance.

All of this was enough to throw him off. Hell, even Barry's death alone would have been enough. And up until now, instead of thinking about what was important and holding on tighter, he had done the opposite, thinking that distancing himself would make things better, easier. But easier on whom and how, exactly?

He pulled out his phone and poised his finger over Madison's name. What could he possibly say to her right now? And it was two in the morning… He tossed his phone on the table, got up, grabbed his glass and the whiskey bottle, turned the lights out, and made his way down the hall to his bedroom.

The room still smelled of her perfume, and he inhaled deeply. She only wore it in the evening because she said she'd rather be flogged naked next to city hall than give the men down at the station the impression that she was a girlie girl. Those were pretty much her exact words. At the time he'd laughed and she'd hit him. He had tried to reason with her that wearing a fragrance wouldn't diminish their respect for her, but she wasn't about to accept his word on that. She said, *What? Perfume one day and manicured nails the next? No. No way, Troy.*

He smiled at the memory, at her stubborn nature—the

same quality that both drew him to her and could push him away depending on how she wielded the power.

He undressed and then poured himself another glass of whiskey before getting into bed. Hopefully the amber liquid would lull him to sleep. And when he woke up, he'd make everything right.

CHAPTER 38

"KNIGHT?"

It was the sergeant's voice. But where was it coming from? He sounded like he was miles away.

She opened her eyes and found herself lying with her head on her desk, facing one wall of the bullpen. She must have fallen asleep. She lifted her head quickly as if to avoid getting caught, but it was obviously too late for that. The side of her mouth felt wet, and she wiped her hand across her cheek, smearing the drool. *Yuck!*

Winston acted as though he hadn't even noticed. "What are you doing here?"

What *was* she doing here? She glanced at her monitor, but it had turned off and her mind wasn't awake.

He looked around her and down the hall. "Where's Grant?"

"He went home." At least she remembered that much…

"I suggest you do, too."

"I'm fine, Sarge."

He let his eyes run over her. "Really? That's your story? Your hair's standing straight up, and you have a sticky note stuck to your face. You sure don't look fine."

Crap. She felt it now. On her right cheek. She pulled it off.

Then she remembered. *The Hellions…*

"What time is it?" she asked.

"After two. That's why you need to go home and get some rest."

Her mind was clearing now. "How did the raid go on the Hellions?"

Winston didn't answer right away.

"What happened?" Based on his avoidance of the question and the pallor of his face, someone had lost their life. Call it a sixth sense or just her experience working around death.

"The raid was a success, but there was a casualty."

Fear pierced her heart. "Troy? Is—"

"He's fine."

She could breathe again, even if only shallow breaths. "Who?"

"No officers."

Now she could get a lungful.

"It was a member of the Hellions' gang."

Her heart sank in her chest. "Who pulled the trigger? Who made the shot?"

"Benson," Winston said, giving it to her straight. "It seems like it was a good shoot. Internal Affairs will most likely just be a formality, but—"

She felt her blood pressure rising, her head feeling slightly dizzy. Troy would take this death upon his own shoulders. "If any of Troy's men pulled the trigger, you can be damn sure it was a good shoot." She was looking in her superior's eyes, and her defensiveness morphed into a deep sadness and empathy for Troy. "Who was shot?"

"Russell Coleman."

"Coleman? Shit!" She stood up and paced the length of her desk. "Now what the hell are we supposed to do? He was a strong lead. He was going to take us to the shooter.

Damn it."

"We can't do anything about the past."

She met her sergeant's eyes. "Please don't. I don't need a life lesson right now."

"Fair enough."

Since when did Winston back down? He must have really wanted her to go home, call it a night, and pick up in the morning. Her grogginess was completely gone now, though, and she remembered why she'd been at the station so late. Obviously she'd wanted to be here and know that Troy had returned safely, but she had also wondered about something else—if Sommer had been right about where they'd find Clark Cousins. "Was Cousins at the Hellions' hideout?"

Winston pressed his lips into a firm line and nodded.

Thank God, something was going right!

"Excuse me," she said.

"Where are you going?"

"To question him."

Winston got ahead of her, blocking her path. "Oh, no you're not."

"What do you mean? Of course, I am."

"He's going to sit behind bars and stew until morning."

"It *is* morning."

"Don't get smart, Knight. Go home. Get some sleep. Come in for nine, and there will be a briefing."

"Fine…" Not that she thought sleep would come, but she'd give it a shot. Bad choice of words, she thought, and Troy entered her mind again. She considered going over to see him, but he was probably already asleep and he'd been through so much. Tomorrow. She'd try tomorrow.

CHAPTER 39

NINE THE NEXT MORNING CAME TOO QUICKLY. Her bed was a lot more comfortable than Chelsea's guest bed and definitely more comfortable than her Mazda. Madison felt like she'd just fallen asleep when her alarm went off. She grabbed a Starbucks on her way to the station and headed straight to the squad room.

The place was standing room only already with members from Major Crimes, Guns and Drugs, Gangs, and SWAT in attendance. It seemed that everyone had beaten her here this morning. She glanced around; she didn't see Troy. She should have gone by to see him last night, to hell with the fact that he might have been sleeping. It would have shown him how much she cared for his welfare.

Winston was at the front of the room and started speaking the moment the hour and minute hands on the wall clock confirmed it was nine.

"As you know, we raided the Hellions' hideout at midnight. Twenty-five people have been arrested. The interviewing process started around two this morning."

Madison glanced at members from the gangs unit. No wonder they looked utterly exhausted.

"It was a success, although one gang member did lose his life."

Madison's stomach knotted into a lead ball at the summation of success given alongside the mention of a casualty.

"The deceased," Winston continued, "was Russell Coleman."

This was news to many, and gasps filled the room.

The sergeant held up his hand. "As we already knew, Coleman didn't fit the description of the shooter and was only claiming to be the driver. We do, however, have another suspect in custody who fits the physicality of the driver. Who was actually behind the wheel at the time of the shooting has not yet been confirmed. Going back to the Hellions, none of the gang members that were brought in resembled the sketch of the shooter, but because we only have the word of one eyewitness on the shooter's description, I think we should keep an open mind." Winston glanced at Madison.

She interpreted his look as calling her out, a questioning of her intuition. But it wasn't that she was attached to Snyder's story so much as she went with what she had to work with.

"We still have not located the BMW," Winston said. "We did, however, seize some cocaine and weapons, including five Glocks. They will all be tested by the lab to see if any of them match the striations left on the bullets from the crime scene." Winston paused as the door opened. He did a double take and heads turned to see the source of his reaction, including Madison's.

Troy.

His glance quickly locked on hers, and he headed in her direction. Madison's heart fluttered as her stomach simultaneously knotted.

Troy stopped beside her, reached out, and brushed

his fingertips along the back of her hand. The softness of his touch made her want to cry, as if all were forgiven between them without a word needing to be spoken. He preferred to make things right with her than be right, too.

She smiled at him, and he reciprocated.

"We also found Clark Cousins," Winston went on. "He was discovered on the second story of the Hellions' hideout. Detectives Knight and Grant will be interviewing him today, but I wanted him to stew overnight. Even a few more hours wouldn't hurt in my opinion."

If Winston thought she was waiting any longer to talk to Cousins, he was sorely mistaken. She'd been patient enough.

When the sergeant was done with the briefing, the room cleared out and she found herself left with Troy. The fact that she wanted to make up with him combined with being here with him now made her mind spin. The words weren't coming. Her pride kept stepping in, telling her that he should make the first move, that he should be the one to apologize. But maybe both of them could avoid that sentiment. They were both hurting over losing Barry; they weren't being themselves. And really, hadn't he made the first step toward reconciliation by touching her hand?

"How are you doing? I mean, in regard to last night," she was quick to add.

Troy took a deep breath. "I'll be okay. I'm just mad that we had to take out Coleman, but we didn't have a choice."

She nodded. "I believe you."

His gaze met hers, his green eyes full of life, as if he was pleased by her belief in him. "Thanks."

"You're welcome." It seemed they were back to that awkwardness that typically existed between strangers.

"You know, if you want to talk about it, I'm here." She started to leave the room. Her emotions were closing in on her, threatening to overwhelm her and making her feel vulnerable.

"I appreciate it," was all he said.

She continued out of the room, pausing at the door, but she knew he was going to let her leave. He could have called her back, said something to smooth things over, told her he just wanted to forget about taking a break, but he said none of those things. Maybe she was a fool for thinking that's what he wanted. She'd known enough men in her life to know that they were out for themselves, not her, and she was the only one who could protect her heart.

CHAPTER 40

COUSINS WAS IN INTERVIEW ROOM ONE, his head resting on the table, when Madison and Terry entered. Madison slammed the door behind them, jarring Cousins awake. There were always two ways to approach an interrogation—as friend or foe. Madison had the foe part down pat.

"Where is your uncle's BMW?" She'd thought about going straight to asking if he shot Barry but skirted the issue temporarily.

"I don't have to talk to you," he said like a spoiled child who was used to getting his way.

Madison smirked at Cousins but let the expression drift to Terry. "He doesn't think he has to—" She smacked her hands to the table, and she lunged across it, her nose inches from Cousins in a flash. "You killed a cop."

So much for skirting around it...

"Nope. You've got the wrong guy." Cousins was as calm as a hardened criminal who had been through all this before.

"Explain why you were found at the known hideout of the Hellions gang, then."

Cousins crossed his arms and sat back in his chair as if getting comfortable.

Two seconds... Four seconds... Six seconds... After

a minute, it was clear Cousins wasn't going to explain himself. She slapped a photograph of Russell Coleman's dead body on the table.

Cousins's eyes drifted to it, but he just clenched his jaw tighter, still remaining silent.

"He was a friend of yours," Madison said, doing her best to add empathy to her words.

"A cop killed him."

Madison didn't say anything. To Cousins, it was just a cop, but to her, she knew there was no way Benson would have taken the shot unless he had no choice. "Your friend held a gun on him." Madison didn't know that for certain, but she was willing to defend her colleague. He'd have matched force against his threat assessment.

"That's what you say, lady." Cousins glanced back at Terry, who was now jingling his change.

"Did you shoot Officer Weir?" she asked.

"Who's that?"

"You're going to play dumb? He was the officer gunned down yesterday morning at Rico's Gas Station. He was a husband and a father of three daughters."

Cousins looked at her blankly. "How sad."

It was taking all Madison's willpower not to strangle this guy. His indifference to Barry's murder stole her breath and ratcheted her adrenaline.

"I'll tell you what's sad…" Madison stood and walked around the table, thinking through her next move, and figured it was best to strike where it would be the most personal for Cousins. "Your uncle's been brought in."

Cousins straightened up. "For what? He didn't do anything."

Madison smirked. "But you did."

He narrowed his eyes. "I never said that."

"Huh." Madison's turn to remain quiet for a bit.

Cousins watched her walk around the room.

"Maybe you'd like a coffee?" she asked, looking from Cousins to the table in front of him. "We could get you a coffee."

"What are you doing?" Cousins pointed a finger at her. "Playing mind games with me?"

"No, not at all." Madison looked at Terry and spoke to him. "I love starting my day off with coffee. If I don't have one, nothing in my day goes right."

"Yeah, I agree with—"

"I didn't kill the cop!" Cousins blurted out, interrupting Terry.

Madison turned serious again and looked at Cousins. "You're going to prison for a very long time." She let her eyes lock with his and held the eye contact for a space of about thirty seconds.

"I should get a lawyer."

She could read it in his eyes, the emptiness of his threat. "Maybe. But you won't."

"Oh yeah? Why won't I?"

"You're innocent. That's what you're claiming, right?"

"Yeah, you've got the wrong guy."

"Hmm."

"Don't *hmm* me. I didn't kill anyone." Cousins's gaze met Madison's briefly before he looked away.

"We know your uncle's vehicle was used in the shooting. Did he give it to you?" Madison looked at Terry. "Or maybe it wasn't Russell who was driving. It could have been his uncle."

"No," Cousins growled.

"Then change our minds, because once my mind gets set..."

"SWAT storms in, kills people—kills Russ—drags me out like a criminal, and…" He paused, not from emotion over losing a friend, it seemed, but more to gather his thoughts.

"We're after the shooter," she stated calmly. Time to retrace and approach things another way. Do her best to relate, see if she could get him to feel like she was on his side somehow. "You give us his name and maybe we can work something out." Not that she had any intention of following through on those words. Promises made to criminals were nothing more than tools to extract what she needed.

"You're going to give me a deal? But I haven't done anything."

"Is that really the story you want to stick to?" she asked, looking him in the eye.

"My uncle wasn't involved. Maybe I was, maybe I wasn't. Cop killers are worshiped in prison. I'd…" A shiver of fear rippled through Cousins's eyes. It made Madison think of the young man who would have faced jail time for shoplifting, how scared he must have been then. Cousins was more bravado than he was actual grit.

"That's what you think? You might want a few minutes to reconsider." Cousins might be respected by his fellow inmates, but the prison guards would make his life hell.

Cousins's eyes snapped to hers, but the action wasn't out of disrespect. It was fear.

"I see that the truth is sinking in. Trust me when I tell you it won't go well for you on the inside."

"Please, I'm too young to—"

"The name of the shooter," Madison spat.

"And we'll have a deal? You'll put in a good word and lessen my sentence?"

Madison managed to suppress a smile. He was obviously guilty of something, so she played along. "Talk to us."

"Russ drove…or so he told me afterward. I wish I'd never even gotten involved."

Madison's impulse was to jump on Cousins's words, but something told her to hold back.

"I'm so stupid thinking that I can even be some tough guy." The front that Cousins had put up since they'd come into the room was quickly disappearing in front of them.

He lowered his head, and tears filled his eyes. "I took my uncle's car, yeah."

"Did he know about it? Why you took it?"

Terry stopped jingling the change in his pocket, and the room fell silent.

Cousins scanned her eyes. "No! No, he didn't. Stop trying to involve him." Cousins jumped in his seat. "He had no idea. I didn't really know what was going on, either."

Madison narrowed her eyes. She was definitely entering the bitchy phase of exhaustion. "Really?"

"I mean it." Cousins seemed to calm himself down and then continued. "He let me borrow the car. He's always believed in me."

It took everything Madison had not to say something that would come across as snide and clam the guy right up. "Tell us what you did with his car, why your uncle has the plates for it but it's nowhere to be found," she said with surprising restraint.

"I don't know where it is."

"You what?" Her voice raised a few octaves, and Cousins pulled back.

He held up a hand for mercy. "I made a deal with

someone." Seeming remorse coated each of his words.

Madison just stared at him, wanting him to continue talking.

"I got word from some guy. He was looking for a car, a gun, and some bullets."

And here comes another version of the *It wasn't me* story...

"He said there was five thousand in it if I could arrange things," Cousins continued.

"Okay, so you gave this guy your uncle's BMW, his Glock, and some bullets in exchange for five thousand bucks? Am I understanding this correctly? And your uncle went along with it?" Brown must have, seeing as he had the plates.

He let out a deep sigh. "Yeah. I had bills to pay. Phil's really too good to me..."

"We'll need this guy's name and where to find him," she said, though she wasn't buying his story. Why wouldn't Brown just lend Cousins the money?

"Uh, that's going to be a problem."

Madison crossed her arms. "And why's that?"

"I don't know him."

"You're going to have to do better than that."

Cousins's eyes drifted to the table but popped up to meet Madison's gaze. "We texted, but I deleted the messages. You guys can recover them, right?"

His phone would have been taken when he was booked. "Possibly. When was it?" Madison wasn't even ready to give herself over to believing him, but it couldn't hurt to look into it. "You can trust me."

"Trust cops? Are you kidding me?"

"Have it your way." Madison went for the door.

"No, wait." He sighed. "Fine. It was last Thursday."

CHAPTER 41

MADISON MADE A CALL TO CYNTHIA to retrieve Cousins's cell phone and see if she could find the deleted messages and trace the sender. But updates went both ways, and the one she received back from Cynthia had Madison's stomach swirling.

"What is it? You look like someone—" Terry didn't finish the sentence when she looked him in the eye.

"Sam's finished firing the rounds from the Glocks collected from the Hellions."

"And?"

She let out a deep breath. "None of them were a match." And surprisingly, it wasn't the fact that they didn't have the murder weapon that was affecting her the most. "What a senseless loss of life."

"Just because the gun wasn't recovered in the raids doesn't mean the members are clear of involvement. We have a recording of Coleman confessing to being the driver. He had to be involved on some level. And if the Hellions were firing at SWAT, I hate to say this, but what did they expect would happen?" Terry looked in her eyes when he made his point.

She appreciated what he was saying; she really did. She nodded. "You're right."

"That's a few times in as many days as you've agreed

with me." Terry smiled. "I've fallen into the twilight zone."

She rolled her eyes. "I tell you you're right a lot."

"Not nearly enough."

"And that's my fault?" she teased. Then the moment of levity disappeared, her mind going back to the interrogation with Cousins and his claim that his uncle knew he took the car. To sell it, no less. Why would Brown let him do that? Were they really supposed to believe that he wasn't involved, that he had no knowledge of what the car was being used for? He had his plates and may have removed them himself. He'd lied about what he'd done with the BMW. Twice. First he said he'd sold it, and then he supposedly had given it to charity.

No wonder there hadn't been a receipt. His nephew was the charity...

But if Brown knew that Cousins needed his car, did he also know about the Glock and ammunition? And again, her mind circled back to why Brown didn't just give his nephew money.

"Brown knew about everything, Terry," she said. "He had to."

Terry tilted his head. Whenever she stated things definitively, her partner met her with skepticism.

"We know Brown's a liar," she went on. "And of course, we still haven't found the vehicle." God, everything would be so much easier if they had. "What we do have is Clark Cousins admitting to taking his uncle's BMW, Glock, and ammunition to sell them. He even said that Brown knew he was taking his car. Brown could have removed the plates from his car himself, and if not, he was obviously aware they had been taken off. He'd have known his nephew wasn't up to any good. Otherwise, he would have left the plates on."

"I see what you're saying," Terry said. "You want to have him pulled from holding? Question him again?"

"No."

"No?"

She shrugged. "Well, not yet anyway. Let him sit. He's waiting for a lawyer anyhow. In the meantime, I want to see if we can get more proof against him."

"What are you thinking?"

"Well, first we need to find out who sent those messages to Cousins."

"Yeah," Terry said. "Assuming there are ones to find."

CHAPTER 42

"HAVE YOU GOTTEN ANYWHERE WITH tracking down the sender of those messages?" Madison asked Cynthia when she arrived at the lab with Terry.

"Do I look like Houdini to you?" she snapped.

Madison glanced at Terry, and both of them approached Cynthia cautiously.

"Are you all right?" Madison asked.

Cynthia blinked deliberately. "Peachy."

Oh, that meant the exact opposite…

Madison turned to Terry. "Can you give us a minute?"

He looked at the two women. "Ah, sure."

When the door shut behind Terry, Madison faced Cynthia. "What's going on?"

Cynthia was shaking her head. "I'm just tired. That's all."

"There's more to it than that, and you know it. Come on, talk to me. Isn't that what you say to me sometimes?" Madison gave Cynthia a small smile.

Cynthia's eyes snapped to Madison's. "Sure, why not?" Sarcasm dripped from the words. "And you're always so forthcoming when you have a personal problem."

Her friend had her there… Madison put a hand on Cynthia's forearm, ignoring her friend's snarkiness. "Talk," she said softly, encouragingly.

Cynthia took a deep, heaving breath. "Lou and I had a fight last night."

"You two never fight." Madison was surprised by how small her voice sounded.

"Well, we did last night. And it was a big one."

Madison was never good at knowing what to say in these situations. She either didn't ask the right questions or she asked too many. She had to say something, though, given the way Cynthia was looking at her. "What was it about?"

Cynthia didn't say anything for a while. "You don't waste any time going for the meat of it, do you?"

"You know me."

"He's just been a real ass this week. Well, ever since Barry died."

Lou sounded like Troy. "He's probably just grieving, Cyn. We all are."

Cynthia shook her head. "I think it's more than that. It's like he's hiding something from me. It's been building for a long time." Her eyes filled with tears. "I think he's having an affair."

"Why do you think—"

"He's secretive. He's up late in the office. I heard him on the phone last night, too. That's what started the big fight."

Oh no... Madison had no doubts about Lou's fidelity. It probably had something to do with the surprise engagement party he'd been working on for Cynthia.

"What was he saying?" Madison asked.

"The door was closed so I just caught bits and pieces, but something about needing to change plans because there was a lot going on."

"And that's all?"

"That's *all*? Maddy, in the past that would have been enough for you to kick his ass and beat the truth out of him."

"Lou's not the cheating type," Madison said quickly and pulled her friend in for a hug. Cynthia felt like a loose rag.

Cynthia pulled back, narrowing her eyes at Madison. "Since when do you have faith in men?"

Oh Lord. She had a point there. Madison was never the type to defend a man. Usually everything was their fault.

"You've really gotten bit by the love bug, haven't you?"

"This isn't about me, Cynthia."

"No, it's not, but you wouldn't normally stand up for a man. Troy's changed you."

"Listen, time has changed me, experience has changed me, not a man."

Cynthia raised an eyebrow. "So you just don't see Lou as the type to cheat?" The heat in her voice, in her gaze, started to evaporate. Her eyes drifted back to her computer screen. "The truth is, neither do I."

"Then what's the problem?"

"Maybe I jumped into this whole engagement thing too fast." Cynthia stated it as if in an attempt at sounding certain, but Madison picked up on her friend's doubt and even her call for reassurance.

"You love Lou," Madison said, trying to keep her face indifferent. But she'd just been put in awkward position— tell her friend and spare her heartbreak or keep her promise to Lou about the surprise party.

"What aren't you telling me? I can see it, Maddy. It's all over your face."

"You're not one to jump into a commitment like

marriage without having given it a great deal of thought," Madison said. "You know that Lou's a good man or you wouldn't have accepted his proposal."

"Madison…"

Uh-oh. She's using my full first name…

"Fine," she said, letting out a deep sigh. "I have something to tell you, but you can't let Lou know that I told you. You have to still act surprised. And I'll be watching—"

"Surprised? What are you—" Cynthia's eyes widened. "He's planning something? Our honeymoon?" She frowned. "I'd love to have a say in what we do. I only plan on getting married once."

Madison was shaking her head and biting her bottom lip.

Cynthia nudged her in the arm. "Speak."

"He's been planning a surprise party for you for months."

Cynthia's jaw dropped slightly.

"Speak," Madison mocked.

"I'm in shock," Cynthia said. "Here I have been accusing him of cheating on me. And it's nothing like that. Did you know about this? All this time?"

"Yeah." Madison looked away, this time ashamed to have hidden something from her friend for so long. "I know you hate surprises, too."

Madison winced, but Cynthia was grinning.

"He's planning a party for me." She lolled her head back and forth. "Sweet. But my lips are sealed." She locked her lips and threw away the key. "He'll never know you told me. I'm surprised you could keep it secret for this long. You said this has been in the works for *months*?"

"Yeah." At least Cynthia was feeling better. Madison

felt awful, as though she'd betrayed Lou's trust.

Cynthia's demeanor was playful now. "You really like him, don't you?"

Madison nodded. "Lou's a great guy."

"Not Lou. Troy."

"What made you take that leap?" She really didn't want to get into her relationship with Troy. It was so complicated. Were they on a break, broken up, or what?

Cynthia smirked. "I talk about my love life but you won't talk about yours?"

"Terry?" Madison called out, projecting her voice over a shoulder so he'd be able to hear her from the hall.

The door opened, and Madison turned back to look at Cynthia and smiled.

Cynthia had a smug look on her face. Madison knew the conversation would be continued, but at least she had a temporary reprieve.

"Cynthia's going to give us some news on the messages." Madison looked at her friend sharply. "Right?"

"Sure."

"Wait, really?"

Cynthia smiled. "I did find the messages."

"And?" Madison asked.

"And what?"

"What did they say?"

"Here. Read it for yourself." Cynthia handed her a printout.

Madison read the text conversation out loud for Terry's benefit:

> *"someone told me you can hook me up. 5k*
> *for 4wheels gun and some bullets*
>   *"who is this*
>   *"5k interested or not*

"interested

"bring $ to mitchell park near swings

"when

"need del on friday in or not

"in."

"Were you able to trace the sender?" Terry asked.

"Yes and no. It was a prepaid phone."

"So you don't know who it was purchased by or registered to?" Madison asked.

"Nope. Not yet anyway. Now get out of here." Cynthia gestured toward the door. "I'll call when I have something."

"How long?" Madison could hear the whine in her voice.

"Long enough." Cynthia shooed them away. "Go. Investigate. Do something."

"We'll be back in an hour," Madison said.

"Make it two and we have a date."

Madison rolled her eyes. "Fine."

She and Terry headed out of the lab. Out in the hall, Terry pushed the elevator to go down to the main level.

"Let's request a warrant for his call history," she said.

"Good idea."

"If we can get ahold of his phone records, we'll find out more about Brown himself, his friends, who he's in contact with."

"And what do you suggest we do now?"

"Go back and talk to Cousins some more. See if we can make him squirm."

CHAPTER 43

CLARK COUSINS'S CHEEKS WERE BRIGHT RED, contrasting sharply against his otherwise pale complexion.

"Please, let me go." His words were pleading and laced with desperation.

"You know we can't do that." Madison kept her tone tight, devoid of emotion as she took a seat across from him.

As per Terry's usual, he took up a spot at the back of the room, standing behind Cousins.

"Did you find the messages? Track the guy down?" Hope lit Cousins's eyes but diminished quickly under Madison's scrutiny.

"You told us that you took your uncle's car, that even your uncle knew about that part. And about the five grand."

"Please just leave my uncle out of this."

At least the kid had some manners. But still...

"Did he know you took his gun and some bullets?" Madison asked.

"No." He ran a hand down his face. "He'd be so ashamed of me."

"Stop the act."

His eyes snapped to hers.

"We found the messages you told us about. Seems odd

that he'd just let you take his car. He probably knew why you wanted everything," she tossed the accusation out there.

"I don't even know who that person was!" Cousins took a deep breath. "And you think that my uncle would knowingly hand over his car so it could be used in a cop killing?" Cousins asked, incredulous. "That I sold it for that purpose?"

"Where did the money go, Cousins?"

"I bought a new video game console, games, a big-screen TV, and a surround sound system. Five grand goes fast."

"And you have receipts for all that?" Madison stood. "You know what, never mind. We'll find out. See, Detective Grant and I, well, we excel at finding out the truth."

Cousins swallowed, his Adam's apple bobbing.

"In fact, we don't stop until we get *all* the answers." She took a few steps, staying to her side of the room to keep an eye on him.

"I don't have anything else to say."

"The first person to start talking gets the deal. Is that going to be you or your uncle?" She let that sit out there for a few seconds and then continued. "Tell us how the money exchange happened."

"I was contacted, asked to get a car, a gun, and bullets in exchange for five thousand bucks. You said you saw the messages."

She pressed on. "How did you get your hands on the money?"

"You read the message," he repeated.

"Humor me."

"It was dropped in a garbage bin at Mitchell Park near

the playground."

"Were you approached because you're a member of the Devil's Rebels?" Her question caught him off guard. He looked from her, to Terry, and back to her. "From what I hear, the Devil's Rebels are just a group of wannabes trying to make a name for themselves on the street," Madison taunted.

Heat flared in his eyes. "That's not what we are."

"Then please, set me straight." Madison glanced at Terry. Cousins was falling apart here. His emotions were easily tipped one way or another with just a little verbal prodding. She didn't even have to point out that he'd said *we*.

"I didn't shoot that cop. Neither did Mike or Travis."

"What about your uncle?"

"No," he spat out. "I'll wait for that lawyer now."

Madison and Terry left for the observation room.

"Did you really need to push him to the point of lawyering up?" he asked.

Sometimes she wondered whose side Terry's was on— hers or the suspect's.

"You could always take a turn at questioning if you want to."

"Yeah, right." He barked a laugh. "You love being in charge."

She narrowed her eyes at him but let the matter drop, her mind back on Cousins. "His asking for one only proves we're getting closer. He's not going anywhere. He has confessed to accepting money in exchange for equipping the shooter with all he needed to take out Barry. Accessory and likely conspiracy to murder will stick if nothing else does. We've got him."

CHAPTER 44

MADISON AND TERRY STEPPED BACK into the lab. "That took a lot less than two hours," Madison said. Cynthia had messaged Madison only forty-five minutes after they'd left her, and she already had answers.

She was sitting in front of her computer and gestured for them to join her. Once they were there, Cynthia pointed to the screen. "The phone was activated a week ago at Sparky's Shack downtown."

Sparky's was an electronic store that carried everything from novelty alarm clocks to computers and TVs.

"The phone was only used to communicate with one number," Cynthia continued.

"Clark Cousins's?" Madison wagered a guess.

Cynthia nodded. "Correct. And the phone was paid for in cash."

"How do you know—"

Cynthia smiled. "Because I'm that good. I called Sparky's, and they parted with the information pretty easily."

Terry's eyes widened. "Without a warrant?"

"I might have said some things that were very persuasive."

Now Madison smiled. "You're not going to share what, are you?"

"A girl has to have some secrets. Anyway, I got more than you probably expected me to."

"Stop stringing us along. You're killing me."

Cynthia smirked and clicked on the screen, bringing up an image. "This was taken from the store's security cameras at the time of the purchase."

"It's the back of the person's—"

The image started moving. It was a video, not a still as Madison had originally thought. As the footage continued, the person turned around, facing the camera. They wore a black hoodie, but the face beneath it wasn't a man's.

Madison stared at Terry in disbelief. "That's Erica Snyder."

Cynthia stood back now, crossing her arms, searching for praise given the twitching of her mouth.

"Awesome job, Cyn," Madison said, but she felt like she'd been socked in the gut. She shook her head. "Everything she told us was probably a lie, including the description on the shooter. She had me believing... God... I need to sit."

Madison dropped into Cynthia's chair, her gaze going to the screen where Snyder's face stared back at her. The entire thing had been an elaborate orchestration to send them away from the real killer. But how did everyone— and everything—tie together?

"Madison? Are you okay?" Terry asked.

"She's been so 'helpful' from the beginning," Madison said in disbelief. "At least after we found her. She actually wanted to be involved in the investigation. She's been in our face the entire time."

"But we know she wasn't in the shooter's vehicle," Cynthia reasoned. "We have her on camera at the other pump."

"We have to find out what her connection is to Barry, then. And to Cousins, to Brown." There was something they were definitely missing.

"All right, well, she told you she'd been dating Sommer, so she probably knew Cousins," Terry said.

Madison looked at him. "Still, how do we get from there to murdering Barry? And why? Nothing about her background stood out. And how does this fit in with the Devil's Rebels, and the Hellions?"

Madison couldn't shake this overwhelming, sick feeling growing in the pit of her gut.

What if everything wasn't as she had originally thought? What if—

"The shooting wasn't gang related," she blurted out. "It was only made to look that way!"

Her heart was beating rapidly. It would explain a lot of things and account for how the investigation kept making these turns, first pointing them to the Hellions, then the discovery of the Devil's Rebels, then to Brown… It was to muddy the path.

"We have a shooter and a driver," she punched out, getting up and taking a few steps. "The shooter yelled out 'Die, cop.'" Another couple of steps. "And four bullets? Why fire another after Barry was struck? It wasn't a drive-by; it wasn't gang initiation. Barry had to have been specifically targeted. But Snyder, Brown, Sommer, and Cousins don't have connections to Barry." She paced a few steps again and stopped.

Snyder had fled the scene. She'd purchased the phone, contacted Cousins and made the request for the car, the gun, and the ammunition.

Everything she'd told them had been a lie. She'd

recognized the decal the second Madison had shown it to her, and it was unlikely she was ever in fear for her life. She probably knew the identity of the driver and shooter. From the time they had found her, she had been manipulating the investigation. But why point them in the direction of the Devil's Rebels or request protection? And why insist on being protected in her own home?

Madison snapped her fingers. That was it! Snyder couldn't get information out to anyone on the status of the investigation from the safe house. "She tipped off Cousins, and that's why he wasn't at his house!"

Terry and Cynthia looked at her, confused.

She explained her thought process quickly and then bolted from the room, shouting, "I've gotta go," over her shoulder.

CHAPTER 45

MADISON PRACTICALLY RAN DOWN THE hallway of the station. She heard Terry calling out to her, but she wasn't stopping for anything. She'd messed up, and she had to make it right. She peeled out of the lot as Terry waved his hands wildly. In the rearview mirror, she saw him put his phone to an ear before running back to the station's door.

Her phone rang on her hip, but there was no point in answering. It would be Terry. He'd be telling her to return to the station, to step back and think things through. But the only thing she could think about was how she'd let herself down, let Joni down, let all of them down. She'd had no idea that Snyder was involved. Her reason for being blind could be explained away, her background was clean, and she'd cooperated. Even though the latter wasn't immediate, she'd seemed like she was coming through.

She made it to Snyder's place in ten minutes, half the time it would've taken if she'd driven at legal speed. There was a cruiser out front, but no one was in it.

That was strange…

Her adrenaline started flowing. Madison slowed down and parked behind the black-and-white. She should call and wait for backup. Maybe paranoia was getting the best of her, though. Just because he wasn't in the car didn't mean he was in danger…

She got out of the department sedan and headed to the front door, ready to draw her gun if she needed to. She assessed Snyder's place. It was a bungalow with a fenced-in yard, and the curtains in the front windows were drawn. No line of sight. No way of knowing what she was getting herself into.

But the front door was closed. If the officer had gone inside, he'd have radioed in that he was going to and he would have left the door open.

She drew in tight to a corner of the house, away from any windows. She didn't need Snyder looking out and seeing her there. Madison pulled out her phone to call it in, not that she really even knew what *it* was yet, but her gut was telling her it wasn't good. The line was direct to the communications and dispatch room.

She hung up feeling ill. Officer Palmer was the one assigned to watch Snyder, and he'd put in the call that he was going to check on her thirty minutes ago.

Backup was being dispatched, and she was told to wait for their arrival. But what if Palmer didn't have that sort of time left?

Snyder could possibly be armed, not only with the Glock from Barry's shooting but with Palmer's weapon at this point, assuming she was able to overcome him.

Madison edged her way around the side of the house, letting herself through a chain-link gate. She was hoping to find an open window somewhere that would give her a view inside the home, or even that would allow her to overhear something. But so far, nothing.

She wrapped around the back side of the house. There was a small patio area and a patio door. Staying close to house, she quickly took a peek.

The good news was that the view through the patio

door was unobstructed.

The bad news was that there were two people inside.

She'd have to look again to get a real feel for the situation. *On the count of three...*

One...

Two...

Three...

She jutted her head around the corner. Palmer was tied to a kitchen chair. And then Madison was face-to-face with Snyder.

Son of a bitch!

The door slid open.

"It seems we have company," Snyder said calmly.

Madison had her gun drawn, but Snyder held one, too. A Glock. Was it the murder weapon? Or Palmer's fully loaded piece?

Snyder was smiling. "I was wondering how long it would take you. Now put your gun down."

Madison assessed the situation. Snyder's eyes were electric, wild as if she'd taken drugs. But besides that, she seemed composed. The gun was steady in her hand. Madison could try to kick it out of Snyder's hand or pull her own trigger, but she'd risk Snyder getting off a shot anyhow. And if Snyder missed, her bullet could travel and hit an innocent civilian.

"Don't even think about it," Snyder said. "I will kill you." The unruffled tone of her voice told Madison that Snyder would have no problem doing so.

Madison heard cars approaching the area and knew that backup was here.

"I'm not going to tell you again."

Madison lifted her free hand in surrender as she bent over to place her gun on the ground. She remained cognizant of Snyder and alert, ready to move if Snyder went to strike. Madison stood up without event.

"Now get in the house."

"No." Madison had a line of sight to Palmer now, and he was looking at her with wide eyes and shaking his head. His mouth was gagged, his wrists and ankles bound to the chair.

"No?" Snyder laughed. "I'm the one with the gun."

"You let him go. Take me, instead."

"This isn't a negotiation."

"You don't want him, anyway. You want me."

It was clear on Snyder's face that she relished the thought of having control over Madison.

"Maybe I want you both."

Madison observed how, as she kept Snyder talking, Snyder kept her hold steady on the gun.

"Why did you kill him?"

"Oh, wouldn't you like to know."

"Well, yes. I asked."

Snyder's smile faded. "You haven't figured it all out yet, have you?"

God, she should have gotten more information before running over here, but honestly, the last thing she'd expected was for the patrol officer watching Snyder to be held hostage.

"What do you want?" Madison asked.

"What do I—" Snyder splayed her free hand across her chest. "I got what I want."

"Then what is all this?" Madison gestured to Palmer.

More vehicles came up on the place. They were just out front. SWAT would have been called in. That meant a sniper. If she could keep Snyder outside talking for long enough...

Was she okay with that idea? Deciding life and death—even guided by the use-of-force model—wasn't a favored position for any cop to find herself in.

But this woman in front of her had been involved with killing Barry. Her *friend* Barry.

"Why did you kill him?"

"You know I didn't," Snyder said, playing innocent. "I was pumping gas myself."

"You set all of this up." Madison was pulling, trying to string together something that would have a semblance of truth to it—or at least hit close enough to get Snyder to open up. "You know who pulled the trigger."

Snyder didn't say anything, a flicker glazing over her eyes.

"But it wasn't Travis… Mike maybe?" Madison kept going. "Or was it Clark?"

"Shut up!" Snyder held the gun in Madison's face.

Something about Clark had struck close to home. Madison put up a hand of surrender, and Snyder lowered the gun.

"You're in love with Clark?" Madison guessed.

"I am not." Snyder jutted out her chin, her eyes filled with tears.

As Madison was thinking about what to say next, she thought through everything she knew about the case. There were so many pieces that still needed to be put together, though. Where was the BMW? Why all the orchestration? Was it just to lead them away from the true killer? How did Snyder connect to Cousins and Brown? Who had handed over the five thousand bucks? Then Madison thought about Russell Coleman.

"You lost someone you cared about recently, too, didn't you?" she asked, finally starting to truly put it together.

"Shut up! I'm warning you!" She jabbed the gun toward Madison again. "You killed him! You damn cops!"

"You were in love with Russell Coleman."

"Don't you dare say his name." Snyder had her gun to Madison's head now.

She could beg, she could tell Snyder that she didn't want to shoot her, but she wasn't ready to call the girl's bluff. She had to show her that she was on her side somehow.

"You hear all the commotion in front of your house? More police are here, and I guarantee you SWAT is here. They will set up a sniper, and they will—"

"Shut up!" Snyder was shouting through clenched teeth, spittle flying.

Madison kept her hands up. "They will shoot you if we stay outside."

Snyder looked quickly beyond Madison. She shoved Madison's shoulder. "Get in the house."

CHAPTER 46

HOW DID MADISON ALWAYS MANAGE to put herself right in the line of fire? Troy knew the answer before the question was even fully formed in his head. She had a talent for running off half-cocked.

He was in the SWAT command vehicle in the front of Erica Snyder's residence. Intel told them that the subject and Madison were at the back of the house. Jay was already getting in position to take a shot.

Several neighbors had reported that Snyder was armed and holding a gun on a woman—Madison.

The thought of that was nauseating. He hadn't even told her how much he loved her. He'd wussed out and let her leave the squad room without making their relationship right.

"Matthews, I have line of sight on the target. Knight is unarmed, and there's a gun on the ground. Confirm that Snyder is holding a gun on Knight. Take the shot?" Jay said over his comm.

Troy took a deep breath. Another death on his hands in less than twenty-four hours… But if anything happened to Madison, he'd never forgive himself. And what about Officer Palmer? Where was he? "Hold off for a—"

"Scratch that. Target has left line of sight."

"What happened?"

"Target and Detective Knight have entered the home."

What was she thinking? He slammed the desk in the command vehicle, his eyes on the phone mounted on the wall.

He picked it up and dialed Snyder's number. It rang repeatedly, and he put the receiver down. He repeated the process five times. The last two times he went straight to voice mail. She'd turned her phone off.

Madison—and likely Officer Palmer—were inside with a cop killer. He paced the vehicle, the other members of his team moving out of his way when he came near them.

"We need all the information we can get on Snyder, and we need it yesterday," Troy barked to his men.

"Her background was clean and she wasn't even a person of interest," David began but fell silent under Troy's stare.

"She was in foster care," Derek offered.

"All right." Troy pointed his finger at the man. "What else? How is she connected with Cousins and Brown? Coleman?" Troy's heart began to pound. Brown had the means—the vehicle, the gun, the bullets. Snyder had the phone that set up the purchase of those items. Cousins had the friendship with Coleman. But Troy was stalling on motive. What drew all these people together to kill Barry? The obvious wasn't there. None of their records showed a connection to him.

He dropped onto the bench next to the table.

"She was Sommer's girlfriend," Jay said, brainstorming with them through the comm. "Cousins's his friend and roommate."

"Keep going, Jay."

"And we know that Cousins and Coleman were friends... With Cousins being found at the Hellions' hideout, he was obviously getting in with them."

"I'd say already was," David added.

"I agree," Troy said.

"All right… So let's look at it from this standpoint," Jay went on. "What made Snyder take Palmer? Know what I mean? She could have gotten away with her involvement in Barry's murder, but she chose to get our attention. Why?"

"She's upset about something," David stated.

Troy looked at him. "That's it! She was personally invested in Coleman. They must've been involved romantically."

"She heard about his death and decided she was going to take action…again," Jay suggested.

"But we know she wasn't the shooter. She was getting gas at the time. And the driver was Coleman."

"So he claimed," Derek said. "Hey, I'm playing devil's advocate here."

"I don't understand why he'd claim something like that if he didn't do it. I think Jay's on to something, though. Coleman's death is the only thing that could've triggered this today. And I have a feeling someone else is involved who we're failing to see. There has to be. We're at least missing our shooter still."

Troy got up and tried Snyder's number again, and it went to voice mail. Again. He called Madison's phone and got through, but it wasn't Madison who answered.

"I'm Troy Matthews with Stiles PD, and I'm here to help you. What's your name?" Always make an introduction and obtain or confirm the contact's name.

"Erica."

"Erica," he began, using her name to establish a sense of camaraderie, "I need to know that everyone is safe."

"Everyone is safe."

"What can I do for you, Erica?" Come across empathic, eager to fulfill the needs of the hostage holder.

"I'm not letting anyone go."

"I never asked you—"

"Bring me the cop who killed Russ," Erica said, and the line went dead.

Troy dialed dispatch. "Clear Palmer's radio."

CHAPTER 47

THE INSIDE OF SNYDER'S HOUSE was laid out simply. The kitchen and dining room were at the back of the house, an arched doorway led to the front sitting room, and a hallway came off the kitchen that probably led to the bedrooms and a bathroom.

Palmer was staring at Madison as if he were trying to communicate something to her, but either he wasn't very good at subtle messages or she wasn't good at deciphering them. Snyder must have banged him up pretty good, too. Fresh bruises colored his forehead.

A phone had started ringing not long after Madison had stepped into the house with Snyder. It was coming from Snyder's pocket, and it wouldn't stop.

Madison knew it was Troy. He'd be outside, ready to negotiate for her and Palmer's release.

Snyder was ignoring it, and it went on ringing for a while.

"Let him go." Madison nodded toward Palmer. "Take me in his place."

"And why would I do that?"

"Because you have SWAT already establishing a perimeter around your place. I guarantee you that you would have been shot in the head if we stayed outside. You trusted me then. So trust me now."

"I don't trust cops."

She sounded like Cousins. Hadn't he said pretty much the same thing?

Her phone rang again, and she pulled it from her pocket and ripped out the battery.

Not a good move…

"Listen, let the patrol officer go," Madison tried again. "You want me. I'm here now."

"I want the cop who killed Russ!" Snyder yelled.

Madison glanced at Palmer. Her heart was racing, and it felt like she was going to black out. "That was me."

"You're lying!"

"I'm not. I did it."

"Why?" Her grip on the gun was no longer steady. "Why do you have to take away everyone we love?"

Madison made a note of her choice of words. *We?* Had Barry been involved in taking someone away from her and another person?

"Tell me why," Snyder screamed. Tears were streaming down her face now.

The situation was getting out of control quickly.

"Do you want to tell me what happened?" Madison offered.

Defiance licked Snyder's eyes. "You know."

"I don't. Please…"

"You're lying." Snyder choked on a sob, and Madison glanced between her and Palmer. The patrolman looked like he was going to pass out. His adrenal glands sure weren't doing him any favors right now.

"I'm not. I promise you," Madison said softly.

If SWAT didn't establish communication soon, there would be a breach and that wouldn't end in Snyder's favor. As if the thought made it happen, her phone trilled on her hip.

"What is that? Oh." Snyder glared at Madison's phone. "Give it to me."

"If you don't talk to—"

"Give it to me," she shouted.

"Here." Madison handed it over. She thought Snyder was going to pull her battery, too, but she picked it up. She said nothing, just held the phone to her ear.

"...Erica... Everyone is safe." Snyder looked Madison in the eye. "...I'm not letting anyone go... Bring me the cop who killed Russ." She hung up but gripped the phone tightly in her hand.

"They're looking for a sign of good faith," Madison said, treading carefully.

"Yeah? Well, they can take this." Snyder spun, the gun aimed at Palmer's head.

"No!" Madison darted forward, knocking into Snyder's side. The gun discharged, the bullet going wide and missing Palmer.

The Glock slid across the floor, and Madison made a run for it at the same time Snyder did. Snyder reached it just before Madison and pointed it at her.

She wondered again if it was Brown's gun or if it was Palmer's loaded service weapon.

Shit, shit, shit.

Troy's voice came over Palmer's radio. "Erica... Are you there? You want the cop who killed Russ? We have him."

Madison stopped moving. So did Snyder, her head turning in the direction of Palmer and the radio.

Snyder went to the radio. She waved the gun from Madison to Palmer's epaulet. "Tell me how to use it."

"We'll need a sign of faith," Troy continued. "Send out

one hostage and I will send him in."

No! What is he doing?

"You promise me?" Snyder asked into the radio once Madison showed her how to work it.

"Yes. Send out the detective."

Madison met Palmer's gaze.

"No," Snyder said.

"Is she unharmed?"

Madison's heart melted at Troy's concern. She sensed his love, his desperation.

Snyder picked up on it, too. "She's special to you."

"I have the cop who killed—"

"Did you hear what I said?"

"Did *you* hear what *I* said? Send her out and—"

"You'll get the uniform."

There was a silence on Troy's end, as if he were considering her offer. "Send him out the front door."

"Five minutes."

No longer interested in the radio but seemingly more interested in meeting the cop who killed Russell Coleman, she turned to Madison. "Grab the scissors in the drawer and don't even think of trying anything."

She followed the direction of Snyder's pointing finger and pulled open a drawer. It was full of junk. "I don't see any scissors."

"They're in there."

Madison moved some things around and found a pair. She held them up.

"Bring them over here. Now."

Madison handed them over. Bullets overpowered scissors as far as a weapon went.

Snyder managed to cut the zip ties she'd used to cuff Palmer with one hand while continuing to hold the gun on him and Madison with the other. "Go. Out the front door."

Snyder didn't have to ask Palmer twice. He was practically running to the front door.

She looked at Madison. "Now sit."

CHAPTER 48

TROY WATCHED OFFICER PALMER OPEN the door and step out into the early-evening air. David, Derek, and Charlie lowered their weapons when it was clear only Palmer was coming out. They shuffled him into the command vehicle.

"Tell me everything there is to know," Troy said, directing Palmer to sit at the table.

"I, uh…"

"You've got to snap out of it. There's another detective in there, and what you tell me could save her life."

"The woman's been drinking," Palmer started. "No drugs, though, I don't think. She's armed. You heard—"

Troy nodded. He'd heard all right.

"She's got Madison's gun and mine."

"Did she have one before she took yours?" Troy asked, thinking about the one used in Barry's murder.

"I think so, but I'm not sure. She came out to the car and told me she swore someone had broken into the house. The second I stepped into the house, she hit me with something hard." Palmer gingerly touched his forehead.

Troy's phone rang, and the caller ID showed Madison's name.

"Hello," he answered casually, not sure if it would be

Madison or Snyder.

"You've got the uniform," Snyder said. "Where's the cop who killed my Russ?"

My Russ…

"Send them in or the detective gets one to the head."

He grabbed a tiny earpiece and was on the move out of the vehicle. He'd been such a shit to Madison the last few days, obsessed and wallowing in his own pain, letting it distort his thinking, his better judgment, but he wasn't going to let Madison lose her life. "He's coming right now."

Troy stormed out of the trailer, and Derek yanked back on his arm. He shrugged him off and headed up to Snyder's front door.

"I'm here," he said, banging on the wood.

"*You're* the cop who killed Russ?" Snyder said through the door.

"I am." *Or as good as…*

Stupid. Exposed. Working from emotion, not logic.

He pinched his eyes shut for a second.

"Come in. Slowly," Snyder told him.

"All right. Coming in now." He turned the handle on the door, wanting to look back but knowing better than to take his attention off what was before him. He was still armed, but Snyder hadn't requested he rid himself of his weapons.

"We're in the back."

Troy heard Madison's voice now. He saw the shadows casting through the doorway toward him.

He held his hands up when he stepped into the room. His attention was on Snyder, but he also quickly assessed Madison's state. Her ankles were zip-tied to a kitchen chair, and more zip ties were on the table in front of her.

"You're armed." Snyder seemed startled at the sight of him, her eyes tracing from his tactical boots up to his eyes. "Hand over your weapons."

"Just on the table?" There was already a Glock sitting there.

"Yeah." She watched him move and he did so cautiously, first placing the phone on the table, and then took off his AR-15, followed by his Glock, followed by his Taser.

Snyder looked to the table with each weapon he put down. He felt Madison's gaze on him. Snyder was distracted and vulnerable, but if Madison risked reaching for a weapon, she risked being shot by Snyder.

"I'm going to kill you, but first I'm going to take something precious away from you. Let you experience real pain."

"You already have."

Snyder didn't seem to expect that. "What do you mean?" She picked up a zip tie and held it between her hands, her hold on the gun compromised.

She was all of a hundred pounds, five foot four. He was over six feet and 200 pounds of lean muscle. Overpowering her wasn't going to be a problem, but he had to make sure he could disarm her safely, which meant he needed a window when she was distracted.

"I know what it's like to lose someone you love," Troy offered, hoping to create a ground for them to bond on, but instead he felt himself choking up, and he flicked a glance at Madison. He'd lost two people.

Snyder kept trying to get a solid hold on the zip tie so she could secure Madison's wrists without taking her gun off them. "Well, I'm so very sorry." Snyder rolled her eyes.

Troy had to act quickly. He made eye contact with Madison, and he hoped she was reading his mind right now. He pushed Madison's shoulders, upending the chair and causing it—and her—to land on its back. He was across the room and had the Glock knocked out of Snyder's hands before she could react.

"No!" Snyder screamed.

He pulled back on her arms and cuffed her wrists. "All secure," he said into his comm.

Madison was looking up at him from the floor, and he wasn't sure if she was going to hurt him or hug him when she got free.

CHAPTER 49

"YOU COULDN'T HAVE HANDLED THAT any other way?" Madison had asked a variation of the same question repeatedly since she'd been freed.

She and Troy were inside the command vehicle, and he'd asked his team if they could have a few minutes alone.

"I'm sorry, babe." He held on to her arms, his huge hands wrapping around her biceps with room to spare.

Did that say something about the size of his hands or her lack of muscle?

She shook away the absurd thought. But she felt so good when he held her like this. It was inviting yet kept her at a distance. And right now a little distance wasn't a bad idea. He had pushed her onto the floor, and her back was killing her. She'd need an ice pack. But he'd also saved her life.

"You're sorry? That's all you have to say for yourself?" she asked, standing strong.

"That's not all."

She raised an eyebrow, waiting for him to go on.

"I've saved your life a couple times now."

She rolled her eyes. "Really? That's what—"

His mouth was on hers before she could finish her thought, and she sank into his kiss, into his embrace.

Awhile later, when she was sufficiently heady, he pulled back.

"If you think you can just kiss me and everything will be ok—"

He took her mouth again and was the first to draw back, smiling at her.

"Oh no. You're not getting off that easy."

His gaze locked with hers, his green eyes doing what they did best—seeing through her.

"Fine," he consented. "I haven't been the nicest person lately."

"You've taken Barry's death hard," she said softly.

"There's something I should have told you before. I'm his children's godfather. I've known him all my life. We grew up together."

Madison nodded, not certain if she should let him know that Andrea had already told her. "Why didn't you tell me before now?"

He shrugged. "It never came up. And with what happened... I'm still trying to wrap my head around it. Barry was the best man at my wedding. I was his best man. We went to college together, then the academy." He expelled a deep breath.

To hear him finally opening up to her was touching her on a deep level.

"I know I've been moody, even distant. I apologize for that. It's just I'm..." He pressed his lips together. "I'm... hurting...so bad."

Madison flung her arms around him and squeezed, wishing to draw out all his pain and take it into her, for her to handle, for her to deal with, just so he didn't have to suffer any longer.

He put his hands on her arms. "I'm sorry I didn't tell

you earlier. I know you're hurting, too. I didn't want to pull you into all my drama, but it seems I did anyway."

"Sometimes you can be stubborn, too," she stated it matter-of-factly, wishing that he had brought all of this up sooner.

"Of the two of us, you should be able to identify the trait."

"Hey." She playfully put a hand to his chest, and he took it and kissed her fingertips.

He lifted his eyes to meet hers. "I love you, Maddy."

Of all the men who had ever said those words to her, she knew in her heart that Troy meant it from the depth of his being.

"Is that what you wanted to hear?"

"Better." She smiled at him.

"I'd like to revisit the whole taking-a-break thing, too."

"Oh yeah?" Play hard to get…yes, that was the best thing to do right now.

"In fact, I think we should take our relationship to the next level."

"The…the…next…?" She was stammering. She snapped her mouth shut. She couldn't breathe. Was it hot in here or… Was he talking about marriage? No, he couldn't be. It was one thing to think about it, fantasize about it, romanticize it, even, and quite another to…

She stepped away from him, but he took her hand and drew her to him.

"Move in with me?" he asked.

She stared at him, certain that she looked like she'd been caught doing something she shouldn't be doing. The words weren't coming.

"Did you hear me?"

"I…" She held up a finger, realization slamming into

her. Love, being together… She remembered what Snyder had asked her. *Why do you have to take away everyone we love?*

"Madison?"

"I heard you."

"Then?" He smiled at her, again, and he rarely smiled—on a good day.

"Snyder—"

"Madison?"

She stepped away from him and was at the door to leave. "I'm going back to the station. Follow me."

CHAPTER 50

MADISON MUST HAVE LOST HER MIND. What was she doing leaving Troy like that, his question hanging out in the open? But they still didn't have their murderer or their motive. Based on Snyder's deceit, she was definitely a player, but she wasn't their shooter.

Madison found Terry at his desk.

"Nice of you to see how I was doing," she said.

He didn't look up from a report he was reading.

"I'm okay, just so you know."

"I see that."

"Actually, you haven't looked at me, so you wouldn't know." And she wasn't completely fine. She had a bit of a hobble to her right now. Something about being over thirty and crashing to the floor, her back slamming into the spindles of a chair…

"I have Brown's phone records," he said, handing her a stack.

She'd had other plans when she'd rushed out on Troy, but she took the printout Terry handed her and headed for her desk.

"We have access to his social media, too," he told her once she was seated, and he looked up. His eyes were focused and sharp.

"I'm sorry," she said.

"You can't keep pulling stuff like that. One day you're not going to be okay. And that's fine, it's your life."

"Nice…"

"It's just…you pull me into it."

"Ah, Ter—"

"Don't even start with the *Aw-shucks* routine. I mean it, Maddy." His tone, his facial expression, all of it confirmed his seriousness.

She nodded. "I promise."

"Good. Now get to work."

She smirked and glanced down at the paperwork. The words Snyder had said weren't far from her mind. But there was one thing that made reports a little less tedious…

She opened a side drawer in her desk and pulled out a Hershey's bar. She flipped the pages on the cell phone history with one hand as she fished around for the chocolate. She found it and peeled the wrapper off without taking her eyes off the report. She had one bite of the heavenly indulgence when her eyes picked up a pattern.

"Terr—" she started, her mouth full of chocolate.

Terry looked around his monitor to see her. His eyes fell to the candy bar in her hand, and he smirked. But now wasn't the time for him to bug her about her guilty pleasure. And really, since when had chocolate become a guilty pleasure? Society's labeling system really needed to be reexamined.

She got up, dangling the report in one hand, holding her chocolate in the other. "He calls this number a lot." She nudged her head toward the sheet, as if that would narrow things down for him. "You see it? It repeats. Punch it into the database. Who's it registered to?"

He leaned back in his chair and looked up at her. "Yeah, sure, I wasn't doing anything." He took the report from her with an eye roll, his attitude all jest.

Terry keyed in the number, and a few seconds later, they were looking at the person whom Brown had plenty of contact with.

"Melody Ford?" Madison said and took another bite of her Hershey's bar.

"The manager from the gas station?"

"That's her." Madison's mind was spinning.

"We did a basic background, but we had no reason to suspect her," Terry said.

She swallowed the mouthful of chocolate. "She wasn't around when the shooting happened… She was supposed to be out of town." She paused, thinking. "What about Brown's social media? Is he friends with her online?"

"Isn't she a married woman?"

"I don't think that matters right now, Terry."

He changed screens and brought up a quick background. He pointed toward the screen. "Yep. Name's Donnie Ford. I remember now. He doesn't have a criminal history."

"Pull up Brown's social—"

"Okay, okay." Terry brought up Brown's Facebook and went to his friends list. Ford's face was looking back at them among the profile pictures.

Madison's insides were twisting. "So what's the connection between Barry, Brown, Snyder, Coleman, and Cousins?"

"You could possibly throw Sommer and Godfrey into the mix, too." Terry's chair groaned as he sat back and rubbed the back of his neck.

Madison's cell phone rang, and she grabbed it before

the second ring. She hung up after a minute and smiled at Terry. "They found the BMW."

"Where was it?"

"Outside the city, tucked away in a ditch under some foliage. Apparently a family stopped alongside the road to let their son go to the bathroom."

It was just a matter of time, and they'd have all their answers. She felt it. Forensics would tie things up in a neat little bow.

"We have to figure out motive…" she said, her mind back on the real reason she'd rushed back to the station.

"What haven't you told me yet?" Terry asked.

"When I was with Snyder—"

"Held hostage by her, you mean."

"Po-tayto, po-tahto." That's what she said now, but at the time, she hadn't been feeling so in control. "She said, and I quote, 'Why do you have to take away everyone we love?'"

"Huh…"

"That's what I thought. She said it in reference to Coleman, but it must go deeper than that. Who is *we*? And who is *everyone*?"

"What do you think she meant?"

"I think that she lost someone and blames Barry for it, and for her to use *we*, it wasn't just her loss. Snyder—and whoever else is involved with this vendetta—planned to kill him and they organized it like a hit."

Terry didn't say anything but slowly nodded.

"Have you ever wondered why it was so easy for Cousins to get his uncle's car, his gun, his bullets?" she asked. "I think he *wanted* him to have them."

"Do you think he set everything up?"

"I don't know yet, but I think we should have his

financial information rushed over."

"I'll get on that right now." Terry pulled his cell phone out.

As he put through the request, she thought over the investigation so far, how everyone had played their part in getting things to this point. Maybe collaborating wasn't such a bad thing. Typically—and no offense to Terry— she'd be fine to operate solo. But sometimes exceptions needed to be made, and sometimes people were stronger with others than by themselves.

When Terry finished with his call, she said, "Let's pull everyone's file, get everything organized in the squad room, and call a meeting."

"Wait, what?"

She smiled at him. "You heard me."

She'd made a promise to Joni, and there was strength in numbers.

CHAPTER 51

MADISON AND TERRY WERE PUTTING up the last couple of photographs on the whiteboard at the front of the room when detectives started coming into the room. Sovereign was the first through the door, followed by Stanford.

Sovereign pointed to the board. "Looks like quite the spread."

Madison stood back and looked at it, marveling at how fast she and Terry had pulled it together.

The board was organized into five columns. In the first one, there were a few pictures of Barry, including one of him from twenty years ago when he had been sworn in as an officer. Beneath that was a photograph of the bloody pavement at Rico's where he'd gone down.

Next over, the heading read, GAS STATION and had DMV photos of Rico Beck, Melody Ford, and Janet Hines. Next, INVOLVED BUT HOW? There were pictures of Erica Snyder and Russell Coleman. Next to his name, the words *self-declared driver*.

Next, three pictures were set out vertically in the order of Travis Sommer, Mike Godfrey, and Clark Cousins. The title was DEVIL'S REBELS.

Beneath that was the last photograph. It was of Phil Brown. Under his photo, she had written CONNECTION? followed by HIS BMW, GUN, AND AMMUNITION. From the photo itself, she had a line connecting to Cousins's photo with the words *uncle/nephew*. There was a second line going from Brown to Ford. EXACT CONNECTION?

More detectives and officers had gathered now, including Troy. He smiled at her subtly before taking a seat at the table. Obviously her playing hard to get and avoiding answering his question didn't bother him too much.

Andrea came in with Sergeant Winston, and he closed the door. His eyes skimmed over the board, and then he looked at Madison and nodded. She just hoped he didn't get used to this amount of communication and cooperation. But enough time had passed, and all of them owed it to Barry to get his killer behind bars once and for all.

She addressed her colleagues. "This is where our case has taken us thus far."

"You're missing the Hellions, Knight." This came from Copeland.

"We all know by now that *that* direction—unfortunately—never produced results," she said. "I left explored and eliminated avenues off the board."

"Yet you have people from the gas station up there?" Copeland asked, his tone incredulous.

"Yes. Let me catch everyone up, and we can put our heads together and give some closure to Barry and his family," she said.

A wave of silence fell over the room.

She let the quiet ride for a while, each officer in the room seemingly weighted down with grief and regret that Barry's killer was still at large.

"Detective Grant and I figure there must have been a hit orchestrated against Barry." She pointed to Ford's photo, then Snyder's, Cousins's, Coleman's, and finally Brown's. "We can make some connections but not all of them are linked. And that's not getting into motives yet… We know that Barry's history and past cases were looked into, and we also know that there was no connection between him and the people on the board. At least nothing that stands out, but we have to be missing something. Snyder mentioned that we took away 'everyone *we* loved.' She made it pretty clear that she and Coleman had a romantic relationship, but she was also referring to someone else."

"Look into her family history, see if she's lost anyone recently," Sovereign suggested.

"But no one in her family history was connected to Barry. So we need to brainstorm that more." A few of the detectives scribbled notes on pieces of paper. "On a different note, Brown's phone records show that he and Ford communicated on a regular basis."

"She's a married woman," Terry added.

"All right, so she and Brown were having an affair," Troy began. "How does that connect to Snyder, who picked up the prepaid phone that led to Cousins taking Brown's car?"

"So none of these people have any relatives who Barry arrested?" a detective asked.

Madison shook her head, summoning her patience. She'd already said that. "Not that we've been able to find yet."

"And the connection between Ford, Snyder, Cousins, Coleman, and Brown?"

"Like I said, we don't exactly know how they all connect yet. We need to figure that out." She paused for a beat. "Now who had the most reason to want Barry dead?

Who, besides Snyder, feels they lost everyone they loved because of him? That's the big question that could lead us in the right direction."

"Can we put Brown in communication with Snyder?" Winston asked.

Madison turned to study the board. They had communication confirmed between Cousins and Snyder, Snyder and Coleman, Cousins and Brown, and Brown and Ford. Cousins claimed his uncle let him have the car, and didn't deny that he also knew about him taking the gun and ammo. But Brown swore his nephew wasn't involved with any of this. Brown and Ford were seemingly having an affair. Brown had to be aware his car was, in the least, being used for something shady, or why remove the plates? If he was just simply helping out his nephew, why not just hand over his car? And that wasn't even touching on the gun and ammo. Brown had to be involved with orchestrating the entire setup, which meant there had to be evidence—or a connection, at least—between Brown and Snyder. Then her mind skipped to Ford. Was she connected to Snyder? She could have been the go-between for Brown.

"Knight?" Winston asked.

Madison then became aware of the detectives whispering in the room, talking to one another. She must have spaced out on them. She turned around, looking at Terry. "Ford and Snyder must be connected."

"Okay, but how?" Terry asked.

"Their backgrounds…" She went fishing through file folders on the table until she had both reports. She put them side by side.

The room went quiet as she scanned the reports. She shuffled through page after page looking for their previous addresses. But something struck her before she worked through them all.

"Wait a second… Snyder was brought into child services as a baby and put into the system. Her mother's name is listed as unknown." Madison flipped to Ford's background. "Ford's mother was Grace Cole…"

What was she missing? She looked up at the room, then back to the laptop on the table in front of her. She pulled up the name Grace Cole. It was the one they'd have searched against Barry, but it hadn't come up with any results. Pulling a report on the woman herself hadn't been necessary, but that's what she was doing now. The results filled up the screen, and she felt her stomach sink. "Grace Cole had changed her name from Grace Boyd."

"Knight?" Winston asked. "Keep talking."

She didn't acknowledge him but searched the system for the name Grace Boyd, and that popped a result. She sat in the nearest chair. "Ford's mother, Grace Boyd, does have an arrest record. Barry was the one who filed it."

"When was that?" Troy asked.

"She was convicted of prostitution two years ago. She served forty-five days but was given three years' probation. But she broke it within the last month. Barry was also the one to write her up and arrest her for doing so."

"I'm still missing Ford's motive, not to mention Snyder's," Sovereign said.

"Grace died in jail a couple weeks ago from a drug overdose. Ford could have held Barry accountable," Madison ground out.

"Okay, but Snyder…" Sovereign repeated.

"Hang on a second." Troy came around to Madison and gestured to the laptop. "May I?"

"Sure."

She rolled her chair to the side to let Troy in. She watched him search the obits, and seconds later, the one for Grace Boyd showed on-screen. She read it along with him. *"...left behind two daughters, Melody and Erica."*

Madison and Troy were looking at each other now.

Why do you have to take away everyone we love?

Everyone being Russell Coleman and Grace Boyd and *we* being Snyder and Ford. Grace Boyd must have been living a rough lifestyle when she'd abandoned Snyder, although she didn't have an arrest history beyond the last two years.

People in the room were talking among themselves. How did everyone else fit into this? Ford had grown up with her mother and had obviously found out about Snyder. Had Snyder pulled in her bad-boy boyfriend, Russell Coleman, and had Ford manipulated Brown? But both men fit the physicality of the driver...

"Ford could have known when Barry filled his cruiser's tank. And she was conveniently away," Winston said.

The black hoodie... Snyder... The small build of the shooter... "Shit!"

"Pardon?" Winston said.

"Ford was the shooter. She wasn't out of town, she'd just shot Barry!"

"Do you have anything to prove your theory?"

"Not yet. But I will."

"And the Devil's Rebels? Why did they even get pulled into all this?" Winston asked, shooting off in another direction.

"Knight?" Troy prompted her to share her thoughts, and whether he knew it or not, he was doing her a favor. The other ones she was having were toxic and self-deprecating.

"We might never know. Maybe the Devil's Rebels are nothing more than graffiti artists? The decal was just something Snyder brought up to throw us off." She hated to even consider that possibility.

"I'm not buying that. She could have just thought it was a good opportunity to bolster the Devil's Rebels' reputation on the street as a gang that should be respected," Terry suggested.

It didn't matter how many times Madison heard the word *respect* connected to the death of a police officer. It never settled with her. It was a twisted and sick perversion to think the two could even be affiliated. Something told her there was more to it, though.

Madison shook her head. "That doesn't make sense. Coleman was her boyfriend and he was in with the Hellions. Why would she want to bolster the reputation of the Devil's Rebels?"

"Maybe the Hellions and the Devil's Rebels have a symbiotic relationship? We did find Cousins there," Troy said.

Madison looked at him and nodded.

"And is Brown connected with the Devil's Rebels beyond his nephew?" Terry asked.

"Besides the decal? It could have been stuck on after they took the car," Madison said.

"So you don't think Brown was personally involved now?" Terry asked.

"Oh, I never said that. It's too coincidental that Ford and Brown were in a relationship, and Brown's belongings were used in the shooting," she said.

She grabbed a whiteboard marker and started to write on the board:

Means = Car, gun, ammo provided by Brown

Motive = Ford and Snyder's mother died in jail, put away by Weir

Opportunity = Ford worked at the gas station where Weir regularly filled up

She was still holding the marker in her hand when she turned to face her colleagues. "I've always hated math, but there is a common denominator here, like I said."

"Ford," Terry ground out, obviously filling in the blank on her equation.

"I strongly believe so."

"Her name isn't noted in means," Sovereign said. "For a common denominator, there has to be something in common for all of them."

"She had a direct connection to the person with the means." She scribbled, *who was in a relationship with Ford*, at the end of the means section. "Ford was an adult when her mother went to jail, and Snyder never even knew her mother and now she never would. They both could have seen her death as a motive to take revenge."

"All right, but answer me this: how did Ford and Snyder find out about each other?" Sovereign asked.

His question stumped her, and she was saved by a knock on the door. Seeing as Winston was standing next to it, he answered. It was Cynthia.

"I have some findings that you'll want to know about," Cynthia said, brushing past the sergeant to Madison. "To start with, a quick look at Brown's bank account shows that five thousand dollars was taken out last Thursday."

"He did pay for the hit," Madison stated, looking at

her partner.

"Brown took out the money and gave it to Ford to give to Snyder," Terry theorized, "to give to Coleman, to give to Cousins by buying the supplies for the hit."

"Wow, this is getting complex," Winston exhaled.

"They were trying to cloud the investigation by complicating the trail," Lou said. "Just like everything else in this case."

"I also ran DNA pulled from Brown's BMW," Cynthia continued.

"That was lightning fast," Madison said.

"That's how I work." Cynthia gave Madison a small smile. "Prints on the steering wheel place Brown and Cousins in the driver's seat. I revisited the city's footage and confirmed that the driver wasn't wearing gloves, so if it had been Coleman, I'd know."

"He must have known about it from Snyder, took the credit to build himself up to the Hellions," Sovereign suggested.

"And got himself killed for the trouble," Troy stated sourly.

"I also ran prints on the three guns that were collected from Snyder's place. Yours—" Cynthia pointed to Madison "—Officer Palmer's, and the one registered to Brown. Brown's was definitely the weapon used to kill Officer Weir. I pulled four sets of prints from the gun— Brown's, Cousins's, Snyder's, and an unknown."

"It's Brown's gun," Madison began. "Cousins could have handed the gun off to Ford...the unknown..." But that didn't explain why Snyder had the gun in her possession. Maybe Ford gave it to her to hide. "And?" Madison sensed there was more Cynthia had to share.

"Not so fast. Casings were found in the car. These, the

eleven bullets from the magazine, and the one still in the chamber had prints and all came back as matches for Brown."

"Brown—not Cousins—loaded the gun for Ford."

"Or for his nephew?" Madison hated complications. "Then Cousins handed the gun over to Ford?"

"So, we still have some question marks. I believe she'll match the missing fingerprints though," Terry concluded.

"I'll get Ford picked up immediately." Winston went to storm out of the room.

Troy caught him before he reached the doorway. "I'd like to be the one to do that, Sarge."

"Me too," Jay Porter said from beside him.

"And me." Marc Copeland took position next to Porter, and then the rest of Troy's team was all there. Even Nick, who would have to stay behind.

"Very well, then. Go."

Troy glanced at her before leading his men from the room. She wanted to follow him and be involved with bringing Ford in, but this was something she knew Troy had to do. She'd have her face time with Ford once they brought her back to the station.

Madison turned to her partner. "We need to confirm who was the driver—the uncle or nephew," Madison said. "We also need to find out what Brown's motive was. We'll need to talk to him again."

"Brown?" Terry asked.

Madison shook her head. "No, the weaker of the two—Cousins."

CHAPTER 52

TROY STOOD AT MELODY FORD'S FRONT DOOR, his heartbeat calm, his stomach clenched. Inside this house was the woman responsible for pulling the trigger that killed his friend, his brother. He knew that her prints would be a match to those found on the murder weapon, and the hunger for retribution washed over him in repetitive waves.

Three of his men were in position beside him, and he'd sent a secondary team to the back door just in case she decided to make a run for it. Melody's husband had already been picked up from where he worked and was being held by a patrol officer in front of the home should they need any incentive for Ford to surrender.

He glanced over at the three men next to him and missed the fact that Nick couldn't be here for this. "Ready?"

They all nodded.

Troy banged on the door. "Stiles PD! Open up!"

There was movement inside, but it wasn't coming toward them.

He banged again and shouted once more.

Everything inside fell silent. That was never good.

"Go in now," Troy commanded the secondary team over the comms.

The back door was rammed through and screams came from inside.

Troy breached the home with the rest of the primary entry team and came face-to-face with Melody, who was standing between them and their secondary.

She was gripping a butcher knife tightly in her hand and swinging it erratically through the air. Her dark hair was tangled and greasy. "Get back or I'll—" She held the knife toward her own throat.

Troy lowered his rifle and held up his free hand to her. "Melody, I'm Troy Matthews."

"I don't care who you are!" Her eyes were wide and wild, but he didn't think she was high or drunk. "You're killers!"

"We're here to help you." The words came out smooth and calm, like a pro, but inside he was quivering with rage.

"You take away everyone we love," she cried out, the blade closer to her skin now.

Troy assessed the situation. She was within ten feet of his men, the distance easy enough to close, to lunge toward them and make a swipe with her blade. Using a Taser could cause an uncontrolled reaction, though, and she could end up killing any of them or herself. And shooting her would leave them with more questions and another life on his conscience. Neither scenario was one Troy was willing to accept. He wanted her to be punished for what she had done, for what she had taken from the world.

"We want to help," Troy repeated, his tone as convincing as he could make it.

"You took her. You took him. Why should I live?"

He assumed *her* was her mother and *him* was Coleman.

The intensity in her eyes had calmed, but there was an eerie serenity to her, and Troy wondered if the threat she'd made to kill herself was more a promise. His mind went to his backup plan. "Your husband. He's why you should live."

She lowered the knife and swiped a hand under her nose. "Donnie? Did you—"

"He's here for you."

"I don't believe you."

Troy spoke through the comms to the officer outside. "Have him come in the front door."

Donnie entered, his gaze going over the room but settling on his wife. "Mel? What's going on?"

"Donnie, leave. I don't want you to see this."

"I'm not going anywhere." The man remained collected considering his wife was holding a knife on herself and standing off against SWAT officers.

"Please." Melody sobbed, cupping her face with her free hand.

"It's not worth it, honey. It's over."

Troy and his team stood back, letting Donnie take over for a while. He knew what his wife was suspected of doing, and they'd prepped him on what they might walk in on—not that they'd known about the knife in advance—but it was unlikely she'd being going down without a fight.

"Please, baby, put down the knife." Donnie glanced at Troy, then back at Melody.

"I hurt." Melody's voice had softened, and she looked at her husband.

"I know, but we'll work through this together." Donnie went to take a step forward, but Troy held up an arm to stop him from getting any closer to her. "You have to put the knife down."

Melody's gaze went to Troy, but he didn't say anything.

"Fine." She lowered to place the knife on the floor, and the second it was free of her hands, Jay retrieved it and Marc was hauling her up and snapping on cuffs.

As Marc led her through the house and out the front door to the waiting cruiser and officer, Troy took his first deep breath in days, but it was hampered under the deadening gaze of Donnie Ford. The man didn't say anything with words, but Troy swore he picked up on communication nonetheless: *It's not worth it, honey. It's over.*

Was it just reassurance for his wife, or had he known what she'd done before they had come for him? Donnie was maybe six foot and probably about 160 pounds—the same height as the shooter. Had he actually been the one to pull the trigger? But then, what would have been his motivation? His wife was cheating on him, and forensics had confirmed her lover, Brown, as the driver. Why would he be in cahoots with his wife's lover? And why was Melody acting guilty?

"We'd like you to come down to the station as we get everything sorted out with your wife." Troy was careful to keep any threat out of his tone, keeping it rather casual.

"Of course." Donnie held eye contact a little longer before leading the way out of the house.

Troy looked at his men, trying to gauge their reactions. Clayton, Derek, and Charlie nodded as if they were picking up Troy's suspicions. No matter how ungrounded they may have seemed...

CHAPTER 53

MADISON ENTERED THE INTERROGATION ROOM armed with a bottle of water and a plastic cup in her hands and a granola bar in her back pants pocket. She'd confirmed with the officers in Cells that Cousins hadn't had food or water for hours, and she was going to work that to her advantage. Going with her gut, she was pretty sure that Cousins was used to being taken care of, pampered. She'd fill that role, attempt to become an ally.

Cousins was already seated at the table and Terry went past him to the back wall when she arrived. Madison didn't miss the way Cousins's eyes went to the water.

"Are you thirsty?" she asked.

"Is my lawyer here?" He spoke with his gaze still on the bottle.

She lowered herself and looked him in the eye. "You sure you don't want anything to drink?"

Cousins crossed his arms.

"Well, I'm thirsty. How about I just pour some for you?" Madison hitched a shoulder. "If you don't drink it, fine, but I'll have some from the bottle."

"Whatever."

Madison made a show of slowly pouring the water into the cup. Then she went at the water in the bottle as though she was parched and let out a satisfying *ahhh* afterward before swiping a hand across her mouth. "Nothing like water. Oh!" She acted as if she'd forgotten temporarily about his cup and put it across the table in front of him.

Cousins looked down at it, then at her, and went for the cup. He gulped it down and set the empty cup on the table.

"We're here as a courtesy." Madison nodded her head toward Terry. "Your uncle is more than just an uncle. He's a good friend to you, isn't he?" She made her voice empathic, as if something tragic had happened to him.

Cousins was peering into her eyes, trying to read them. "Yeah."

"Unfortunately, we've found out something and he's in big trouble."

The kid glared at her. "Oh, don't pretend you care about him."

He'd seen through her act, but Madison also picked up on the fact that his uncle being in big trouble didn't seem to faze him.

"Did you want more water?" she asked.

"No," he snapped. "What do you want from me?"

"We need to know your side of things. See, evidence is pointing toward your uncle being a cop killer. You do remember our conversation about what happens to cop killers in prison, right?" Madison remained calm but poignant.

Cousins angled his head. "What do you think you have on him?"

"We have proof that your uncle took out five thousand dollars cash from his personal bank account… The same amount given you for the car, gun, and bullets."

"You think he bought his own stuff? That's crazy. And why would he want to kill a cop?"

Did he not know, or was he pretending not to know? Either way, the thought sank in her gut.

"The DA's looking at it as him paying for a hit on the cop. It's not looking good." Madison was doing her best to remain detached and not give the impression that his last statement had thrown her off. "You admitted to picking up the money, to buying things like video games and a television with it. You made that money disappear."

"That doesn't look good for you, either," Terry added.

Cousins looked back at him.

"I'm thinking your uncle told you to spend it up," Madison said. "Am I right? He didn't want you holding on to it. He's taken care of you for a long time." She was rolling with it, following her intuition. The relationship between this uncle and nephew seemed closer than blood. They were bonded for some other reason. Then it hit her. The decal on the BMW... They thought the driver or shooter had placed it there, but what if—

Madison looked at Terry. "Detective, will you join me in the hall?"

He looked at her quizzically and then followed her into the hall.

"We've been blind," Madison said. "We were so fixed on the decal being placed on the BMW by the perpetrators *after* they picked up the vehicle, but what if it's not that at all? What if Brown is actually the leader of the Devil's Rebels? His car, his decal. It was already all there."

They stared at each other in silence for a few seconds.

"He could be," Terry consented. "Travis Sommer could be Brown's second-in-command. But why would he have Snyder send the text message to Cousins?"

"Cousins would have found it odd if Sommer got the message."

Terry shook his head. "Not following."

"Well, obviously Cousins was the one with access to the car, et cetera."

"Okayyyyy." Terry dragged out the word. "We know Cousins is hardly an innocent in all this. His fingerprints are on the gun."

"It could have simply been from handing it over."

Terry angled his head to the left. "Really?"

"Trust me, I'm not trying to give him an out by any means."

"All right. So what are you thinking?"

She thought back to the interrogation room, how it seemed that Cousins was likely used to being taken care of, how even Pope told them she'd get in fights with Brown over Cousins's innocence, how Brown had said his nephew was as innocent as he was, how he hated Russell Coleman. They couldn't tie Coleman to the BMW at all, though, so what made Coleman boast about driving the car?

"Coleman just took it upon himself," she said aloud as if Terry could hear her thoughts. "I was just wondering what made Coleman boast about driving the car."

"You think he lied?"

She nodded. "I believe so. It was to build up his own reputation with the Hellions. Cousins probably figured out that his uncle's car, gun, and ammo were used in the shooting and talked to his friend Coleman."

"Well, Cousins was picked up in the Hellions' hideout, so we know the two were in communication. He could have just been visiting."

"Or maybe he was getting in with them?" She wasn't even sure whether it mattered.

"Going back to Brown, we need to figure out his

motive."

"And you heard Cousins? 'Why would he want to kill a cop?' I honestly don't think Cousins was in on this from the start." She walked a few steps, hoping something would shake loose.

Terry paced next to her. "He could be lying."

She shook her head. "I believe him."

He stopped moving and stared at her blankly. "Then how do you expect to find out Brown's motivation?"

She came to a standstill. "I have no doubt that the more recent situation with Ford and Snyder triggered something in Phil Brown, but I don't think it was just a matter of him setting things up for a girlfriend. I think it involved losing someone he loved. 'Why do you have to take away everyone we love?' She said *We*, Terry. This was larger than Ford and Snyder's mother. Brown might not have had a history with Barry, but he's the one who paid for it. Ford and Snyder's loss and hatred toward Barry could have reopened a buried hurt for Brown."

"All right, so he set everything up, to…we'll say, get even…for Grace *and* for whoever he lost? He lost his parents. Could that be it?"

"They died in a car accident. I think there's another loss we're not yet aware of." Her mind was whirling, but the thoughts were hard to hold on to.

"And how do you intend to find out? I really don't think he's going to tell you."

"Melody Ford."

CHAPTER 54

MELODY FORD COULDN'T HAVE BEEN sitting in the interrogation room for even ten minutes before Madison stormed in with Terry. The woman who had seemed so genuinely concerned when they'd first met her glared at them as they took their positions. But there was something different in her eyes. She appeared broken now. No longer was there the posture of a confident woman, but rather the shell of one.

Troy had told them she'd threatened to commit suicide and that he'd believed her. But that's what guilt could do—snake through your system and devour you from the inside. Madison found it hard to empathize as she sat across from Ford.

Madison opened the folder on the table in front of her. "You know why you're here."

"I do."

"Did you kill this officer?" Madison pushed photographs of Barry in uniform across the table.

Ford didn't even look at them but kept her focus on Madison. "You take away everyone we love."

And there was that statement again. Troy had mentioned Ford saying it at the house, as well.

"Who is *everyone*?" Madison asked, choosing to delicately dance around this interview.

Ford blinked slowly. "My mother."

"Your mother wasn't well."

"You lie," Ford spat.

"She had a hard life and—"

"And it ended because of you! Because of cops who locked her up. She wasn't strong enough for jail!" Tears fell down Ford's cheeks.

Madison let her cry and, in that time, reflected on the woman across from her, how she'd been the one to take Barry down, how she'd wielded the power of God, and how she was going to pay severely for doing so. It would take all Madison's strength to demonstrate caring at all about Ford's loss, but that's what it would likely take to keep Ford talking.

"I can only imagine that it must have hurt…losing her," Madison said. She'd demonstrate empathy, but there was no way she'd offer an apology, even an insincere one.

Ford swiped away her tears. "I was robbed of my mother." Her voice had softened, seeming to become reflective. "I didn't even know that I had a sister until…"

Madison straightened up, realizing their reunion was one thing they had yet to figure out. "Until when?" she prompted, her interest genuine.

"I was going through our mother's things when she first went to jail, and I found a photograph of a baby." Ford paused, tracing a fingertip over her lips. She dropped her hand. "I knew it wasn't me so I asked her who it was."

"That's how you found out about Erica."

Ford nodded. "I was so excited to have a sister after being the only child for most of my life. Mom wasn't happy, though. She didn't like having that part of her life brought up again. She'd given up Erica because she couldn't handle a baby back then." Ford's mouth curved in a subtle smile. "But Mom came around to the idea of meeting her grown daughter. And they hit it off." Ford's eyes turned dark now. "But when she broke parole and was carted back to jail, she couldn't take it. She'd only been reunited with her long-lost daughter for less than two years. It broke her heart. No one cared about Mom excerpt for me and Erica, and I say that she died of a broken heart in prison. All because some zealous cop put her back behind bars." Ford hissed the last statement.

Madison tamped down her anger. None of this was Barry's fault. He was doing his job. The only one to blame for the mother's death was the mother herself. She took a few deep breaths. "You mentioned cops take away everyone *we* love. Who is *everyone* and who is *we*?" Madison asked, hoping to move things forward and maybe even uncover Brown's motivation for setting up the hit.

"My sister, for one. She lost her mother, and now her boyfriend."

"Who else?" Madison pressed.

"Phil. I'm sure you know that he and I were having an affair," she stated unapologetically.

"Who did Phil lose?"

"He lost his parents to a car accident… But it's your fault he didn't know his sister."

His sister… Terry had mentioned Phil had one. What was her name again? *Ah.* "Kara Brown?"

"No." Ford curled her lips. "His other sister. It turns out his mom had a past life that she had withheld from her family. It wasn't until she died and included the sister in the will that he found out about her."

Madison sat up straighter and leaned forward. "What's his sister's name?"

"Emma Sutton. But you're not going to find her in any file attached to Phil. Emma was the result of a rape when Phil's mom was a teenager, but she didn't give her away. Police took Emma from Phil's mom. Said it was because she was on the streets and in no position to take care of a child."

"How did Phil react when he found out about his sister?"

"I didn't know him then, but I know he felt like he'd missed out on having a relationship with his sister. Really, by the time he found out about Emma, it was too late."

"Too late?" Madison tossed a quick glance at Terry, who'd remained silent for this interrogation—no jingling change, not a word spoken.

"The system had eaten her up," Ford went on, "and years of sexual abuse had landed her in a mental ward of a psychiatric hospital. Her mind's so gone, she might as well be dead."

Madison nodded.

"See? Police killed her, too. At least that's how Phil came to see it."

Instead of viewing the police as saving his mother's life and making his possible, Brown was fixated on the fact that his sister was taken away and her life destroyed. He failed to see the truth that the blame for any abuse rested on the shoulders of the foster parents.

Tears fell from her eyes. "I guess when Mom died, it brought everything up for him again."

"So you both decided to avenge your loved ones by killing Officer Weir?" That had to be one of the toughest questions she'd ever had to ask.

Ford met Madison's eyes. "They saw how much pain I was in and they wanted to make it right."

Make it right? By killing an innocent man?

Madison was screaming inside but managed to calm herself down as she focused on Ford's use of the word *they*. Was it Brown and Snyder she was referring to or someone else, as well? Her thoughts shifted to Ford's husband, Donnie. He had no criminal record, but for some reason, Madison had this niggling in her gut. Maybe it was because Troy had voiced his suspicions about the man's innocence, letting her know he'd told Ford that it wasn't worth killing herself and that Donnie had managed to quickly deescalate the situation and was the right build for the shooter.

There was a knock on the door, and Madison pried her eyes from Ford and got up to answer it.

Cynthia stood on the other side of the door, extending a folder to Madison. "The results on the unknown fingerprints."

Madison sensed the findings without needing to look. The answer was in her friend's intense eye contact as she handed them over.

Terry stepped up behind her, both of them standing in the doorway now. Madison glimpsed over her shoulder at Terry briefly, and then, taking a deep breath, she opened the folder. And there were the results, right in front of them in undeniable black-and-white.

"Thank you, Cyn," Madison said as she and Terry backed up into the room.

"I did it. I shot the cop." Ford's eyes were going rapidly from Madison to Terry, Terry to Madison, Madison to Terry.

"No, you didn't." Madison kept her tone gentle yet firm.

Ford began crying. "He only did it because he loves

me."

"He killed a police officer, Melody."

"Donnie found out about Phil, about the affair, but he didn't care. He just wanted me to be happy again. He said he'd take care of things. He must have found out that Phil…" She paused as if trying to ascertain their knowledge of his character. "That Phil is the kind of guy who can make things happen."

"What kind of things?"

"You know…shady things, not necessarily legal things."

"All this was Donnie's idea, then, or Phil's?" Madison asked, gauging Ford.

"Donnie just wanted me to come back to him, to make things better. I might have said something about killing the cop who locked up my mom, but I would never have gone through with it." She added softly, "But he did. For me. That's how much he loved me."

"He committed murder, and your sister conspired and helped facilitate it." Madison was beyond dancing around the matter and glanced at Terry to indicate it was time to leave.

They reached the door when Ford yelled out, "Don't take them away from me!"

Those words echoed in Madison's head as she left the room, and they'd probably haunt her for a long time to come. It was that mentality that had started all this: that the police were somehow responsible for taking people away from their loved ones. Ford would be facing time in prison for being an accessory to murder after the fact, but she just hoped that Ford wouldn't find the gumption to act out violently toward police officers when she got out.

Chapter 55

THE NEXT DAY, Madison got out of her Mazda and walked around to the passenger side where Troy was exiting. They were at the curb in front of the Weir house.

She put her hands on his shoulders and looked him in the eye. "Are you okay?"

He leaned forward pressing his forehead to hers. "I'm going to be... What about you?"

"I'll be fine," she responded instinctively and realized quickly that she'd meant what she said. She had made good on her promise to Joni and got justice for Barry.

Brown would be facing life in prison, as would Snyder. As for the rest of them—Sommer, Godfrey, and Cousins—they were all facing accessory to murder charges, as Madison and the Stiles PD were able to provide enough evidence that the three roommates were well aware of what had been taking place. And in Cousins's case, he had accepted money in exchange for providing the means to carry out the murder, but he ended up making a deal that gave up his uncle as the driver. He only realized how everything was used after the fact. Cousins also confirmed that the Devil's Rebels was Brown's gang and that the murder, in addition to getting even for the perceived slight by law enforcement, had a side benefit of building up the street cred for the

Devil's Rebels.

Barry's funeral was scheduled for Wednesday, the following day, and at least he would be going in the ground with his killer and those who conspired against him going to prison.

Troy pulled out a small box with a bow from a coat pocket. "Have you given any more thought to—"

Her eyes went to the box. What was he asking her? Was that a ring box?

I thought he just wanted to live together.

She met Troy's eyes and licked her lips. Her heart was racing, and her palms were sweaty. Had the original question changed?

"What's that?" She pointed to the box.

He gave her a subtle smile. "Answer my question and find out."

"And the question is—"

"Really, Maddy? You're killing me here. Will you move in with me?"

Relief coursed through her. She could resume breathing now. But was she truly ready to take this step? The last time a man had asked her to live with him, the relationship had come to an end before she had acted on the invitation. Going further back in her dating history to Sovereign, the situation had turned out even worse.

"Maddy?"

"Yes." She grinned.

His gaze latched onto hers. "You'll mo—"

"Yes!" she interrupted.

Holy crap! Their relationship was officially on to the next level...

Her mother would be so happy to see at least some commitment from her daughter. She might even be able to overlook the fact that he was a cop for a while. But all those thoughts disappeared when Troy kissed her.

When he pulled back, he handed her the box. She eagerly took it from him and tore the ribbon off. Placed on the silk inside was a key. She looked up at him.

"You didn't think it was going to be a ring, did you?" His voice was teasing, as if that would be the last thing she'd ever think about, but the way his facial expression became serious, he'd read her mind. He must have seen that the thought of being engaged didn't seem quite as scary now as it used to seem.

"No. Heavens, no." She smiled at him, tucked the box into her pocket, and looped her arm through his. She nudged him toward the front door.

Footsteps approached from inside, and the door opened.

Joni's eyes were full of tears. "Madison? Is it true? I just heard…"

"We caught them, Joni," Madison said softly.

"Oh thank God." Joni stepped back inside the house, motioning for Madison and Troy to enter. She wrapped her arms around Madison, holding her briefly but tightly. Then Joni went to Troy. She put her hand to his cheek, and he pulled her in for a hug.

Troy didn't cry, not a single tear, but Madison sensed his pain and regret for not coming by to see Joni sooner.

Joni kissed Troy's cheek before leaving his arms.

Then Allison came into the room and ran toward him, her arms wide. "Uncle Troy?"

Troy looked at Madison as the girl's arms wrapped around his waist, and even now he didn't let tears fall, but his eyes were wet.

Joni's other daughters must have heard Allison and

came running toward the door. They piled on behind their older sister in hugging Troy. After they hugged him, Allison and the girls hugged Madison.

Up until then, she'd been doing a good job keeping herself together. But with the love of Barry's family so strong amid facing such loss, she was overcome with emotion. Tears fell down her cheeks, and she found that she wasn't in a hurry to wipe them. She simply let them fall.

Joni was dabbing a tissue to her nose. "Come in. Tell me everything." She pointed toward the living room. "Would either of you like a drink? Something to eat?" She looked directly at Madison and mouthed, *A cigarette?*

Troy turned to Madison. "What?"

Madison shrugged, smiled, and waved him off.

"Girls, why don't you go play?" Joni said. "We're going to talk for a while. Allison, would you…?"

"Okay." Allison gave Troy one more hug and left, her younger siblings in tow.

Madison sat where she had days ago when this nightmare first began. It was hard to grasp time, as it had a way of feeling as though infinity lived in a second. What was short felt long, and what was long felt short.

Troy took a seat beside her and put his arm around her, and Madison leaned against him.

Joni swallowed hard from her place in the reclining chair. "Tell me everything. Who did this to my husband and why?"

Madison nodded and went on to tell her everything about the case.

"So this lady Erica?" she asked unsure.

"Yes."

"She and the lady who managed the gas station were

half sisters? And they killed my Barry…" She paused and dabbed her nose again. Tears fell down her cheeks. "He was the one who arrested their mother, and she killed herself in jail because of Barry."

Madison nodded. "Their minds are messed up, Joni."

"Given her lifestyle…and that she was a prostitute, she probably overdosed because she was getting high for pleasure," Joni said, hot anger lacing her words.

"We don't know that for sure," Madison said gently. "Her daughters looked at it—"

Joni held up her hand. "If their mother was in jail, she deserved to be. Barry was a great cop."

"No one doubts that, Joni," Troy said.

Joni nodded. "So they will all be charged?"

Madison told her how everything had played out from that standpoint.

"This Donnie guy is the one who actually shot Barry?" Joni looked confused, and Madison had to admit there were a lot of intricate parts to this case.

"Yes." There would be no advantage to revealing his motive.

"What made that other man set everything up? The car, gun… What did my Barry ever do to him?"

"Sadly, nothing. But he was having an affair with the gas station manager, and when everything came out about her mother, the past came back to haunt him." Madison explained about Brown's sister Emma.

Joni was crying now and glanced at Troy.

"You're not alone. You know that, right?" Troy asked. "And I'm so sorry I didn't get here sooner. I wanted to be strong for you, but I wasn't feeling so—"

Joni got up and walked over to hug him. "Thank you for being here now and for your part in solving all this."

"Of course." His voice was gravelly.

Joni walked back to her chair and sat down. "They had quite a complicated plan going."

"They figured if they threw out a lot of variables we'd never get to the truth," Madison said.

"Thank God you did. And thanks to your partner, too, Maddy. All of the Stiles PD, really. I owe all of you."

A few tears fell down Madison's cheeks at Joni's sincere gratitude, and Troy rubbed her arm. She put her life on the line every day without thought to consequence and without concern for her own safety. It was the last thing on her mind each morning when she grabbed her badge and headed out the door. She just wanted to serve, to make a difference, to change lives, to bring about justice for murder victims. And in this moment, she felt like she had accomplished just that. If only for right now, she would let the appreciation for what she did sink in, and not discount all that she sacrificed and put on the line. Really, she wouldn't want to live her life any other way.

Chapter 56

Madison had attended line-of-duty funeral services in the past. *Intense* was one way of describing them. A punch to the gut was another. And with each service came the all-too-true realization that it could have easily been her in the casket instead of her fallen brother or sister.

The day of the funeral was sunny, and colored leaves blew, carried on a cool breeze. The service started with a convoy procession through the downtown core, and the community came out to show their support for the officer who had fallen in the line of duty, who had made the ultimate sacrifice.

Madison and Terry were part of the motorcade, of course, as were most ranked officers in the Stiles PD. All officers were in dress uniforms whether they helped manage the crowds or took part in the procession.

Civilians waved American flags from the sidewalk, and the crowd, despite its size, was quiet—eerily so. It was a dark reminder that what had transpired was final. It had taken someone they loved away from them.

Joni, her girls, her parents, and her in-laws were in a black limo directly behind the hearse.

They were all headed to the cemetery where they would say their final good-byes.

Madison wanted to do nothing more than cry as she

drove the department sedan, overwhelmed with emotion by the way the community had come together to honor the brotherhood of blue. Somehow, she managed to suppress the tears, to keep her eyes on the road and her mind on Barry, smiling slightly as she conjured up good memories.

Terry sat next to her, as silent as she, likely lost to his own thoughts, his own memories, his own emotions.

The procession wormed into the lane toward the cemetery. It wouldn't be long before they'd be lowering Barry into his final resting place.

There was a fire truck on each side of the cemetery entrance, the back ends of the rigs to the drive, their ladders extended in the air. Attached to the ladders was a banner that read, IN MEMORY OF OFFICER BARRY WEIR, A FALLEN HERO.

MADISON SCANNED THE GATHERED CROWD. She saw her fellow officers with the Stiles PD, those from surrounding communities, and those with the Stiles FD. While those here mourned the loss of their brother, officers from surrounding communities were asked to step in while they remembered Weir.

She spotted Price, one of the paramedics who had arrived at Rico's to help Janet Hines. Chelsea and her husband were also in attendance, and so was Terry's wife, Annabelle.

Joni and her daughters were in the front row with her parents and in-laws.

The casket was braced above the ground, where it would soon be lowered to its final resting place. An American flag was laid over the lid. Bouquets and floral arrangements lined the perimeter of the box on the ground. Their perfumed fragrance was strong, bringing with it the sour alert as to their purpose here: a life had been lost.

Terry joined his wife, and Madison and Troy were in the third row near Andrea and her husband. Next to the burial site, officers in dress uniform were standing at attention.

The crowd was silent.

Breaking the still, a dispatcher's voice came over the speakers. It would also go out over all officers' radios.

"Dispatch to 235."

A pause and then she repeated, "Dispatch to 235."

Pause.

For a third time, "Dispatch to 235."

A longer pause.

"Dispatch to 235. Come in Officer Weir." The dispatcher's voice broke.

Silence.

"Attention all units, there is no response from 235. Officer Barry Weir was killed in the line of duty on Saturday, September 24 at 6:10 AM. 235 is now 10-7."

Out of service.

Tears slid down Madison's cheeks and her heart raced in her chest, yet her breathing slowed.

Three tones sounded over the speakers to notify on-duty officers that the radios were back for active communication.

As a priest spoke a sermon, Madison was caught up in an overwhelming moment of thoughts of life and death, of mortality, of what really matters in life and what doesn't. She was crumbling apart, her body shaking, and sobs heaved in her chest, heartbreak burning in her throat and lungs.

When the priest concluded, officers took the flag from the coffin and folded it thirteen times to form a triangle and passed it off to Joni.

A helicopter flew overhead, the whirling blades drawing everyone's attention briefly up to the sky. Bringing them back a moment later was the cry of Sergeant Winston, marking the start of the 3-volley salute. "At attention!"

Seven officers holding rifles stood in a row.

"Right face!"

The officers turned to their right.

"Ready!"

The officers cocked their rifles.

"Aim!"

The officers lifted their rifles toward the sky.

"Fire!"

The sergeant and officers repeated this two more times.

"Ready, aim, fire."

A brief silence was followed by the sound of bagpipes playing "Amazing Grace."

Madison looked heavenward, not necessarily believing in God or religion, yet putting faith in the existence of a Greater Being, even at a low time such as this when most blamed him—or her.

The clouds moved across the sky, and she thought of her friend. She squeezed her eyes shut and then opened them again.

Rest in peace, my brother. You may be lost, but you will never be forgotten.

Be certain to catch the next book in the Detective Madison Knight Series!

Sign up at the weblink listed below
to be notified when it's available for pre-order:

>> http://carolynarnold.net/mkupdates/ <<

You will also receive:

*Any updates pertaining to upcoming releases in the series
(cover art, book description, firm release date)*

Access to sneak peeks

*Behind-the-Tape™ insights giving you an inside look at
Carolyn's research and creative process*

Letter for Law Enforcement

This book is dedicated to all the fine men and women who serve or have served in law enforcement and in memory of those who have made the ultimate sacrifice.

While some of you may view being a law enforcement officer as a job, there are many of you who feel it is your calling. You respect that the departments in which you serve are businesses, but that's not what drives you. You wouldn't live your life any other way.

You make your communities a safer place to live.

You put your lives on the line every shift.

You run toward gunfire while the rest of us run away.

You do all of it not for the praise or glory, but for your love of people.

Your job is most often a thankless one, but you carry it out anyway.

You are making a difference. It is because of you that the world isn't in complete chaos, why there is some order and justice to be found.

You appreciate that how we live our lives affects more than just us and our community. It has a global impact.

For all of this, I thank you, and the world in its entirety should thank you, too.

You and your contribution will never be forgotten.

Acknowledgments

My love for law enforcement officers runs deep, and without them this book wouldn't even exist. Their insight and experience, their sacrifice of their time to answer my many questions, has made this book what it is.

Carl J. Harper, thank you for working through my pages of questions on ERS (SWAT) procedure. Your taking the time to gather such detailed responses really helped me to fully understand their roles and how they would go about doing things. And even after typing out pages of answers, you were still open when more questions popped up.

Stacy Eaton, you've been a tremendous help for years now by answering my questions as they come up, even reading through manuscripts to check that I had my procedures and terminology correct. Thank you.

I also would be amiss not to thank and acknowledge the amazing officers at London Police Services. Taking part in the Citizen's Academy was a real treat. I was a part of the action on my ride-along with Greg Blumson on the scene of a death investigation. I put my hands on weapons and equipment used by various units. I toured the ERS and the Command Center vehicles. I met incredible people! Catherine Fountain, Tom Allen, Colleen Kelly, Andy Bakker, Angus Campbell, Chris Riley, Brad Lobsinger, Sam Page, Gary "Buzz" Bezaire, Ryan Valiquette, Jamie Porter, Marissa Thorburn, Sylvain Leclerc, Ryan Scrivens, Travis Wintjes, David Payette, Dave Ellyatt, John McDonald, and Chief John Pare. Being taught by you, being around you, was an amazing experience that has only added further credibility to my work. Also, I would like to thank Chris Carne for taking my husband on a ride-along and providing information on warrants and more. Laurie Legg, from the Forensic Identification Section with the Criminal Investigation Division, helped me get my facts straight with ballistics. Thank you. Terri Jackson, thank you for letting me watch you work on-scene and for giving me a tour of the I-dent vehicle. Greg Parrott, you approached me and offered to help me if I had any medical situations arise in my books. Little did you know that at the time I was working on a book in which someone passes out. Your EMS knowledge enabled me to add more depth to that scene.

Danielle Poiesz, your amazing talent for crafting my words, challenging me, and bringing out the best in my writing is appreciated, even when there are times I need to step away for a bit and drink a tea. Also, thank you to Morgan Marsicano, who proofread to ensure the final manuscript was perfect.

CAROLYN ARNOLD is an international best-selling and award-winning author, as well as a speaker, teacher, and inspirational mentor. She has four continuing fiction series—Detective Madison Knight, Brandon Fisher FBI, McKinley Mysteries, and Matthew Connor Adventures—and has written nearly thirty books. Her genre diversity offers her readers everything from cozy to hard-boiled mysteries, and thrillers to action adventures.

Both her female detective and FBI profiler series have been praised by those in law enforcement as being accurate and entertaining, leading her to adopt the trademark: POLICE PROCEDURALS RESPECTED BY LAW ENFORCEMENT™.

Carolyn was born in a small town and enjoys spending time outdoors, but she also loves the lights of a big city. Grounded by her roots and lifted by her dreams, her overactive imagination insists that she tell her stories. Her intention is to touch the hearts of millions with her books, to entertain, inspire, and empower.

She currently lives just west of Toronto with her husband and beagle and is a member of Crime Writers of Canada.

CONNECT ONLINE
carolynarnold.net
facebook.com/authorcarolynarnold
twitter.com/carolyn_arnold

And don't forget to sign up for her newsletter for up-to-date information on release and special offers at carolynarnold.net/newsletters.